I WILL SAVE YOU

MATT DE LA PEÑA

I WILL SAVE YOU

DELACORTE PRESS

Grateful acknowledgment is made to Hal Leonard Corporation for permission to reprint lyrics from "I Didn't Understand," words and music by Elliott Smith, copyright © 1998 by Universal Music-Careers and Spent Bullets Music. All rights administered by Universal Music-Careers. International copyright secured. All rights reserved.

Delacorte Press is a registered trademark and the colophon is a trademark of Random House, Inc.

Visit us on the Web! www.randomhouse.com/teens

Educators and librarians, for a variety of teaching tools, visit us at www.randomhouse.com/teachers

Library of Congress Cataloging-in-Publication Data
Peña, Matt de la.
I will save you / Matt de la Peña. — 1st ed.
p. cm.
Summary: Seventeen-year-old Kidd Ellison runs away to work for the summer at a beach campsite in California where his hard work and good looks lead to friendship and love but painful past memories surface in menacing ways.
ISBN 978-0-385-73827-9 (hc) — ISBN 978-0-385-90719-4 (glb) —
ISBN 978-0-375-89742-9 (ebook) [1. Emotional problems—Fiction. 2. Schizophrenia—Fiction. 3. Mental illness—Fiction. 4. Cardiff by the Sea (Encinitas, Calif.)—Fiction.] I. Title.
PZ7.P3725Iam 2010
[Fic]—dc22
2010021186

The text of this book is set in 11.5-point Garamond BE Regular.
Book design by Angela Carlino

Printed in the United States of America

10 9 8 7 6 5 4 3 2 1

First Edition

for Caroline

You once talked to me about love
and you painted pictures of
a never-never land
And I could've gone to that place,
but I didn't understand
I didn't understand

—ELLIOTT SMITH,
"I Didn't Understand"

I was on the beach with everybody else, all of us in hoodie sweatshirts and flip-flops, waiting for the grunion to run how the papers and news-show people all talked about.

It only happens a few times a year, late at night, and goes like this:

Post–full moon and after high tide the entire beach goes silver like a thousand tiny mirrors with female grunion fish riding swells onto shore and scurrying up the sand and digging in with their tails, and then the males, sometimes seven or eight at a time, wrapping around the females and releasing their milt and then all of them scurrying back to sea together, leaving their eggs buried in the sand to hatch during a future post-full-moon high tide.

I read it in the paper at the campsite coffee shop.

In one picture from last summer the whole beach was shimmering, like a rich woman's dress going down a red carpet. Before I left the shop, Lea, one of the workers, cut out the picture for me with scissors and now it was with me on the beach, folded up and stuck inside the pages of my philosophy of life book. Next to the good-luck tiger whisker I planned to give Olivia.

I flipped the book open and looked at the picture and the whisker and got excited all over again.

Since the entire event was supposed to last less than a minute we were all just standing around, waiting, saying how cool it was gonna be, even Mr. Red, my boss, and Peanut, the campsite dog.

Then I looked up the cliff.

And I saw it. . . .

Devon sitting with Olivia at the top of the stairs, talking close like flirting people talk.

I choked on breath.

I almost squatted down on the not-yet-silver sand 'cause my knees went wobbly and I couldn't tell which way was up, like when a wave takes you underneath and spins you around the ocean's washing machine.

Olivia and Devon.

Together.

The beach sky was black except for a moon oval that lit up their position on the cliff like a stage spotlight in some romantic play, and I set right off for them, my heart knocking in my chest and stomach and even my neck. My philosophy of life book shaking in my hand. I walked at first like everything was normal 'cause I knew if Mr. Red thought something was happening he'd call me back and take off his old sombrero and fire off question after question ("What's going on, big guy? You all right? Somebody stressing you out?").

When I made it around the bend I jogged, then I ran up the stairs, two at a time, thinking I had to get to her before something happened and what if something happened.

I saw them through the bushes and stopped cold.

Peanut ran into the back of my leg.

Devon slowly tracing the mark on Olivia's cheek, the one she showed *me,* and her just letting him.

"You can't do it," I said under my breath.

Olivia didn't turn to look at me.

But Devon did.

Devon stared and even got a tiny grin on his face and I

told him: "Get away from her!" But he didn't get away from her. Instead he ran his fingers through her long blond hair and leaned in to whisper something in her diamond-earringed ear and then kissed her a real kind of kiss, like two people who were committed together as a couple.

She kissed back.

Somebody else's tiger whisker was already pinched between her thumb and forefinger. A shopping bag and card by their feet in the dirt.

My whole body lost its feeling and then went jumpy, like I was freezing cold, but I was in my hoodie sweatshirt and warm. I clenched my jaw to stop its chattering and made my face into steel. Then I crashed through the bushes and started marching toward them, one foot up and down and then the other up and down like I was going into a war, wearing my fatigues and a rifle on my shoulder, never taking my eyes off Devon, who was still looking back at me even though he was kissing Olivia.

I stopped in front of them and Olivia still didn't look at me. I was some kind of ghost that made no tracks in the sand, or that Jesus poem "Footprints," but then I reached out and took Devon by the hood of his sweatshirt and moved him away from the only girl I've ever loved or ever will.

I shoved him from the steps toward the part of the cliff where the fence was weakest. I should know 'cause I fixed the whole thing with Mr. Red earlier in the summer and this was where we ran out of material and had to just leave the old part. This was where Mr. Red shook his head and told me, pointing at the fence, how the only thing between some person and falling forty feet down the ice plant face of the cliff to the beach and his most likely death was whether or not he was stupid enough to test it.

I walked me and Devon toward that test, him by the hood of his sweatshirt and me gritting my teeth, still clutching my philosophy of life book, meaning this more than anything I'd ever meant, and Olivia screamed: "Oh, my God, Kidd! What are you doing!"

"I can't let anybody hurt you," I told her.

"Kidd! You're scaring me again!"

When I turned and looked at her, something wild leapt in her eyes, out-of-control flames that no amount of fireman's water could've ever extinguished or even slowed down.

My heart lowered its head, ashamed.

Olivia.

For a second I got confused and thought, Am I maybe wrong to do this?

"Please!" she said. "Kidd!"

"I have to make sure you're okay."

"Why do you keep saying that? Nobody's hurting me."

But I already had Devon's back against the part of the fence that wasn't new, and he was grinning in my face 'cause of his death drive, and he told me: "So, here we are, eh, Kidd? I knew you'd show up."

His laugh.

Him looking down the cliff, at all the people on the sand.

"You still don't get it, do you?" he said. "All of these people here, man. They think they're better than us."

I was only half listening, though, the other half still seeing Olivia's trembling lip behind me, which made me think of my mom's trembling lip when she sat across from me at the kitchen table the day I turned ten, seven years ago. Saying how I was a man now and how I deserved the truth about my genes and what was about to happen with her and my dad. I remembered her long-nailed fingers digging into her own hands and her right knee going up and down and up and down, the poor man's shake Mr. Red calls it whenever he catches mine doing the exact same thing around his campfire—usually 'cause I'm thinking about myself and if I'm good enough for Olivia.

My mom looked at me that birthday morning like she was telling me something brand-new about my dad, and to protect her feelings I acted like I didn't know.

"I'll do it," I said to Devon, making my face into the hardest possible frown.

"You won't."

"I will."

"You won't."

"I have to."

Peanut stared up at me, his tongue going and one of his ears standing in a point like it was hearing something too high for humans.

"Kidd, stop!" Olivia said.

She took two short breaths and told me: "Just—just come back here a minute. I wanna talk to you."

Olivia was pretending calmness now, her voice quieter and deeper and more desperate. Her eyes darting in their sockets and her lip still going like my mom's lip when she sat me down in front of my ten-candle cake and said how I had a right to know and how I was a man now.

"They may have just stuck you in this special program at

school, honey, but I know you're just as smart as you ever were. Now I want you to listen, okay?"

Her pushing loose strands of long black hair behind her ears and glancing at the ceiling and taking a deep breath. When she looked back at me her eyes all jittery and building tears.

"This is who you are," she said. "And you can never forget that."

I watched that first tear slide down my mom's cheek and fall onto the collar of her light blue shirt in a circle, that part going instantly darker.

Below me and Devon the ocean massive and making its constant fuzzy sound and yawning up onto the already wet sand and then rolling back into itself, all its secret eternity buried beneath and calm like Olivia was pretending to be calm behind us, and its whispering of how meaningless the three of us were above it on the cliff, the sand still not silver like the picture folded in my book, but dull and gray and sad.

I stood there, gripping Devon's sweatshirt.

My philosophy of life book, on the ground now, with all my answers and me with no time to read 'em.

"Please," Olivia said in a tiny voice.

"You won't," Devon said.

"I have to," I said, and I drove him harder into the weak part of the fence until it broke like I knew it would break and I shoved him down the cliff and watched his body bounce-tumble-fall-stretch-fetal-thud into the thick sad sand and lay motionless, and everybody who was once waiting for grunion was now racing to his side and touching his arm, his back, his leg, and looking up the cliff at me and Olivia.

Peanut took off down the stairs.

I studied Olivia's hysterical crying face as she hurried to the edge of the small cliff and crumpled to her knees, sobbing and looking down at Devon's limp body and screaming "No!" and then looking at me and shouting my name, "Kidd!"

Over and over like that.

"Kidd!"

"Kidd!"

A bad feeling slowly dripping into my stomach, warm, and how I couldn't move or feel anything.

But then I pictured what Mr. Red said. "A man's gotta take care of his woman." I'd just put it as #5 in my philosophy of life book.

And that was all I did.

Take care of Olivia.

The human crowd now gathered around Devon and flashlights shining and combined talk rising up to us and fingers pointing and cell phones opening and going to people's ears. Olivia sobbing, her long blond hair now back under her ski cap, the flap again covering the mark on her cheek.

My heart hanging from the edge of the ice plant cliff by its fingertips and slipping.

I stepped back and watched it all like a show on TV, and right that second it happened. . . .

The grunion came from the ocean.

All at once they wiggled out of an especially heavy swell and rode up onto shore, blanketing the sand like real-life glitter and everybody who was touching Devon turned to watch the silver fish digging into the sand and circling around each other and some scurrying all the way up to people's flip-flop feet and climbing over Devon's motionless body.

And me on Mr. Red's secret part of the cliff, above everything, out of breath and in awe, thinking how could such a good thing like a sparkling beach next to the girl of my dreams come at the exact same time as such a bad thing, my ex–best friend, Devon, broken in the sand 'cause I pushed him and the sound of sirens in the distance and Olivia burying her face in her hands, sobbing.

Before all the silver had time to fade back in the ocean I closed my eyes to keep freedom pictured in my head and waited for them to come take me away.

I WILL SAVE YOU

I keep picturing it over and over in the pitch black of solitary confinement. With my arms and legs strapped down and my head taped in place so I can't move or barely even breathe.

I see me pushing Devon off the cliff.

Him in the air reaching, ricocheting off the ice plant cliff, hitting the sand, people circling his crooked body.

The grunion coming from the ocean.

Olivia crying in her hands.

And every time I picture it a worse feeling goes in my stomach, like my whole body is unbalanced, or when you drop straight down in your roller-coaster cart and everybody has their hands up, screaming.

Except for me there's no end of the ride where I can get off and just sit on an empty bench with my soda watching people. This kind of roller coaster keeps going.

'Cause what if I was wrong about Devon?

What if the whole time he wasn't trying to hurt her, he just loved her? Same as me. What if *that's* the reason he was always wandering around alone in the middle of the night like he was depressed?

And what if Olivia actually loved him back, and I got in the way of people's fate?

That doesn't make sense, though. 'Cause he kept telling me she thought she was better and he would use his gun on her.

And Olivia liked *me*.

She even said it at Torrey Pines Beach while we sat together on her special rock and watched the sunset colors spread over the ocean.

They put me in Horizons after my mom died 'cause they said I had post-traumatic stress. They believed it was the reason I was always so tired and confused and bad to myself.

But right now it's even worse.

I can't think.

I can just stare at the total darkness in front of me, which feels like being inside a black hole. Or if your boat drifted into the Bermuda Triangle.

Solitary confinement is like you don't exist.

If I had my philosophy of life book and a pen I'd try to write about what happened on the cliff, and how maybe now I understand why some people have to be put in jail. They've shown they're capable of crossing a line, like pushing another person off a cliff, and maybe it wasn't even for the right reasons, which shows you their judgment, and what if they did it again.

But I can't write anything 'cause the police didn't put my book with me.

That's the first thing I checked when I woke up in this blackness. I tried to reach, but my arms were strapped too tight. My whole body ached after I just barely shifted, parts I'd never even thought about like in between my fingers and behind my knees.

The police must've pounded me with their billy clubs when they loaded me into the back of their squad car and drove me to prison. They probably thought I was evil for what I did to my best friend. Everybody probably did.

Even Olivia.

But they didn't know Devon.

They'd never heard him talk about rich people, especially girls. They'd never seen his gun or how he made a throat-slashing sign at Olivia or how he'd stand there staring at her tent in the middle of the night when she was sleeping.

They'd think different if they knew.

I wake up and try to reach out my hand again, to feel for my philosophy of life book, 'cause I need it, but I still can't move. The straps feel even tighter. My breaths barely have room. And it's still the blackest black you could ever picture, like everything got burned up.

I keep thinking if this is the form of torture that happens in solitary confinement, even though you're not supposed to torture people in the United States.

And then it really sinks in.

Where I am.

Strapped down in a bed behind bars.

Locked up.

And all my mom ever said was for me to be a good person. And be polite. And respect my elders.

I imagine her looking down from heaven right now. Her only son in solitary confinement, being tortured. And I see from her expression how heartbroken she is. Tears running makeup stains down her cheeks and her chin quivering and her eyes so sad, like two cat's-eye marbles nobody wants to shoot for.

Just thinking about my mom crying makes my lungs start going too fast. Like I've just sprinted up the campsite stairs. And now I'm gasping for air and my heart's pounding my ribs and it feels like I'm lifting out of my own body, floating above my prison cot. . . .

I'm hovering by the ceiling now.

Next to my mom.

We're both watching me lay here, unable to move, chest

going up and down and up and down, too many times a second. We're cringing at the welts on my arms and legs and face where they clubbed me.

And this loud ringing noise starts in both my ears.

Little gusts of wind pass over my skin like prison ghosts are moving all around my cell. They're waiting for me to die so they can take me to what comes next for a person who pushed his own best friend off a cliff.

And my mom's sobbing and holding them away and saying for me to hurry and remember.

Philosophy 1:
About Being Awake

Dear Kidd:

You have to always remember the time you escaped Horizons with Devon and ended up at that street fair downtown and how you and him had to pee so bad you couldn't even stand still. It doesn't seem important just thinking about it, but it goes exactly with what Mr. Red said about not sleepwalking and knowing you're alive. . . .

You and Devon slipped past the night watch, remember? And hopped a bus all the way to the Gaslamp District and walked through the different booths where bands were playing and people were drinking and laughing and dancing. And you drank that huge Coke and had to pee. But when you looked at the line for the portable bathrooms it stretched all the way around the block. You turned to Devon and without even saying, you and him walked up the street together looking for any random place.

There were people everywhere, though, way more than what's in Fallbrook. You went into a liquor store with elephant tusks over the doorway, but it didn't have a bathroom either, not one you were allowed to use, and by that time your bladder was so full it was pounding and you could barely walk. Devon held on to one of the magazine shelves and said it was the exact same for him.

The back door was open a crack and it looked like there was a little yard and Devon nodded and you peeked at the worker who was busy with a customer and you snuck out there behind Devon and went to the opposite part of the wall from him and unzipped your zipper and started going, your eyes making tears 'cause it was the most total relief you'd ever felt, the thin yellow puddle rolling between your shoes just barely missing them and going in the grass behind you like a contaminated ocean for the ants. . . .

On my first day working at the campsites Mr. Red told me how most people are asleep even when they're awake.

We were in the main campsite restroom, the one right by the coffee shop, mopping where a toilet overflowed all this nasty brown sewage and both of us were making disgusted faces and holding our noses and mouths as far back as possible.

"Trust me, big guy," Mr. Red said, wiping his frown on his shoulder and spitting in the toilet. He was as old as most people's dads, with floppy blond hair and tan skin, and he always had a grin on his face like everything was funny. My old counselor, Maria, said people always looked twice at Mr. Red when they passed him 'cause he was so handsome and he resembled a famous actor.

He looked at me and then looked back at the mess. "Monday through Friday. Pretty much everybody I know, Kidd. They walk around half conscious."

I kept mopping the floor and listening.

"They flip it to autopilot," he said. "You understand what I mean by 'autopilot,' right?"

I nodded, picturing a plane soaring high above the clouds and the pilot just reading a magazine or eating soup, even though I knew that wasn't what Mr. Red was saying.

He set his mop back in the bucket and dug his leather surfer hands in the back part of the toilet, started messing with pumps and hoses. "See, when people grow up and get a job, Kidd, life gets kind of monotonous and ordinary. All the possibilities dry up." He wiped his face on his shoulder again. "So, what do people do? Learn how to shut off their minds. Sleep-walk through the weekdays."

He looked up and said: "Why do you think I started drinking in the first place, big guy, for my health?"

I smiled 'cause Mr. Red was smiling.

He shook his head and put his right foot up on the toilet seat for leverage. "Shoot, Kidd, soon as quitting time came on Friday I'd hurry off to the bar and wake up on whiskey. Couple years like that and I couldn't wait until weekends anymore. Wednesday seemed close enough. Then Tuesday."

He looked at me and shrugged with his eyes, then went back to what he was doing. "According to my sponsor, Bill the Deacon, that kind of thinking is what landed me in rehab. I tried to explain how the only time I saw colors was after I'd knocked down a couple Jamesons, but Bill the Deacon just shook his head and told me I was deceiving myself. Bill's a big heavyset dude from Iowa, by the way. Former deacon. Used to milk cows and rake hay and drive a tractor in his downtime, the whole thing. Only deacon-farmer I've ever met. Now he sells pharmaceuticals out of a white van in La Jolla. Anyway, according to Bill the Deacon, drinking's just another form of sleepwalking. And all those colors I thought I saw, they were an optical illusion. Like looking at yourself in the funny mirror at the fair."

I pictured my mom drinking wine from a box. How she'd nod off in her rocking chair, in front of the flickering TV, knitting needles loose in her fingers like sharpened pencils and her head leaning forward in super slo-mo and her catching it, leaning forward again in slo-mo and her catching it.

I stood there mopping the murky brown water. Remembering my mom.

"Point is, whenever I gotta mess with crap like this," Mr. Red said, pointing all around the sewage. "No pun intended. You know what I tell myself, Kidd?"

"What, sir?"

"I say: 'All right, Red, maybe this isn't your number one choice. But at least you're awake enough these days to smell it!'"

He laughed hard, his shaggy blond hair falling in front of his blue eyes. He moved it away with the back of his wrist and stopped doing what he was doing and looked at me. "By the way, I don't know if I like you calling me sir, big guy. Makes me feel like a venture capitalist."

"Yes, sir."

"Oops, there it is again."

"I mean, Mr. Red."

He tilted his head and frowned. "Mr.?"

We looked at each other.

I thought how my mom always said to have respect.

He was quiet for a minute, just frowning at me, and then he coughed into his shoulder and said: "Anyway, sometimes I still dream about it. How warm a swallow of Jameson felt going down. The sweet aftertaste. The beautiful women who sat beside me on barstools and told me their lives."

He spit into the toilet again. "Sometimes I wonder: is an occasional glance at a funny mirror really such a bad thing?"

He shook his head, put the lid of the toilet back on, and wiped his hands down the sides of his work shirt and shorts. "Promise me you won't tell Bill the Deacon what I just said."

"I won't."

"Good man."

A smile went on his face and he said: "Look, you get my point, right? About handling the different jobs you'll be doing here? Some are a little less glamorous than others."

I nodded, thinking how I'd rather do any job than be stuck inside the faded pee-colored walls of my bedroom at Horizons, where the people constantly watch you and make you do therapy and take medicine.

Mr. Red play-punched me in the shoulder, said: "Maybe you *are* a little rough around the edges like they say, Kidd, but I'll give you this. You listen. I don't know how it is for anybody else, but listening goes a long way in my book."

I put my mop in the bucket and squeezed out dirty water and said: "What book do you mean, Mr. Red?"

He checked his waterproof watch, said: "Come again?"

"You said your book."

He smiled. "Just a figure of speech, big guy. It's the way I see the world. Everybody has a way they see the world, right?"

I stayed looking at my mopping and didn't say anything. I didn't want Mr. Red to know I didn't have a book with the way I saw the world.

Figuring Out a Name

Soon as I got off work that night I went to Campsite Coffee and bought a blank notebook and a special pen from Lea and went back to my tent, where I was gonna live for the whole summer, and stared at the cover for the longest time, trying to think.

I listened to people talk as they walked along the path

outside my tent. Mostly kids. A girl voice said some girl named Blue looked too skinny. And maybe that was why she always went to the bathroom after she ate.

Another girl voice said she brought a big bottle of aloe this year.

A little later a man's voice said: "She's not depressed, Mary, she's insecure. There's a difference."

A woman's voice answered: "She's sixteen and she's a girl, Ron. What do you expect?"

"Jesus, why do you think I'm taking her to New York?"

"I understand, but until then . . ."

Their voices trailed off and I looked back at my book and right that second a name popped in my head:

Kidd's Philosophy of Life Book.

I laid in my tent that night, on top of my sleeping bag, writing my first-ever philosophy about how people are asleep even when they're awake and about seeing colors and being on autopilot. I addressed it to myself, like a letter to me, thinking I could read it later on and remember all the important things I learned from Mr. Red.

As a regular person.

Outside of Horizons.

And then, I don't even know why, but I started writing about this time me and Devon had to run for our lives out of this liquor store downtown.

. . . You weren't even close to being done peeing, though, when you heard a deep growling sound and when you turned around there was a huge pit bull crouched down and showing his teeth, saliva dripping onto the grass exactly how it'd be in a cartoon. And remember how paralyzed your body got? It was frozen. You couldn't even breathe air in your lungs.

Devon shouted: Come on!

You zipped up midflow and raced back through the liquor store with the rabies dog chasing you, barking so loud you couldn't even hear what the liquor-store guy was yelling. You and Devon flew out the store and up the street, not looking back or stopping or saying anything until you were at least fifteen blocks away.

Then you ducked behind that big black truck and leaned over laughing and trying to catch your breath. And even though it probably doesn't seem like that big of a deal now, getting chased by a dog and having to stop your pee in the middle, to this day you've never run so fast in your life or laughed so hard. You just sat there on the sidewalk next to Devon, bent over laughing and laughing and laughing. People walking past gave you dirty looks probably thinking you guys were on drugs or crazy, but it's just how close you came to getting attacked by a killer dog in the middle of peeing in his yard.

Maybe it goes exactly with what Mr. Red said today: that you should always remember how awake you feel when you're running or laughing with Devon or even when you're just cleaning a campsite bathroom as part of your job. You always have to remember how lucky you are, to be away from Horizons. And to be free.

And alive.

And awake enough to smell everything.

I can't remember what happened after the grunion came. I don't know if Devon died when he hit the sand, or if Olivia understands how I did it for her, or if anybody saw the police club me and push me in their backseat with handcuffs. I have no idea what I thought about as I stared out the window while they drove me here.

Either I blocked it out or they gave me drugs like the ones I got at Horizons after my mom died and they said I had post-traumatic stress.

I've been laying here this whole time, in the dark, trying to remember the summer and everything that happened before I pushed Devon off the cliff. Like my mom said. 'Cause then I could know if I was right.

But so much of my mind is missing.

And the way I feel is missing, too.

That's why I think they gave me pills. It's the same as after they sat me down and said my mom was gone and gave me drugs that would supposedly make me better. Except I didn't feel better at all. I just got hollow, like a chocolate bunny in your Easter basket. Which is how I am right now.

You know those stories they have about cats coming up to babies' pillows when they're asleep and stealing their breath? That's what it feels like with me. Only the cat that came to *my* pillow left my breathing alone and stole how I feel.

What I Remember About My Mom

All you can do in prison is think. And your mind goes to bad places if you let it think whatever it wants, so you have to picture certain things. Most of the time I try to remember the summer, before the grunion night, to decide if I was right about Devon. But today I've just been laying here picturing things about my mom.

How she never looked you in the eyes when she talked to you. She'd stare at the top of your forehead. Or in your hair. Or at something past you.

She never picked up the phone. She'd stand there watching it ring, waiting for the voice-mail light to start flashing.

This time we did miniature golf and she hit a hole in one and all the spotlights came on and the workers announced it over the loudspeaker and gave us a bucket of free tokens. How on the bus ride home she told me she just aimed for the green wall, that was her secret, nobody else knew to aim for the green wall, and she called me her good-luck charm.

The last letter she wrote. Me memorizing every word.

How she'd fall asleep in front of the TV and I'd wake her up and take the empty wineglass from her hand and help her to her feet and watch her stagger to her room. Me carrying her glass to the sink, staring at the red stain at the bottom, wondering what was gonna happen to us.

Me as a little kid waking up and finding her standing over me as I laid in her bed. Looking at me. Saying: "You can still sleep, baby. Mommy's just watching you."

My dad coming over and them smoking on the fire escape. Laughing and sitting close. Him staying over. The next morning her dancing to the radio in the kitchen, making pancakes and bacon. Bringing out our plates, setting them down. Rubbing Dad's shoulders while he took his first bite and then winking at me.

Me standing behind her in court when she got the restraining order. And then later that night how she let him in 'cause he said he was sick. Pulling money from her secret cookbook stash and slipping it into his hand. Them hugging and crying and her telling me: "Go on back to bed, baby. Mom and Dad are talking."

Her on her knees by the bed in her room one morning, praying. Then when she saw me, acting like she wasn't.

But mostly I remember every morning before school. How she'd say "Hey, honey!" just as I was walking out the apartment door. And me stopping and turning around and saying "What?" And her saying: "I love you." And me rolling my eyes like I just wanted to hurry up so I didn't miss the bus. I'd start going again and she'd say "Hey, honey!" and I'd say "Mom, come on!" and she'd say "I love you," and I'd pretend I was so annoyed 'cause she was wasting time and I had to go catch the bus. And how secretly it was my favorite part of every day.

Philosophy 2:
About Saying the Truth to People

Dear Kidd:

You should always tell the truth to people you care about, even if they won't like what they hear. You just have to say it. Like Mr. Red does with all the women he meets. Like Mom did when she sat you down and tried to tell you about your dad and your genes.

Except with that time, even though she was telling the truth, you already knew 'cause your last memory was when he showed up at your apartment in the middle of the night and started banging on the door and begging for money and saying: "Jesus Christ, Darla! Open the door! I'm dying out here!" And your shaky-hands mom undid the locks, slowly, and cracked open the door, slowly, and told him in a trembling voice how he had to go away and about the neighbors and the restraining order, but he pushed himself in and went down on his knees and begged for just a little money, as much as she could spare, he needed it so bad, she didn't understand how his body felt, he probably wouldn't survive even one more night.

You snuck out of your room, remember? And watched everything from the hall. How Dad grabbed the hem of Mom's nightgown and put it to his face and breathed it and said how nobody could understand how bad he was 'cause they'd never felt it for themselves and they'd never been inside his body. She was the only person who cared at all, the only person who was willing to sacrifice for him.

You can never forget the serious look on Mom's face that night. Like she knew she was wrong to let him in, and she knew something bad was about to happen, something that would change things forever. . . .

Five blond girls were sitting in a circle of lawn chairs, talking and laughing and eating colored cereal out of plastic bowls with their fingers. I watched them from the railroad tie on the next campsite over, waiting for Mr. Red to come out of his tent and for us to start working.

It was my fourth day, and I was still getting there an hour early for two reasons. First, I was so excited to have a real job I could barely sleep (which was weird 'cause during my last six months at Horizons all I did was sleep). And second, I was so thankful Mr. Red hired me in the first place and I thought the best way to show him was to always be there when he came out of his tent.

One of the blond girls got out of her chair and stood on a skateboard with her cereal bowl, looking back in the tent and saying: "Come on, Olivia. You can't stay in a tent the rest of the summer." Her friends said stuff, too, and then everybody shrugged and the girl on the skateboard stepped off and sat back in the chair with her friends and they kept eating their cereal.

I was watching them, thinking how they were the kind of pretty you could never actually meet, when Mr. Red's voice scared me.

"There he is!" he shouted.

I spun around.

He climbed out of his tent yawning and stretching, wearing a T-shirt that said CARDIFF BY THE SEA, which is where we were, and black surf trunks that went down to his knees and no shoes.

"I see you, Kidd," he said. "Dawn patrollers have hardly set their boards in the water and here you are ready to mop more sewage."

"I'm ready, sir," I told him, standing up.

"Fortunately there won't be any actual mopping today." He held open his tent flap and out of it climbed a black-haired woman in a long white T-shirt, holding an open duffel bag with a black dress hanging out. She stopped and pushed the dress the rest of the way in and zipped the zipper.

Mr. Red looked at me and shrugged.

"Donna," he said and pointed to me. "I want you to meet a colleague of mine. Mr. Kidd Ellison from Fallbrook, California. Dude would cheat his own grandmother out of a game of speed chess, but he works his butt off around the campsites."

"Hi there," Donna said, smiling at me.

"Hi, ma'am," I told her back. And then I turned to Mr. Red and told him: "I never cheated you in—"

"Come on, Kidd," he interrupted. "We don't need to rehash this again. One minute I have you down four pieces, the next you're knocking off my queen and I'm mated." He shook his head and turned to Donna. "I've played a lot of speed chess in my day, babe. A board doesn't change that quickly without a little foul play."

"I don't know, Red. Kidd doesn't look like the cheating type to me."

"It's all an act."

They both sort of laughed so I laughed, too.

• • •

How I Got the Job in the First Place

Me and Mr. Red met at Horizons in Fallbrook when he used to come visit Maria, this nice counselor lady who worked there. He'd show up on most Sundays and we'd all watch football games on TV and throw the Frisbee and eventually me and him started playing speed chess and I always beat him and he always said I cheated.

Then before last summer started two things happened. First, Maria got laid off because of the economy and they only had two counselors working at a time. And second, Mr. Red filled out some paperwork for me to have a job with him for the summer, and even though he said he'd bring me to my counseling as much as they wanted, they rejected him. He appealed and had a meeting with the board of directors and explained how it'd be great experience that I could take into the workforce. But the directors turned him down again saying it was too far from their headquarters and how I was an "at-risk" case and needed closer supervision, at least through the completion of my therapy program.

Mr. Red came to see me right after, this time without Maria even being there, and told me everything they said and how sorry he was.

A whole year passed.

Then at the start of this summer I packed a bag without even asking, snuck out at four in the morning and hitchhiked all the way down to the beach.

When I finally made it to the sand, the sun was just starting to rise. I sat and watched it for a while and thought about my new life. Then I walked north along the tide with all the morning joggers and people walking their dogs, asking every few miles how close I was to Cardiff by the Sea, until eventually I found the campsites and this lifeguard named Christian took me to Mr. Red, who was eating breakfast on the campus picnic table with a pretty black woman.

When Mr. Red saw me he stopped his chewing and looked all around like spies might be watching from the bushes. I told him I didn't want to live at Horizons anymore, I wanted to work, and I'd almost finished my program, and besides I was almost eighteen and on the Internet it says kids are allowed to work as soon as they're sixteen and they can even be emancipated if they want which means you don't have to have parents anymore, not even foster ones.

When I finished talking Mr. Red sat there for a while looking between me and the black woman.

He smiled and nodded his head, said: "To hell with the system, big guy. Welcome to San Elijo Maintenance."

Mr. Red's Position on Women

Mr. Red led Donna to the shiny black Jetta parked in front of the coffee shop. I watched them kiss goodbye and her climb in and shut her door and drive off, waving.

When he came back to where I was he was carrying his beat-up sombrero in his right hand. He put it on his head and told me: "Another day, another dollar, eh, big guy? How's it feel to be on an official payroll?"

"It feels great, sir—"

"Look," he interrupted, poking his finger through one of the holes in his sombrero. "We might as well get this out in the open. I'm friendly with a number of women. I understand your loyalty probably lays with Maria. As it should. She was your favorite counselor and a fine Mexican woman."

I looked at the ground and pictured Maria, the only thing I liked about Horizons.

He led me toward the campsite work shed, where we got out our tool belts and he put on his work boots with no socks. "I want you to understand something, Kidd. Everything between her and I is on the up-and-up. We may have parted ways for the time being, but we still talk. Maria's aware of the other women, and the other women are aware of Maria." He paused, looking at me, and then said: "And I thought we were dropping the whole 'sir' thing."

"Oh, yeah."

He made a face and slapped me on the back. "You want me to lay out my position on females, big guy?"

"Okay," I said.

We walked up toward Campsite Coffee, where Mr. Red gets his morning coffee, and he held up a finger and said: "Hold that thought."

He opened the door, and we walked in and the woman was already holding a medium cup out for him. "Lea," he said, taking the cup. "How's my girl?"

On my first day Mr. Red told me how Lea was just a year out of business school at Stanford and she and two other girls had bought the campsite store and turned an ugly, boring store into one of the hippest coffee spots along the 101.

Lea put her hands on her hips and said: "I'm mad at you, Red."

"Me?"

"What happened to our trip to Legoland?"

Mr. Red squinted his eyes like he was thinking. "Oh, Lea. Last week got really stressful here. Ask Kidd."

Lea turned to me, and I shrugged.

"Me and the big guy were stuck mopping sewage in the girls' bathroom."

"Blah blah blah."

"Not a pretty sight. You women are deceiving."

Lea rolled her eyes, said: "By the way, wanna know what I overheard?"

Mr. Red was stirring sugar into his coffee.

"Some of the girls were talking about your new assistant here. Saying how handsome he is. What are you gonna do if Kidd steals all your women?"

Mr. Red turned to me. "Hear that, Kidd? Lea just made a pass at you."

I looked at Lea and she rolled her eyes and laughed a little.

"Don't worry," Mr. Red said. "I plan to teach Kidd everything I know."

Lea took my hands, said: "Be sure to listen, Kidd. Then do the exact opposite."

She smiled and let go of my hands.

Outside Campsite Coffee, Mr. Red told me: "As I was saying, I have a tough time with the whole monogamy thing."

He veered us off the road again, toward his tent.

"Don't get me wrong, I recommend it for ninety-nine percent of the population. But I've been divorced three times, Kidd. *Three!* I'm only thirty-six years old. Let's crunch the numbers on that: twenty-seven the first time, add nine, divide by three, that's only three years per 'I do.' A guy can only bark up the wrong tree so many times, right?"

I shrugged.

"And it's not like I don't explain my position to every woman I meet."

He stopped suddenly and looked me in the eyes. "Look, Kidd, you're not some kind of moralist, are you?"

"I don't think so," I said.

"Are you affiliated with a fundamentalist church?"

"No."

"Do you sympathize with the banning of books?"

"No."

"Have you ever donated money to the NRA?"

"I never had money."

"Good," Mr. Red told me, and he started walking again. "Way I see it, Kidd, communication is the key. You can be anything you want in this country as long as you're honest about it."

He looked up at the pack of blond girls in the campsite next to his. They waved and he waved back and then he turned to me and said: "Wait a sec."

"What?"

"Kidd . . . you're not a virgin, are you?"

My eyes went wide and I opened my mouth to say something, but nothing came out.

"I'm staring into the eyes of a damn unicorn."

"I was gonna say–"

He waved me off. "Look, it's none of my business, big guy. Like Lea said, you're handsome enough. It'll happen."

I looked at the ground.

It's not that I hadn't thought about girls before. Or that I didn't like them. It's just at Horizons I never had enough time by myself to actually talk to one. And I wasn't brave like Devon, who snuck out late to meet with them.

"Okay," Mr. Red told me. "Maybe I chose a drastically different path when I was your age. I mean, I knew *dozens* of girls by the time I was your age. But that doesn't mean my way's the *right* way. Apples and oranges, big guy."

Mr. Red dipped into his tent and came out with two ripe bananas. "Speaking of fruit," he said, and handed me one and we both peeled them and started eating as we walked down the long campsite stretch. He said since there wasn't a whole lot that needed fixing before his lunchtime surf session he'd give me a tour of the campsites.

We walked past every campsite plot and he told me the best and worst things about each of them and how much they cost per day and how they held a drawing to determine who got which spot. He explained that most people stay a week or two, but that some groups, like the blond girls across the road from his tent, keep a campsite all summer. The girls and their parents come and go throughout the day since they all live in the neighborhood. Sometimes they sleep at home, he said. Sometimes they're gone for chunks of time because they go on real vacations to Hawaii or Europe or the Caribbean. But throughout the summer they always have a place to crash at the beach.

Me and Mr. Red walked along the fence by the edge of the cliff and up and down all the staircases that led to the beach and he told me how many steps each one had and which sections would eventually need to be renovated and what materials we would use and which finishes hold up best in oceanfront conditions. We passed a scraggly-looking dog laying in the dirt near the shed and Mr. Red told me his name was Peanut and how nobody knew exactly when Peanut showed up or how old he was or what breed he was; he'd just become part of the campsite setting, like a mascot.

Peanut raised his scruffy head and looked at me and then lowered his head back onto his paws and closed his eyes again. I'd never seen a dog so old and tired-looking.

Then Mr. Red led me to his favorite place to check out waves, a hidden patch of fence behind two thick bushes. You wouldn't even know it was there unless you thought to duck under this overgrown bush. He told me he kept it wild like that so it would stay his secret spot, and how he'd even stashed a couple beach chairs so he could sneak back here at night to watch the sunset.

"Well, look at this," he said under his breath, staring out over the ocean and nodding his head. "Surf's picking up."

"Yeah," I said, trying to look where he was looking.

Then Mr. Red went quiet.

I looked back and forth between him and the ocean, trying to figure out what you were supposed to look at when you checked out waves. All you could really see were a few people out in the deep part sitting or laying on their boards, waiting, spread out from each other, not talking. Sometimes small swells of water would roll in slow from way out and lift the surfers slightly and set them back down. The swells would gain momentum as they went closer to the sand, rising up at the last second and crumbling into whitewash and spreading over the beach like a blanket and then sucking back into the ocean. Other times the swell would be bigger and it would rise up earlier and one or two of the surfers would face the shore and paddle to catch it and spring to their feet and slash back and forth on the face of the wave as whitewash crumbled behind them like it was chasing after. And at the end of their ride the surfers would crash or just dive off on purpose and turn around and start paddling back out to where the rest of the surfers were still waiting and looking out over the back of the ocean.

We stayed there for a long time, me and Mr. Red, and he never took his eyes off the water. I thought about telling him thanks for showing me around and giving me this job in the first place and telling me his advice about girls, but he looked so focused on the waves I decided to just be quiet and let him look.

> . . . Mom promised Dad again and again she didn't have any money and how she couldn't even afford to pay bills, and he stood back up and pointed a finger in her face and called her worthless and a whore, and when she brushed away his finger he yelled at her so loud she started crying. He said as a matter of fact he saw her in La Jolla walking with some guy in a fancy suit who got into a BMW. She promised it wasn't her, but that just made him more mad. He told her to shut up and when she pushed his finger out of her face again

he gritted his teeth and did something you'll never forget for the rest of your life.

He punched Mom in the face with a closed fist.

How a guy would hit another guy.

The crack so loud it hurt your ears and you felt it in your bare feet through the floor and your body got paralyzed and your mind stopped thinking and all you could do was stare at what was happening.

Mom crumbling to the living room floor without sound, her body slumping against the wall, blood coming from her nose and mouth and trickling down her chin and her eyes going in the back of her head. You were so scared looking back and forth between them that pee went down your pajama legs warm and darkened the rug by your toes and you couldn't move or breathe or think.

You were only nine on that night, but you'll never forget.

Dad turning around to leave, him crying, too, like he was already sorry, and then him looking at you, looking down at your pee. His chest going in and out and in and out and yours not moving. When he looked up at your face again his eyes stayed stuck on yours for the longest time—even now, all these years later, with you in this campsite tent on the beach, in this new life of freedom, the sound of the actual ocean outside and your pen scribbling in this philosophy of life book.

Sometimes it feels like his eyes are still on you. Exactly how they were that night. The last time the three of you were in the same room. Dad's chest breathing and yours not moving and Mom knocked out against the wall and then later the paramedics would rush her out on a stretcher and put her in an ambulance that had its lights going but no sound. And later when the doctor stood over her in the hospital room reading her chart and asking questions and writing things down in a file and sometimes looking at you.

When Dad finally turned to leave the apartment that night you concentrated on how the back of his head looked walking away 'cause you knew you'd never see him again and you never did.

Dreams from Solitary Confinement

There are dream voices in here. That's something I never would've thought, but it's true. Or maybe it's a real dream. But it doesn't feel like a dream.

I'll just be laying here and I'll hear a voice start going, sometimes a man and sometimes a woman. I don't always understand what they're saying because they sound far away, like if I'm in one room and whoever's talking is down the hallway or on the other side of my cell wall.

But mostly I swear it's a girl saying the words from my philosophy of life book. Like I was just hearing the words I put about my dad hitting my mom and him leaving and me and my mom going to the hospital.

When I hear something from my book I stay super still and listen, pretending it's Olivia's voice and that we're laying together on the beach in the middle of the night. I pretend she's reading to me 'cause she's knows the police didn't put the book with me.

I can't really tell who the voices are, though, 'cause they keep it so pitch black in solitary confinement.

You know how after you're done using the bathroom in the middle of the night and you flip the lights back off and everything goes so dark you can't see? You always have to wait like five or six seconds before a few shapes slowly come into view. Then a few seconds after that you can see enough to walk back to your room and climb in the right bed.

Well, in solitary confinement it's like those first few seconds of dark, except it's all the time.

You can't see shapes no matter how many seconds you wait.

You can only hear dream voices.

What I Know About Devon

How he's lived in group homes and foster homes ever since I've known him and since he can remember. Twice he even got sent to juvenile hall, though he didn't have to stay long.

He swallowed a whole bottle of sleeping pills when he was fifteen. In his group-home bathroom. Passed out in the tub. His counselor found him and called 911 and the ambulance rushed him to the hospital where they charcoaled his stomach and saved his life. And when I visited he wouldn't look up or say what happened or even why he did it.

This one time in an arcade in Fallbrook when a big Samoan guy said it was his game, not ours, and shoved me out of the way and put in his quarter. Devon smacking him on the top of his head and everybody stepping back and watching the big Samoan sock Devon in the side of the face and throw him into the wall. Devon getting back up and the Samoan socking him in the mouth, lines of blood going down Devon's shirt and him out cold on the floor. But Devon got up and laughed and charged the Samoan again, and the Samoan smacked him in the ear. Everybody telling Devon to just stay down, the Samoan was gonna kill him. Even the Samoan said to stay down. But Devon kept getting up, over and over, smiling through bloody, broken teeth, charging this guy he knew he could never beat. He didn't stop until the cops came running into the arcade with their clubs raised.

• • •

How Devon's always looking at girls or talking about girls or saying what he just did with some tattooed girl he met behind the liquor store down the street from Horizons.

Days when he seemed so happy and had a hundred ideas for what we should do. Always saying how he was gonna be a fireman when he got older. Or a private detective. Or an NFL announcer. Or a movie director. How fast he'd talk those days, hardly taking a breath, and all he wanted to do was wrestle or shadowbox or play basketball at the park with whoever was there.

Other days when he wouldn't lift his head to look at me or answer my questions or even say what was wrong.

How much he hates rich people. 'Cause according to him they hoard their money and possessions and use them to feel better than people like us. He thinks worse about people with money than even my dad.

How so many times I wished Devon wasn't my friend 'cause of all the bad stuff I end up doing when he's around. And how my therapy person made me promise to keep him out of my life. But then other times when I'd think how good it is to be with another person so you don't have to feel so lonely.

I'll **never forget seeing** Olivia the first time. It was a Saturday, and even though I knew how weekends were different from weekdays, that day I didn't even think about it and the morning started out like any other morning, with me on Mr. Red's railroad tie an hour early, in front of his tent, waiting for him to come out so we could start working. Only this time the campsite dog, Peanut, was waiting there with me, sitting in front of my feet and breathing with his mouth open.

I touched his old head and told him: "Hey, boy."

He licked my hand and went back to breathing with his mouth open and staring at me.

When Mr. Red unzipped his tent flap and stepped out to stretch he didn't say "There he is!" like he usually did. He got a frown on his face and just stood there staring between me and Peanut.

"What's going on, Kidd?"

I looked at him confused. "I'm here to work."

"You realize today's Saturday, right?"

"Yeah."

He glanced toward the ocean and then looked back at me and said: "You've never had a job before, have you?"

I shrugged, told him not one I got paid for.

He looked at Peanut, who was now laying next to me. "And what's *he* doing here?"

I shrugged.

He shook his head. "Not the best-looking dog, eh?"

I looked down at Peanut. He was brown with short shaggy hair and some patches missing and even with his mouth closed you could still see some of his teeth 'cause they were so crooked and one ear sort of stood up and the other flopped down. His eyes were cloudy, too, like one of those snow globes after you shake it up.

Mr. Red held open his tent flap and a different woman came out, one I'd never seen before. She had short black hair and about twenty earrings in each ear and a big tattoo of the sun and moon together on the inside of her forearm.

"Michele," Mr. Red said, pointing at me, "I want you to meet a colleague of mine. Mr. Kidd Ellison from Fallbrook, California. Pizza of choice: Hawaiian. Ice cream: Neapolitan. Color: magenta."

"Hi," she said.

"Hi," I said back. "But my favorite color's not—"

"Trust me," Michele said, pointing her thumb in Mr. Red's direction, "I never believe a word that comes out of this one."

"Yes, ma'am," I said.

"Listen, Kidd," Mr. Red said, "when your boss says you have weekends off, that means on Saturday and Sunday—the *weekend*—you don't have to show up for work."

"Oh, yeah," I said.

He pulled his phone out of the back pocket of his trunks and checked a text, then he flipped it closed and looked up at me again and said: "Now go on, Kidd. Get out of here. Enjoy your Saturday."

I nodded and smiled, turned and started walking away. But I only got like three steps before I spun around and asked Mr. Red where I should go.

He looked at Michele and then looked back at me. "Come on, Kidd, use a little imagination. You got one of the best beaches in the state about twenty-five feet away. Or there's a park across the highway."

"What about a museum, Red?" Michele said. "There's that quaint little gallery on Birmingham."

Mr. Red rolled his eyes. "And by quaint she means miniature and creepy."

Michele stared at Mr. Red for a while, and then she punched him in the shoulder. "That is *so* rude."

He laughed and said: "Come on, Michele. The big guy doesn't wanna go to a museum."

She put her hands on her hips, said: "How do *you* know?"

"He'd be bored to tears."

"Oh, is that right?"

"You don't understand the male mind, Michele. Guys wanna be outside. We wanna surf or throw the football around. Scope out chicks in bikinis. Men seek fresh air, Michele. Adventure."

"First of all, Red, museums aren't boring. They're just beyond your primitive intellect—"

"*That* weak little museum?"

"And maybe Kidd appreciates art. Not all guys spend every waking minute either surfing or thinking about surfing or ogling every set of boobs that passes through their line of vision."

"Really?"

"Really."

Mr. Red shrugged and turned back to me. "Look, Kidd, go get some ice cream across the street or rent a kayak or buy yourself some jeans at one of the surf shops along 101. That pair you wear every day could probably use a breather, don't you think?"

I looked down at my jeans.

Mr. Red loved to mess with me, but I didn't care. I actually thought it was funny. It's so weird how when you like somebody they can make fun of you all day and you'll just sit there and crack up.

"You got money in your pocket now, buddy. Live a little."

"I know," I said, and I started backing away again, but as soon as I turned around to leave Mr. Red called out my name.

"Tell you what, tomorrow morning—which, by the way, Kidd, is yet another day off. You don't work weekends, okay? *No trabajas.*"

"Yes, sir."

He made a face.

"I mean, Mr. Red."

"Tomorrow we'll rent you a foam board and I'll take you surfing."

Michele cleared her throat.

Mr. Red looked at her, then looked back at me. "Guess I already have plans for tomorrow. Maybe next Sunday? I'll have you doing off-the-lips by lunchtime."

"Okay," I said, and after I looked at Peanut I went away from them for real.

Me Trying to Figure Out What to Do

After I left Mr. Red and Michele and Peanut I wandered all over Cardiff by the Sea looking at stuff and thinking how different it was from Fallbrook, where some people rode horses along the side of the road or drove huge trucks with stuff airbrushed on the side, like two girls sitting back-to-back in bikinis.

In Cardiff people wore flip-flops and shorts that weren't cutoff jeans. And everywhere you looked they were riding beach cruisers with surf racks or jogging or walking their dogs or sitting barefoot in beach chairs on the sand, sipping coffee and looking at the paper.

And you could tell they had money.

I went down on the beach and picked through these big clumps of fly-infested seaweed collecting broken seashells and tiny polished rocks and pieces of ocean-worn glass and then I left them all in a pile by an abandoned sand castle wondering if some little kid like I used to be would find them and think it was a treasure.

I went past these two surfer girls putting on wet suits and they said hi to me and I said hi back, trying to be like I wasn't shy. But really my entire back felt hot from their eyes and their most likely judging of me. I knew they could tell I was from Fallbrook and that I'd just come from Horizons, where counselors don't let you do anything by yourself, which makes you seem weird to regular kids.

When I turned around, though, the girls weren't even looking my way.

I walked back up to the campsites and past Campsite Coffee and the main restroom and out the gate and across the two-lane Highway 101. On the other side was this little valley that had train tracks in the middle. I slid down the cliff on my hands and shoes and walked along one of the metal ties for a while. Then I climbed up the other side and wandered into the park Mr. Red was talking about.

I went past the swings, picturing how my mom used to

push me when I was little. I walked the wrong way up the slide and sat there watching a mother squatting next to her little toddler, helping it try to take steps, its tiny hand wrapped around her middle finger and both of them smiling.

Two old guys with baseball caps were throwing horseshoes back and forth on my other side. They'd yell out the score after every shot and sometimes go to their cooler and pull out a water bottle and drink from it and then put it back.

Eventually I ended up sitting in this grassy area near some bushes, watching guys play basketball. I kept thinking of my best friend back in Fallbrook, Devon, and how different we were. Like, he wouldn't just sit here watching, like me. He'd walk down to the court and ask if he could play, too. And after a few games they'd all be laughing with each other and slapping fives.

My therapist always told me it was unhealthy for me to have a friendship with Devon. She said he was a bad influence, which is true. One of the things she made me do for my program at Horizons was have a talk with Devon to tell him we couldn't hang out anymore.

I was just sitting there, watching the guys play, picturing me and Devon's talk and wondering if everybody felt lonely on their day off, when something happened.

Without really thinking anything, I turned and looked at the swing set.

And I saw a girl.

She was just sitting on a swing, reading a book, barely swaying, but my chest got this weird feeling, like when you stare into the eyes of a little baby and the baby looks back up at you and you can feel how pure and innocent it is, so much it makes your stomach feel empty–probably 'cause you realize you used to be pure like that, too, and now you're not.

But I'd never had that feeling from a girl.

Love at First Sight

She was barely rocking, and she was holding on to only one of the chains with a sweatshirt-covered hand and staring down at her book. I moved behind the bush some more so she wouldn't catch me watching. She had on a ski cap even though it was hot, and the blond ponytail that came out the bottom was long and straight and beautiful. She had a short flowing green dress on over jeans with a faded surfer sweatshirt and tons of rubber bracelets on her one wrist that was showing and she was concentrating on what she was reading.

It was so weird what happened to me. I had that chest thing like I just talked about and my skin felt warm and even though I hadn't eaten all day it felt like I'd never be hungry again.

She looked up at me.

And she waved.

My breath instantly stopped and I ducked farther behind the bush and stayed hidden for the longest time, perfectly still, feeling my heartbeat in my throat and staring at this one fallen leaf. It was brown at the very tip and a tiny ant was walking around it in circles, sometimes stopping and feeling with its antennae, then walking in circles again.

I looked slowly past the bush, and her eyes were back on her book, and I let myself breathe.

• • •

For the next half hour I watched her like that, until she got off the swing and put her book in her peace-sign backpack and walked out of the playground.

I followed her, far enough behind that she wouldn't know I was there, but close enough so I could always see her long blond hair swinging with her steps.

I trailed her out of the park, ducking behind cars every few seconds, past storefronts like the ice cream shop Mr. Red talked about and all the clothes stores and then to this street that went across the 101 back toward the campsites. She went in the entrance, which surprised me, and after waiting a little I went in, too.

When I got through the gate there was no sign of her. I'd waited too long and messed it all up. 'Cause what if I never saw her again?

I remembered how Maria taught me about fate and how there's somebody out there for everybody, even people who seem like they're always alone. But what if you wait too long to go in the campsite entrance?

Could somebody ruin their fate?

All of a sudden she jumped out from behind the big tree in front of me and yelled: "Boo!"

I jumped two feet and spun around, and she bent over laughing, holding her hand over her mouth.

She looked up at me and said: "Oh, my God! You totally should've seen your face."

Then she turned and ran away, still laughing, and I just stood there watching as she got farther and farther away from me and then ducked around a corner near Mr. Red's campsite, out of sight.

I tried to think what just happened.

Her eyes big and green.

Her face white and perfectly smooth.

I hadn't lost my fate, I thought. It was just hiding behind a tree.

I backed up a few steps and sat on the bench near Campsite Coffee and thought how my stomach ached, but I didn't want the ache to go away. I thought how weekends really are the best part of your week, like Mr. Red said, 'cause when you get a break from working you can explore new places and walk along the train tracks and almost meet a girl.

I imagined talking to her next time. I had to sound smart. And normal. I had to make her think I was a regular kid.

I breathed in the salty ocean air, feeling so excited in my stomach and feeling instantly older.

Dreams from Solitary Confinement

I'm asleep and dreaming right now, but it's the kind of dreaming where you know it's dreaming, and since you want it to keep going you refuse to open your eyes and just lay there and watch.

Like it's a movie in your head.

In this one I'm sucking in my breath and slipping through solitary bars and floating above the empty prison yard, over armed guards positioned in their towers, up into the night-time clouds.

I'm looking down on scattered freeway cars whose headlights shine beams of light into the pitch black. Over sleeping houses and empty store lots and lonely train tracks. All the way to the campsites, where everybody who saw me push Devon off the cliff is tucked safely inside their tents, sleeping.

In my dream I slowly lower onto a beach towel spread for me on the sand.

And there's Olivia.

Waiting.

She's looking at me with sadness in her eyes, her hair and ski cap hiding the left side of her face like always and her faded sweatshirt covering her wrists. Green eyes clear like glass and cutting into my chest.

I open my mouth to tell her I'm so sorry, and how I never knew if she liked Devon, too. But dreams are wordless in solitary confinement. At least mine are.

'Cause nothing comes out, not even a sound. I'm mute.

Olivia continues talking, and I realize she's been explaining something this whole time, even before I landed from the sky.

I look all around to see who she's talking to.

There's nobody.

She's talking about the people from Horizons coming and how they told her everything about my psychology and what happened with my parents. At first, she says, she didn't believe them; she even *blamed* them. But now she's not so sure. The only thing she's sure about is that she's made a vow to stay here with me until I get out, as long as it takes, even if she misses going to New York and the big appointment her dad made.

And she's stubborn, she says.

I look out toward the buzzing ocean, too dark to see, and I think how it must be midnight in my dream.

What's Olivia doing on the beach this late? Without anyone to protect her from drunk college guys or whoever else. I hear a low horn sound, like maybe there's a ship somewhere out there in all that dark.

And right then it hits me—the worst possible thing about being in prison:

I can't protect Olivia.

She takes a drink from her water bottle and clears her throat. There's something she's decided to tell me about, she says. Something important. Something she's never discussed with anybody.

But tonight she's going to explain it.

To me.

I look in her eyes and watch her mouth move.

Sometimes we have to be patient, Kidd. There are things people will want from us that we won't be ready to give. Like with showing people my face.

She smoothes her ski-cap flap and says: *But what I wanna tell you about tonight is what happened with me and the piano.*

In my dream I open my mouth to tell her how great she is. How the song she played me at the music store is my favorite one in the world. But no words come out. So I just keep looking in her eyes and breathe.

You remember what I told you about surfing, right? So what if you didn't stand up those first few times Red took you. Surfing's not some stupid race. I told you maybe you'd stand up the next time. Or the time after that. And you did, remember? You stood up that Sunday morning Red pushed you, and I even got to be on the beach to cheer you on.

She puts her hand on my knee.

My point is, you stood up eventually. At your own pace. And you'll stand up again.

I lower my eyes to the sand.

In real life I never stood up.

We both look to the water. A tiny moon piece glowing quietly behind thick fog and invisible waves moaning before us and a dot of a ship way out to sea. The midnight cold kept away by us sitting so close on Olivia's towel, our sweatshirt shoulders almost touching and her hand on my knee.

She rubs her eyes with balled fists and clears her throat, begins explaining about the piano. She was a little girl when she started, five or six, and she was a natural. At first she was on her dad's old Casio keyboard, but when he saw how quickly she took to it he went out and bought her a baby grand and hired a renowned private instructor named Hans, who'd once performed with the New York Philharmonic.

He would come to our house twice a week, she says, staring down at her flip-flop feet. *Wednesdays and Saturdays. I picked up everything incredibly fast that first year, and Hans would praise me and tell me I was one of the most gifted students he'd ever taught. Dad would stand there with his arms crossed, beaming with pride.*

Before bed my parents would sometimes ask me to play whichever piece I'd just learned, and they'd clap when I finished, and I'd bow. I felt so important as they led me to my room and tucked me in. The sound I'd made was so beautiful that the mark on my face disappeared. I wondered what my older sister thought as she sat all alone on the other side of the wall. An ordinary girl doing ordinary homework. No applause.

I'd lie in bed dreaming of performing onstage in New York. My parents sitting center orchestra. The standing ovation I'd receive. People turning to my dad as everybody filed out of the packed amphitheater, saying: You must be so proud. So talented and beautiful. My parents smiling and nodding and thanking them all for coming.

But after that first year a weird thing happened. I stopped improving so quickly. I was trying just as hard, practicing just as many hours, but Hans wasn't praising me as much. My dad no longer beamed as intensely. I was only seven years old, Kidd, and I was washed-up.

But here's what I've figured out. Back then, that was all I played for. Praise. And as soon as I started getting a lower dose, I stopped dedicating myself to the practice.

The following year it got worse. I started dreading the hours I was expected to sit on that rigid bench, fingers on those icy keys. I dreaded Hans standing over me with his arms crossed, shaking his head whenever I hit a wrong note. At night I'd lie in bed fantasizing about all the ways I could quit. I started intentionally making mistakes. When Hans asked me to perform a basic run, something I'd mastered long before, I'd strike a series of wrong keys and act oblivious to the hideous sounds I was making.

Olivia picks at the corner of the towel.

She looks at me.

It went on like that for over a year. Until Hans moved back to Long Island to care for his sick mother. When my dad brought up finding a new instructor I cried and begged him to let me stop. I'll never forget the look on his face that night. It was beyond disappointment. It was repulsion. Dad was humiliated to have a little quitter for a daughter.

But then the strangest thing happened. When I didn't have a lesson hanging over my head I found myself drawn to the piano again. My parents would go to a friend's for dinner and I'd sneak over to the baby grand and run my fingers along the keys. And I'd play. Whatever I felt like playing. Mostly I'd just make stuff up, silly little songs like the one I played for you at the store. But I also started learning again. I'd pull out my old lesson books and work through them one page at a time.

In my dream Olivia takes my hands and puts them in hers and rubs warmth into me.

The difference is I no longer played for an instructor's praise, or for my parents' approval. I played for me. Do you understand what I'm getting at, Kidd?

I nod but she's looking at the sand.

I'm gonna be honest with you, she says. *I still can't comprehend why you would do something like this. I honestly can't. But I know as soon as you come out you'll explain it all to me. And I promise, Kidd. I'll be here.*

Waiting.

In my dream I wanna tell her how confused and worried I am. About everything. I don't know if I should have pushed Devon. And if Devon actually died. And I don't know how long I have to be in prison. Or if I *ever* deserve to be free.

Go home, I wanna tell Olivia.

Please.

Go to New York for your appointment.

You're too smart and talented and beautiful to wait for someone like me.

I don't deserve to be sitting next to you, Olivia. Not even in a dream.

And right as I'm thinking all this, a strong wind comes and starts pulling me away.

Olivia's face gets worried.

She reaches out her hand for my hand.

But it's too late. I'm already sucked back into the clouds; I'm flying back over the train tracks and the dark park and the scattered freeway cars.

And now I'm squeezing back between my prison bars and laying on my cot, my head settling on the pillow and the straps instantly wrapping back around my arms and legs and forehead.

When I open my eyes, having left my dream, I'm all tied down in the dark and totally alone and it feels like dying.

The second time I saw Olivia was on the campsite steps. It was a few hours after Mr. Red tried to teach me to surf, and I couldn't stand on my board. I went to his secret place where he checks out waves, thinking I could write in my philosophy of life book about how hard it is to learn surfing, and how I hated making Mr. Red frustrated.

But I kept thinking about other things instead. Like fate and girls that could make your breathing change, and was it some group of people in the olden days that decided what pretty looks like, or were we all just born knowing?

Mostly, though, I was thinking about the girl I'd seen on the swings.

Again.

Since the day she tried to scare me, she was all I'd thought about: during work and when I fell asleep at night in my tent and first thing in the morning and when I brushed my teeth in the drinking fountain outside the bathrooms and while I read magazines in Campsite Coffee and while I sat on the railroad tie next to Peanut, waiting for Mr. Red to come out of his tent so we could work.

But for some reason I couldn't write about her.

Every single thing I put wasn't what I meant, so I had to keep ripping out pages and starting over.

I was just about to rip out my fifth straight page when out of the corner of my eye I spotted the real-life version of her coming up the beach stairs with two friends. She stopped and held a camera up to the sunset and took a picture.

My eyes felt like they were popping out.

I couldn't move.

She was wearing ripped jeans and the same sweatshirt and red ski cap with the earflaps covering part of her face. The two other girls had cameras, too, and after a few seconds I realized they were two of the girls who ate cereal in the campsite near Mr. Red's.

The girl in the ski cap walked a few steps lower with her camera and looked out at the ocean for a while, then she brought her camera up and took another picture and lowered it again and just stared.

I looked at what she was looking at, thinking if that connected us. She was seeing this same sun falling into this same reflecting ocean. These same puffy clouds trapping these same colors and making them seem darker and less real. These same seagulls gliding through this same sky, barely flapping their wings and turning together in a V shape just over the water's surface.

I thought how if two people see the exact same thing, at the exact same time, their minds probably store the same memory, even way into the future, and that's something in common.

"Aha!" a voice said from behind my back. "I knew it!"

I spun around. "Mr. Red."

"Oh, man," he said with a big smile. "Looks like we got ourselves a little hand-in-the-cookie-jar moment, eh, Kidd?"

"What do you mean, sir?"

My heart was beating fast.

"I mean this." He pointed at me and my philosophy of life book and then at the girls on the stairs. "You. Up here. Staring at the ladies."

I looked down at the girls and then looked back at Mr. Red. "I was watching them take pictures–"

"Go 'head, big guy," he said, waving me off. "Spin it like a politician."

"What?"

"Look, your secret's safe with me."

I stayed staring at him.

"I got a pair of binoculars in the tent, big guy. If you wanna get your money's worth."

He laughed.

Me and Mr. Red Have a Talk

I turned back to the staircase. The ski-cap girl was now watching her friends. One of them had climbed onto the handrail and the other was holding her steady by her waist and they were both giggling as the girl on the rail slowly brought up her camera and tilted it sideways and aimed it at the sinking red sun.

She took a picture and jumped back down.

"Which one is it?"

I looked at Mr. Red. "Which one's what?"

"Don't play coy," he said. "Last I checked it was okay for a young guy like yourself to dig on a female. Which one do you like?"

I looked back at the girls. "I saw the one with the red cap last weekend."

"Yeah?" he said.

I nodded.

"You talk to her?"

"Not really."

"Not really," he said. "Now, what's that supposed to mean?"

"I followed her into the campsites. But then I didn't see her anymore until she jumped out from behind a tree and tried to scare me."

"That's good, big guy!"

"It is?" I said. I looked back at the girl, wondering how many people she'd tried to scare.

Or if I was the only one.

Mr. Red slapped me on the back, said: "I'd go get us a bottle of champagne to celebrate except I don't drink anymore."

"Why's it good?"

"She was flirting with you, Kidd."

I made my face into a frown like he was crazy.

Inside, though, my stomach had butterflies.

Mr. Red took off his beat-up sombrero and held it by his side and looked at the girls. "Name's Olivia, by the way. Her and her friends' parents have been renting that same campsite every summer for the past five years."

"You know her?" I said.

"I know everybody here. It's part of the job. Fix things and be friendly."

"Olivia," I said to myself.

Mr. Red smiled. "Guess you guys didn't get to that part."

Right then his phone started playing a Bob Marley song. He put his sombrero back on his head and pulled his phone from his pocket and looked at it with a confused face.

He muted it and put it back in his pocket and said: "Look, Kidd, about surfing this morning. I apologize for getting so frustrated. That had nothing to do with you."

I felt bad for letting Mr. Red down. All he wanted was for me to stand up. Once.

And I couldn't do it.

"Been a long time since I taught somebody how to surf," he said.

I looked at Mr. Red.

"Didn't teach it right that time, either." He looked at the ground and shook his head.

"I had fun, sir."

"You did?"

I nodded. "Thanks for taking me."

He sort of smiled halfway and looked back at the ocean. "How about we try it again sometime. I promise I'll be more patient."

"Okay," I said. "And I promise I'll do better."

He smiled and pulled off his sombrero, ran his fingers through his wavy blond hair, then put his sombrero back on.

"Hey, Kidd," he said. "Can I ask you something?"

I nodded.

It was the first time I'd seen Mr. Red look serious.

"You think they'll come looking for you? The folks from Horizons?"

I pictured the counselors and therapists and the board of directors. For a second I got a bad feeling, like I should be hiding. But then I thought about when a kid named Jonathan left. They didn't find him for over a year. And that was only 'cause he got real sick and went to the emergency room and when his name came up there was something about him being gone from Horizons.

"I hope not," I told Mr. Red.

"Me too," he said. "I like having you here, big guy. I've never had a partner who works so hard."

"Thanks, Mr. Red."

We were quiet for a minute and then without looking at me he said: "You miss your friends back there?"

"I never really thought about it."

"No?" Mr. Red went closer to the fence and looked at the girls, who were now sitting on one of the steps, talking. They couldn't see us, 'cause of the overhanging bush.

"I think it's important for people to have friends," Mr. Red told me. "At least one or two you can BS around with. I can introduce you to some of the surf knuckleheads that hang around the campsites. Or what about Olivia? Girls count, too."

My stomach felt nervous with him just mentioning Olivia. "Hey, Mr. Red," I said.

"Hey, Mr. Kidd."

"Did something happen to her?"

"You mean the ski cap?"

"Yeah."

He looked toward the girls again and then looked at me and crossed his arms. "She didn't used to wear it." He paused. "Girls are complicated, big guy. They can get hung up on stuff."

His phone started playing that Bob Marley song in his pocket again and he pulled it out and looked at the number and this time he flipped it open and said hello.

A surprised look went on his face and he said: "Jacky Newman? That you, girl? I haven't heard that sexy accent since Cabo. Where you been hiding?"

He stood there, listening and nodding his head.

"Of course," he said. "Yeah, yeah, let's do it. Why don't you swing by here around eight or so. I'm just off the 101— Listen, hang on a sec."

Mr. Red turned to me, cupping the phone, said: "Gotta grab this, big guy. Tall brunette I met at a bar in Mexico last summer. She's in town all the way from Charleston, South Carolina."

I nodded, trying to think how far South Carolina was from Cardiff. I'd never even been past downtown San Diego.

"I'll let you get back to stalking, big guy. See you Monday morning?"

He pulled his hand from the receiver and said: "Jacky! Damn, girl, how are you? I can still picture you up on that bar at Frederico's, doing a Jäger shot off the plastic swordfish. Ha-ha. Of course I remember. . . ."

His voice trailed off after he ducked under the bushes, out of sight.

I turned back to the stairs and the girls.

I watched them for a while, wondering why Mr. Red would say that thing about me having friends. I always tried to act happy around him. And excited to work. Which was true.

But maybe he could tell how I also felt by myself sometimes.

Actually, a lot of times.

I opened up my philosophy of life book and read what I'd just written about the ski-cap girl, Olivia, and I couldn't believe how wrong it was. I was about to rip out my page when I heard a second voice from behind my back:

"Ha! I knew it!"

I spun around thinking it was Mr. Red again, but when I saw who it was my heart stopped.

I couldn't believe my eyes.

Devon.

Seeing a Ghost

He pointed at me and laughed, said: "Dude, Special, check you out, man. You're totally spying on those chicks."

He looked the exact same.

"What a perv," he said.

I closed my book and made myself start breathing again. "I'm not a perv," I told him.

"Oh, you're not?"

"I'm just watching what they're doing."

He laughed again and shook his head, and I just stared at him for a couple seconds. It was so weird to have Devon standing right in front of me.

I hadn't seen him in almost two years, since the day I told him exactly what my therapist at Horizons *told* me to tell him. How we couldn't be friends anymore. And it wasn't personal. It was just part of us getting older and growing in different directions and becoming our own people.

"Dude," Devon said. "What do you think a perv does?"

He snatched my book and flipped it open, and when I tried to take it back he pushed my hand away. "Check this out, you're describing every single thing about the one in the ski cap."

I took back my book and closed it, held it behind my back. "Where'd you even come from?"

"Same place as you," he shot back. "My mom's uterus."

"I mean today," I said. "How'd you find me?"

"Don't worry about it, Special. You know I got detective-type skills. The real question is, when did you turn into such a perv?"

"I'm not—"

"Last I remember, you didn't even like girls. You thought they had cooties."

"I never said they had cooties."

Devon could make me more frustrated than any person I'd ever met.

He walked past me and looked at the girls on the stairs. "The other two are way hotter," he said. "If you like boring-ass blondes."

I looked, too.

"Why you writing about the one in the ski cap?"

"Maybe I wanted to."

Devon turned back to me shaking his head. "Dude, you're like the exact same, aren't you? Pretending to be all naïve and dopey so nobody expects anything from you."

"That's not true—"

"It's such an act, Special. Please tell me you at least realize it's an act."

I didn't say anything.

"You've been playing this stupid game since I met you. Remember, Special? That day you couldn't even read a letter from your own mom? Thank God your boy Devon was there to save the day."

I glared at him.

He knew I hated anybody talking about my mom.

I turned to look at the girls, thinking more about Devon's

reaction when I told him we couldn't be friends anymore. I figured he'd yell and call me a traitor and maybe even try to hit me or something.

But he didn't.

He just smiled and said I was making a huge mistake and how as soon as he walked away I'd be totally alone, and he turned out to be right.

I turned and watched Devon watch the girls.

Here's the thing about him. Even though he constantly smiles and talks loud and everybody thinks he's so much fun to be around, really he suffers from depression. Like the time he swallowed an entire bottle of pills and they had to charcoal his stomach. Or before that, when the Horizons people found him on top of the school building across the street and he threatened to jump. Or this time with him hitting his head in the shower, over and over, until the entire tub was bloody and the counselors had to hold him down on the tile.

Devon turned back to me, said: "Actually, Special. I take it back."

"What?"

"She's not that bad. The girl you wrote about."

I instantly got a bad feeling in my stomach.

"For a rich chick." He was staring at Olivia. "But what's up with that ski cap? It's summer, man. What's she hiding under those flaps?"

I looked at her, too. "She probably just likes the hat."

"I bet her face is beat the hell up or something. Good from afar but far from good, know what I mean?"

I stared at the side of Devon's face for the longest time, then I told him: "How'd you find me anyway?"

He shrugged. "I heard you ran away from Horizons."

"From who?"

"You weren't even done with your stupid therapy, were you?"

"Almost."

"I wonder what they'll do if they catch you," he said. Then he grinned and shoved his hands in his pockets.

"Where you staying?" I asked him.

"I got my lodging covered," he said. "Quit worrying about me, money. What you should be worrying about is the people from Horizons showing up at your tent. Or if that surfer burnout guy you hang with secretly wants to molest you."

"Mr. Red?"

"Yeah, man. That's one bitter dude. Who knows how that shit's gonna play out."

"He's not bitter."

"Are you kidding? The guy obviously couldn't handle the pressures of being a pro surfer and quit. And then he felt like such a loser he turned to drugs and alcohol and became the burnout he is. I bet he took a job here to try and relive the glory days, which probably weren't even that glorious."

"Mr. Red's not like that," I said.

"And all those chicks I heard about, man. You gotta wonder. What's he trying to prove to himself about his sexuality?"

"You don't even know him."

"You're right," Devon said.

"Exactly."

"But I watch people, Special. I observe."

I felt myself getting irritated and confused, exactly how I

always get when I'm around Devon. He tries to spin things around so I can't think.

"You get what I'm saying, don't you, Special?"

"No."

"Yes, you do."

"No, I don't."

He laughed and looked at the girls again.

How I Got the Name Devon Calls Me in the First Place

We were sitting at the kitchen table together, eating cereal, him reading the back of the box and me the front. I was brand-new to Horizons and he'd already been there for years. He lifted his head and set down his spoon with a look like he'd just thought of something smart.

He told me how the cereal we were eating, Special K, was probably invented especially for me because ever since what happened with my mom I was mostly in remedial classes at school, which was only one step away from special ed, and if you took the first half of special ed and added my first initial it would say Special K, just like the cereal.

He laughed and laughed and said how that should be my nickname, and then he went back to eating his cereal and reading the back of the box.

I still remember that day I promised myself I'd never become friends with Devon, but for some reason I did anyways.

He's called me Special ever since.

I was just about to tell Devon how wrong he was about Mr. Red, when he looked over my shoulder and said: "By the way, you're going about this girl situation all wrong."

"What?" I said.

"You don't just sit up here like a weirdo, writing about the girl, you introduce yourself. You say hello. Like this."

He pushed past me and went to the edge of the fence and megaphoned a hand around his mouth and shouted: "Hey! Yo!"

All three girls looked up at us.

"Get any good shots or what?"

"Maybe," one of the girls said back. "What's it to you?"

Devon smiled, said: "I was just thinking how you should probably take one more."

The girls looked at each other and then the same girl said: "Dude, who *are* you?"

"I'm saying. You should probably get a quick shot of a brown boy like me so you have some variety." Devon ran his fingers through his hair all dramatically and then jumped up on the waist-high fence and balanced himself in a squatting position and slowly spread both his arms out wide and smiled.

The other two girls looked at each other like Devon was a freak, but Olivia actually stepped forward, smiling, and snapped a few pictures.

Soon as she lowered her camera Devon acted like he was losing his balance, and after waving his arms around for a couple seconds he fell backwards accidentally-on-purpose and hung onto the fence and slowly lowered himself onto the dirt, back first.

The girls all laughed and Olivia called out: "I should've got a shot of *that*."

"It's all good over here," Devon shouted, giving them two thumbs-ups. "Everybody's okay. Nothing to see."

The girls laughed a little more.

He brushed the dirt off his butt and shouted: "All I ask is those pictures don't show up on the Internet!"

"How much you gonna pay us?" one of Olivia's friends shouted.

Devon pretended to get serious and said: "That's blackmail!"

"More like a business opportunity!"

Everybody smiled, including Devon, and then he waved them off and walked back over to me and said: "See that, Special? Simple little interaction goes a long way with chicks. Especially rich, sheltered ones. Then you walk away. Next time they'll know who we are, and *they'll* be first to say hi. Trust me, rich girls love a challenge because they've been handed everything their entire lives."

"I don't know," I said.

"You also don't come off like some perverted freak mute."

"I'm not a mute."

"*I* know that," Devon said. "But they don't."

I looked at the ground.

He brushed his butt off some more and then tweaked his body so he could see the back of his own legs. "Anyways, I gotta go," he said. "What are you doing tomorrow?"

"Working."

"Ooh, fun. What are you doing after?"

I shrugged.

"Good, I'll meet you out front of that stupid coffee shop they have here. I wanna swipe some new clothes from a few of the surf shops I saw on the way over. And I need my partner to watch the door for me."

I stared back at him, remembering what my therapist always said about the company people keep and how sometimes the only difference between a good citizen and a criminal is who a person chooses to surround himself with.

Then I thought about what Mr. Red said about having a buddy to hang around with.

I looked at the girls who were now walking up the steps together.

"Come on, Special," he said. "Be my road dog again. I miss you, man."

I knew it would end up bad.

Still.

I told him: "I guess so."

He play-punched me in the arm and smiled big. "It's good to see you, dude. It's been, what, like a year and a half?"

I shrugged.

"You know, just because somebody's little business card says *Therapist* doesn't mean you have to take every single thing they say as the gospel. Those people are human beings, too, right?"

"I guess so."

"And humans make mistakes, right?"

"Maybe."

"Well?" he said, holding his hands out and shrugging like he just made an incredible point.

Then he spun around and ducked under the overhanging bush like Mr. Red and was gone.

I waited three hours after work, but Devon never showed up. He didn't show up the next day either. Or the day after that. I didn't see him again for over two weeks, when he unzipped my tent door one night and stood in front of me out of breath, saying how sorry he was for ditching me and how he had a perfectly good excuse but wouldn't bore me with the details.

After he was done apologizing he asked if I talked to those rich girls since he last saw me. I told him not really.

"What do you mean 'not really'?"

"I saw them a few times."

"And?"

"We waved."

"That's it?"

I nodded.

"Dude, this isn't 1845. You don't have to ask for parental permission just to talk to a damn girl. Jesus."

I decided not to tell Devon about the other stuff that had happened since I saw him. How I'd started sleepwalking again. How I'd wake up in the middle of the night on the beach. Or in the campus bathroom, on the cement floor. Or near the railroad tracks. Or in the park.

That morning I'd actually woken up on the roof of Campsite Coffee, feet dangling off the side and a banana peel in my hand.

I didn't tell Devon about my sleepwalking 'cause I knew he'd remember how I used to do it at Horizons. And he'd say how those therapists obviously didn't do such a great job fixing me after all.

"Is it really that hard to say hi, Special?" He shook his head. "Maybe a comment about the weather?"

I shrugged.

"You didn't even talk to the one with the head injury?"

"She's not injured."

He waved me off and told me to hurry and get ready 'cause we had a bunch of stores to hit before they closed at seven.

I stood up and looked at him, and this weird feeling came over me: I didn't really know Devon anymore.

"Special," he said.

"Yeah?"

"Why you looking at me like that?"

"I'm not."

"You are."

I shook my head.

My stomach felt off balance.

He took a deep breath and blew it out slow, said: "Trust me, Special. We know each other just as good as we ever did. It's all psychological."

My eyes went wide 'cause he totally read my face.

Mr. Red always talks about that, how people's faces tell more about what they're thinking than their words. I never really thought about it before, but maybe he was right.

"Dude, come on," Devon said. "We don't exactly have time to break down our entire friendship right now."

He picked up my duffel bag, unzipped it and dumped everything out, then he went out of my tent door and I followed him.

• • •

How It Went with the Surf Shops

Next thing I knew we were stealing clothes from a bunch of stores along the 101, right across the street from Cardiff Reef Beach.

More like *Devon* was stealing.

I was just watching the door to make sure nobody came in, like a cop or security guard, and if they did I was supposed to start whistling "Mary Had a Little Lamb," but I never had to whistle 'cause nobody like that ever showed up. Mostly I just looked between the highway and the parking lot and Devon in the store as he sifted through the different racks of clothes.

Devon's shoplifting theory was this: as long as you act like you know what you're doing people will leave you alone. He says the worst thing a thief can do is think of himself as a thief. You'll automatically feel nervous and people will pick up on it and they'll start watching you to find out why.

"You know what's my secret weapon with shoplifting?" Devon said as we were walking toward our second store.

"What?" I said.

"Smiling. Who would suspect me of stealing if I look like I just hugged my damn mom?"

And that was exactly how Devon looked all through our first three stores. He'd hold up a pair of shorts, smiling and singing with whatever song the store was playing. Or he'd talk to the workers about how their summer was going. Or he'd laugh with them about all the tourists who must come in with cameras strapped around their necks, especially foreigners. After a while he'd say the shorts weren't exactly what he was looking for, but instead of putting them back up on the rack he'd slip them into the half-open duffel bag on the sly and move to the next rack.

Whenever he was done "shopping" he'd tell the worker how there was nothing worse than leaving a store empty-handed, and he'd laugh at whatever they said back, even if it wasn't a joke, and tell them he'd probably be back in as soon as they got a new shipment. Then as he was going past the alarm he'd wave at the person with his duffel-bag hand, which would raise the bag just over the sensors, and he'd walk out all calm and motion with his head for me to follow and I would.

We'd wander behind all the stores toward the lagoon, where there was nothing but bushes and birds and bad-smelling stagnant water that had collected from the ocean on the other side of the highway. We'd head for this one small bush that had purple flowers, where Devon was stashing all the stuff he stole. He'd open the duffel and pull out his new items and admire them for a minute and then add them to his stack, telling me to quit acting all offended when he and I both knew deep down I had as much thief in me as he did, maybe more.

On our way to the next surf shop I'd explain to him all the reasons why that wasn't true, and he'd just roll his eyes and tell me: "Why are you here, then?"

"What do you mean?" I'd say back.

"You didn't *have to* come, right? But you did."

I wouldn't know what to say back, since I was so tired from sleepwalking, so I'd just keep following.

Everything went that same way, Devon smiling while he stole and me watching the door, until we got to the fifth store and then it changed.

First of all, the worker wasn't some young beach girl like at the rest of the stores. She was a tall parent-aged lady who had slumped shoulders and a permanent scowl on her face (I wonder what Mr. Red would say *that* kind of face was saying). From the second Devon stepped in the store she never took her eyes off him.

I started getting nervous.

At one point I even whistled the start of "Mary Had a Little Lamb," but when Devon looked up at me and I motioned toward the worker lady he just rolled his eyes, then went back to sifting through a rack of jeans.

I turned back to the parking lot, thinking about Devon's psychological disorder, the one my Horizons therapist explained during one of my appointments with her. She said Devon had a strong death drive, which made him do risky, self-destructive things because, unconsciously, he thought ending his life was the only way to restore order in his idea of the world.

The second she explained that, I knew it was right.

How I Know Devon Has a Death Drive

Devon says his first childhood memory is him in a group home with some counselor standing over him explaining how to mop the bathroom tile. He knows he was born to a mom and dad, like any other kid, but he doesn't remember them. He said he knows it's a defense mechanism, but he doesn't care. He doesn't need anybody.

Also, Devon once told me he hardly even considers himself a real person 'cause if he disappeared one day nobody would call an AMBER Alert or even wonder where he was.

Maybe a counselor would eventually have to do some paperwork but that's it. According to Devon the definition of being a real person is if somebody would notice when you're gone, like that saying about a tree falling in the forest.

Devon claims one day he'll be the falling tree.

And since nobody will be there to hear it, his life won't really have made a sound.

Sometimes he tries to say it's the same with me, and that's why we understand each other, and why we're friends, but he's wrong about that.

First off, I had a real mom and dad. For over half my life. And even though my dad sometimes hit me and my mom, I still remember good things like him teaching me how to throw and how to fix the leaking pipe in the kitchen. And my mom took me everywhere she went and always said she'd do anything for me.

Actually, the only person I know who's like Devon is my dad. According to my Horizons therapist he had a death drive, too, and that's why he did drugs and committed domestic abuse and lived with all those different women.

My therapist says I was most likely drawn to Devon because his behavior felt familiar.

I even tried to explain that one time to Devon, but he covered his ears and acted like he was singing "The Star-Spangled Banner."

As I stood just outside the store, watching an old man open his car door, I thought how maybe Devon was right about me secretly wanting to steal. Maybe everybody did. Even A-plus students. Maybe we want to do even worse things, like smack somebody in the back of the head just to see what happens, or jab a tree branch through a store window to see the glass shatter, or throw a rock off a bridge to see which car gets hit on the freeway and if it causes an accident.

Regular people may think these things, too.

But Devon actually *does* them.

He's missing that part of your brain that worries about getting caught or hurting another human being.

I looked in the store again and it was a perfect example. You could tell by Devon's face he was actually *happy* the store woman was following him around the aisles. He held up a pair of dark jeans, and put them up to his body and looked in the mirror. Then he turned around and looked right at the saleswoman and said: "Excuse me, ma'am, may I try these on?"

He scooped up the pile of clothes he'd picked out and stayed staring right in her eyes, smiling.

She scowled back and took the jeans and the rest of the clothes in his arms and counted them and said in an irritated voice: "I'm sorry, sir, but you can only try on five items at a time. You have eight."

Devon picked five from the pile and looked up smiling and said: "How about just these then, ma'am? Are these okay?"

The woman rolled her eyes and led Devon to the dressing room and opened the door and held it for him and said there was a five-minute limit in the room and to please leave his duffel bag outside.

Devon bowed and set down the duffel and then as he went into the little room he looked at me and winked. I turned around fast and stared at the street so the saleswoman wouldn't think I was with Devon.

After a minute or so I turned back around. The lady stood there for a while, checking her watch every ten seconds.

Another customer walked in, a woman in a fancy tracksuit who had two little boys with her, and the saleslady looked at Devon's door again, and at her watch, and then she went up front to where one of the boys was looking at stickers through a glass case. She told him to please not put his face against the glass, and the boy's mom pulled her son's arm away from the case and told him not to touch anything. Then she tried on a pair of sunglasses and looked at herself in the circular mirror and pulled them off and held them to the side while she looked for another pair.

I kept staring at the dressing room door, waiting for Devon to come out, but it stayed closed for the longest time.

I was just about to go back to the lagoon by myself, to wait, when I heard somebody say: "Psssst."

I spun around.

Devon.

He was outside, squatting under the store window and laughing without sound. The five clothing items stacked in his lap.

I looked in the store again and the saleslady was knocking on his dressing room door, my duffel bag still sitting there.

I turned back to Devon, whispered: "How'd you get out?"

"I got my ways, Special."

He motioned with his head for me to follow him and I did, and as we were fast-walking away the store woman came rushing out of the back door and shouted: "Hey! Come back here! You didn't pay for that!"

Me and Devon took off sprinting across the parking lot, weaving through cars and ducking behind a restaurant called Kai's. We looked at each other, both of us breathing hard, and he held up a finger and ducked his head around the restaurant to look at the store and he said: "She's gone."

"Probably to call the police," I said.

"Probably," Devon said, and a big smile went on his face.

"What are we gonna do?"

He looked around the restaurant again and then told me to follow him and we sprinted back through the parking lot and down into the lagoon. When we got to our bush we were still breathing hard and Devon was laughing.

"Dude, Special," he said between breaths. "That's my favorite. When some lady acts like she's gonna chase me down in flip-flops."

"What if we got caught, though?" I said.

"We didn't."

"I know. But we could've."

"But we didn't."

I took a deep breath and said: "Why don't you care?"

He shrugged. "Dude, we just won't go back to that store. It's no big deal. Considering there are about ten on this block just like it."

"I know, but . . ."

I tried to think what I could say that would make him realize it wasn't just that, it was everything, but my mind was working too slow.

"Besides," Devon said, sliding his stack of clothes out and adding the ones he'd just taken. "Look at all this gear. You can't tell me we didn't need new clothes."

I looked at Devon, surprised he said "we" and not just him.

He smiled and said: "You're my boy again, aren't you?"

I told him yeah.

He looked back at the clothes. "Here, we have"—he counted through the stack—"fifteen things. We'll just take turns picking. You go first."

"Me?"

"You need new stuff more than I do, Special. That crap you're wearing is straight welfare."

I looked at my clothes and then looked back at Devon.

"What'd you think, I was just stealing for myself?"

I shrugged, said: "I didn't think anything."

"Well, go on, dude. Pick something."

I looked at the stack, remembering what Mr. Red said about giving my jeans a rest. I took a new pair.

"There you go, Special," he said. "That's the spirit."

We took turns picking through the rest of the clothes and then Devon walked me back to my tent, talking about the rush of taking things and not paying a dime, especially when you had money in your pocket like he did.

He pulled his wallet and opened it and showed me all the twenties and put it back.

"Where'd you get that?" I said.

"Come on, dude. I'm a businessman."

"You don't even have a job."

"Jobs are for punks."

Then he went on and on about how the rich kids in Cardiff all got stuff from their parents and since we didn't have parents we had to take stuff for ourselves.

"I'm not gonna sit here waiting for somebody to come along and make things fair," he told me, shaking his head. "Hell no. I'm gonna make fair happen for myself. Know what I mean?"

He talked about the rich and the poor for the rest of our walk back to the campsites. I didn't say anything else, just nodded occasionally and let him talk. And when we got up to my tent he said he had to go handle something and we slapped five.

"Find you in a few days, all right?"

"Okay," I said.

"Maybe we can go to the beach and check out the chicks." He lifted my chin and said: "Hey, Special."

"Yeah?"

He grinned, let go of my chin.

I fake-smiled back.

Devon pointed at the stack of new clothes in my arms, said: "Don't be wearing those with a bad conscious either. They're yours now."

"I know."

"Enjoy 'em."

I nodded.

"We didn't steal today, Special. We just made life a little more fair."

"Okay."

He turned and walked away.

Philosophy 3:
About How a Bad Thing
Can Turn Good

Dear Kidd:

You have to find out about a book by this guy who had a stroke and was paralyzed and wrote the whole thing by blinking with his only eye that worked. Olivia talked about it just now, during the first time you ever had a conversation with her, so it has extra meaning. Also, you have to figure out if something good can come from something bad 'cause she asked about that, and you couldn't think of how to answer 'cause you didn't want to say anything wrong.

Actually, being in this tent now, and writing . . . it could have something to do with Mom and that time in the hospital, after Dad hurt her in the living room. Remember?

Mom finally told the doctors she'd see you, and the nurse came and got you and you followed her into Mom's room and got so scared looking at her in that hospital bed, hooked up to all those tubes and hanging bags of liquid medicine. Her face black-and-blue and swollen, almost like she wasn't really your mom, but a car-wreck costume somebody made her wear. Your stomach felt instantly sick. Her head was all bandaged on one side and a cast on her left arm, and when her eyes turned to you she tried to make a smile but it didn't even look right. It was crooked. And she said: "Oh, no. Honey, don't cry. Mommy's okay."

You wiped your eyes and looked at the floor and she said: "Mommy's still here, isn't she?"

You nodded and stared through blurry eyes at the lines between the black-and-white tiles.

"Honey, I want you to look at me." You looked at her. "Sometimes things happen that we don't necessarily want to have happen. Obviously I didn't choose to end up in this hospital bed, right?"

You shook your head, wiping your face on your shirt.

"But I'm here. And now I have to make a choice. I can either lock myself in a room when I get home and sulk and say 'poor me,' or I can look myself in the mirror and accept what's happened and come up with some sort of plan that will prevent it from ever happening again."

She touched her head bandage and cringed a little and then looked at you and made herself smile again. "I've done a lot of thinking about this. And a few things have become very clear. I have to be a stronger person. And I have to do a better job of protecting you. I thought I understood this two days ago, but I didn't. And we paid for it. Both of us. But I'm going to tell you something very important, honey."

She lifted your chin and said: "I will never.

Ever. Let this happen again. Do you hear me, baby? Never."

You told her okay and looked at her bandages again, and right then the doctor walked in the room holding a clipboard and closed the door behind him. He smiled on his way to Mom's charts and told you: "Hey there, little buddy. You must be—"

"It's not my name anymore," you interrupted, so he couldn't say the name your dad gave you. 'Cause you were so mad.

He looked at Mom and then looked at you again, nodding, and said: "No problem, son. It's nice to finally meet you. . . ."

I was stacking and restacking all my new clothes when Mr. Red came by and stood at my open tent door and said: "Knock, knock."

I quickly hid my stolen pile from view and told him: "Hey, Mr. Red."

He nodded his head for me to come out so I got up and stepped through the door and stood there looking at him. It was the first time I'd ever seen Mr. Red wearing long pants and shoes that weren't flip-flops, and he wasn't wearing his beat-up sombrero.

He'd even combed his hair.

This time he was with a beautiful tall blond woman wearing a short black dress and high heels and a thin silver necklace with a cross at the end. Her smiling face was like a fashion magazine.

I felt bad about Maria.

"Claudia, I'd like to introduce my partner in campsite crime, Kidd Ellison. Kidd takes his steak rare and his potatoes mashed and his caramel lattes with extra whip. Kidd, Claudia."

"Hi there," Claudia said.

"Hi," I told her back.

Mr. Red looked past me, into my tent. "Good work, big guy. Finally got yourself some new duds."

"I bought 'em at this clothes place," I said. "I went yesterday and paid with my own money. What I made here."

"That's usually how it works, partner."

"I got new jeans like you said."

"These campsite girls won't have a prayer."

"I think he's cute in the clothes he has on," Claudia said. "You didn't tell me he was so handsome, Red."

I turned to her, embarrassed, and said: "Thank you, ma'am."

She winked at me and smiled and then she looked at Mr. Red, who was shaking his head. "Well, isn't this a touching little Hallmark moment," he said. "Look, Kidd, Claudia and I are about to do some serious fine dining. You ever heard of the Chart House?"

I shook my head.

"Four-star rating in Zagat's, and Cardiff doesn't have any fives."

Claudia rubbed his arm and said to me: "Isn't Red sweet? He's taking me to a real restaurant this time, like a grown-up. He's so proud of himself."

They both smiled and Mr. Red told me: "Anyway, I came by to tell you about this bonfire a group of guests are having on the beach tonight. Everybody's invited—"

He cut himself off and tilted my head to the side. "Hold up, Kidd. What the . . . ?" He pointed at my neck. "Is that a hickey?"

"What?" I said, moving my head out of his hand.

"Don't embarrass him," Claudia said.

"Big guy, you been doing work out here when I'm not looking?"

"No," I said.

Mr. Red stepped back and looked at Claudia and they both laughed a little, Claudia quickly covering her mouth. "It's none of your business, Red," she told him.

"It's not a hickey," I said.

Mr. Red looked at me for a while, smiling. "I know, I know," he said. "Curling iron got you, right?"

"What?"

"Nothing."

I was about to say something back, but he waved me off. "Look, Claud's right. It's none of my business. I just wanted to encourage you to check out that bonfire. Go represent Campsite Maintenance."

I looked toward the ocean, thinking about my neck and picturing thousands of people talking to each other around a fire.

Mr. Red clapped his hands together softly and said: "I've also received confirmation that a certain someone will be in attendance."

"Who?" I said.

"Who do you think?"

"Olivia?"

"In the flesh, big guy."

"Ooh, is that your girlfriend?" Claudia said.

"No, ma'am, I barely just met her."

"Look, Claud, Kidd likes to go at his own pace, okay? Quit putting so much romantic pressure on everybody."

Claudia smacked him on the shoulder with her handbag.

"Where on the beach?" I said.

"Follow the large orange flame," Mr. Red said, holding Claudia's wrists so she couldn't hit him a second time. They were both laughing. "Go check it out, buddy."

"Why aren't *we* going?" Claudia said, pulling her hands out of Mr. Red's grip.

"Because I'm hooking you up with the surf 'n' turf."

"It's not because you're embarrassed of me?"

"Claud, look at you. Look at this dress. You're the most beautiful woman in North County."

"Ah, that's sweet, Red." She turned to me. "Your boss can actually be sweet sometimes."

Mr. Red took Claudia's hand and said: "Check out the bonfire, Kidd. Could be nice."

I told him I would.

They waved and started walking toward Mr. Red's old Bronco. Claudia leaned her head on his shoulder. He opened her door and let her in and closed it behind her and then turned to me and said: "Hey, Kidd."

"Yeah?"

"Talk to her, okay?"

"Okay," I said.

"Just tell her hello. Introduce yourself."

"Okay."

He walked around to his side and opened his door, but before he got in he looked over the faded black hood and said: "And throw on some of those new duds."

"I will."

"I bet you'll look super *GQ*." He stood there a sec, looking at me, then he laughed a little and tapped his hood and said: "Check out the two of us, big guy. Getting dressed up to impress women."

"Yeah," I said.

"They're really something, aren't they?"

"Who?" I said.

"Women."

"Oh, yeah," I said. And I felt bad about Maria again.

He nodded his head awhile and then got in his Bronco and closed the door and drove off.

After Mr. Red and Claudia left I went back into my tent and changed into new clothes like Mr. Red told me, and looked at my neck in my mirror. There was a dark, circular rash-looking thing, and I didn't know where it came from or how long it had been there. It didn't hurt when I pressed it. I stared at the rash for a while, confused, wondering what made me have one. Maybe a certain bush rubbed against me. Maybe it happened when I was sleepwalking.

Then I just sat on my sleeping bag for the next two hours, watching the sun disappear outside my tent door and trying to talk myself into going to the beach.

Finally I made myself a deal. If I got up and went down the stairs I could just look at it for a while, and see Olivia, and then come right back up to my tent and go to bed and hopefully not sleepwalk into another poisonous bush.

The Bonfire

A big crackling flame coming out of a homemade pit and two older guys sitting on stools playing acoustic guitars and singing and everybody else in little groups eating off paper plates and drinking from red cups and talking and laughing, their chairs all facing toward the bonfire or each other or the ocean.

I sat leaning against the cliff, by the stairs, watching them, sometimes looking down at my clothes, my brand-new jeans and new collared shirt. It didn't even feel like me anymore. I watched the bonfire again, thinking how it'd be if you could actually turn into the person your clothes made you seem like. Then you could go over to whatever party was happening like you totally belonged and have as much fun as everyone else.

I remembered how when I was little my mom would sometimes do a barbecue in the alley behind our apartment complex and some of the neighbors would come down with plates of their own marinated meat and coolers of beer and lawn chairs. My mom would cook all their food on the grill, wearing her favorite checkered apron, and everybody'd be talking and laughing with each other, just like this, and I'd be right with them.

I was staring at the bonfire, thinking of those alley barbecues, and my mom, and what it felt like to be inside a party, when I noticed two girls walking toward me.

I looked over my shoulder.

There was nobody.

I watched them and whispered in my head: "Oh, no. Oh, no. Oh, no." Over and over. 'Cause I knew it was the two girls that were on the stairs taking pictures with Olivia, but I didn't know what they were gonna say. And when it came to girls I wasn't like Devon. It always felt awkward.

One of them was wearing a flowing brown dress and as she walked she sipped from her plastic cup. The other one was wearing jeans and a sweatshirt and she had a red cup in each hand and she was saying something to the dress girl.

Then they were in front of me.

"See, told you it was him," the sweatshirt girl said.

"You were right."

I stood up and leaned against the cliff and crossed my

arms, but it felt awkward like that so I uncrossed them and pushed off the cliff and stood regular.

"Hi, again," the sweatshirt girl said.

"Where's our money?" the dress one said.

"What?" I said, and then I smiled 'cause I figured out she was just saying a joke about Devon.

"We can still post those pictures, you know."

They both laughed and the sweatshirt girl held out a red cup and said: "Here, we brought you a present."

I took the cup and told them thanks and looked in it.

"You work with Red, right?"

"Yes, ma'am."

The girl in the sweatshirt flipped her long blond hair from one shoulder to the other and said: "We've seen you. I'm Jasmine, by the way, and this is Blue."

"Hi," I told them.

"And it sounds a little strange calling Jasmine 'ma'am,' don't you think? Considering she's not some old lady."

I nodded and leaned against the cliff again and then pushed off.

"I bet I'm actually younger than he is," Jasmine said. She looked at me. "How old are you?"

"Seventeen."

"Okay. Same age." She turned to Blue. "He looks older than seventeen."

"Right?"

"We thought you were, like, nineteen or twenty or whatever."

Blue took a sip from her cup and wiped her mouth with the back of her hand and said: "Anyways."

I looked in my cup again.

"It's fresh lemonade," Jasmine said. "Blue's mom made it."

They both looked at each other and giggled a little and Jasmine said: "Plus a little bit of vodka Blue just mixed in."

"You do drink, don't you?" Blue said.

"I guess so." I smelled in my cup.

"You guess so? What's that supposed to mean?"

"I mean, yes, ma'am," I said. "I mean, I do drink. Yes."

I'd never drank before.

Jasmine turned to Blue and said: "He's, like, uberpolite."

"Right?"

"Anyways," Jasmine said. "Take a sip and tell us if it's the perfect blend or not."

I did and it tasted like regular lemonade except after I swallowed, it made my whole chest and stomach feel warm.

I took another sip.

"Well?"

"It tastes good."

"That's because we mix the perfect drink," Blue said. "We've been making them for everybody."

"So, are you gonna tell us your name or what?" Jasmine said.

"Should he?" Blue said. "I kind of like calling him OCM." She looked at me again. "That's what we call you, by the way. OCM. Operation Campsite Maintenance. You're like the mystery boy of the summer."

"Don't you want to know his name, though?" Jasmine said.

Blue looked at her and rolled her eyes. "Okay, fine, tell us your name."

"Kidd," I said.

"Kid?" Blue said. "Like, 'Hey, check out that kid building a sand castle'?"

"Except my name has two *D*s at the end. And the *K*'s capitalized since it's my name."

They looked at each other and burst out laughing and then Jasmine said: "Where'd you get a name like that?"

I shrugged. "My mom."

Blue smiled at Jasmine and said: "Who am I to judge? My mom named me Blue."

"That's true."

I didn't tell the girls how my dad gave me a regular name when I was born, but I changed it forever, two days after Mom died. I didn't say how "Kidd" was the first thing that came into my head when Devon (who was standing in my room at Horizons, holding my mom's letter) asked what my name was.

Ever since then I told everyone to call me Kidd and they all did.

Except Devon.

Blue looked over her shoulder at the bonfire party, and then she looked back at me and said: "So, why are you sitting way over here? Don't you think it's, like, a little antisocial?"

I shrugged and said I was just sitting here. I didn't tell them I was waiting to see if Olivia came.

"Come with us," Jasmine said. "There's still food."

"And later some of us are going on a spooky midnight walk. It's a ritual, after every time we have a bonfire."

"No parents allowed."

"And no flashlights."

"We just follow the North Star, like in biblical times."

"Right?"

They both giggled again and Jasmine said: "Come on."

I followed them over to the bonfire, secretly looking all around for Olivia, but she wasn't there.

The girls introduced me to everybody. To friends I was "Kidd." To parents I was "the Guy Who Works for Red." They were all super nice and one lady even handed me a plate of barbecue chicken and a corn on the cob and told me I was too skinny and needed to eat. When I took it and told her thank you, ma'am, the girls giggled and Blue said: "Congratulations, you actually picked an appropriate context for the word 'ma'am.'" And they both giggled some more, and as they explained it all to the woman who'd just given me the food I looked everywhere around the bonfire but Olivia still wasn't there.

Jasmine and Blue sat me next to a group of surfer-looking guys and they said hey and I said hey back, and then the girls went to help clean up. I ate my food and drank my special lemonade and listened to the guys talk about surfing and surfboards and which campsite girls were the hottest this summer. I looked at whoever was talking and laughed whenever they laughed, but inside I was thinking about myself and how I was just sitting here with all of them, in the middle of a party, and I didn't even feel that nervous. It was amazing. I sipped more lemonade and felt the warmth and thought how coming to the campsites this summer was the best thing I could've ever done, even if Devon *did* find out where I was. At Horizons I never would've had the chance to meet people my own age.

A guy named Jackson, who had long blond hair with green at the bottom, asked me if I was the one who worked for Red and I said I was. Everybody said how great Mr. Red was, and they said he used to be an amazing surfer, too, maybe the best to ever come out of North County. Two of them, Rob and Jeff, even had posters of him on their walls, from when he was pro, and they talked about which ones and what magazine they came from. Then this guy Frankie said it was too bad about what happened with his son, it's probably what made him quit, and everybody told him to shut up about that and said how rude it was to bring up somebody else's personal life.

"What's that even about, Frank?" Jackson said. "You gossip worse than a skirt."

"You've been vibing people all night," Jeff said.

"Dude, I was just saying."

"Mellow out," Rob said.

Jackson tossed a broken shell at Frankie and said: "Yeah, guy, or beat it."

It was quiet for a while after that and then they started talking about their own surfing again, and girls, and "paddling out to the kelp beds," which they told me they did for the first time last summer.

I listened and drank my lemonade and felt the warmth and thought how Mr. Red never said anything about having a son.

I wondered why not.

I wondered what was so sad you shouldn't talk about it. Then I thought of what happened with my mom.

Our Midnight Walk

After the parents packed up what was left of the food and folded all the chairs and tables and marched back up the stairs to their campsites, Jasmine told everybody we would leave as soon as Blue got back. A few minutes later she did.

And Olivia was with her.

She had on her ski cap and her favorite sweatshirt and jeans, and when she walked past me she smiled.

My stomach instantly got butterflies and I took my last drink of lemonade and threw away the cup. I felt how warm it was going down and then concentrated on the feeling in my head, which was so light and airy, and I remembered how Mr. Red said it made him see colors and how Bill the Deacon said those colors were a mirage.

I looked for rainbow colors all over the beach but it was still just gray and dark-looking. Maybe the colors Mr. Red meant were inside the person, I thought, like your imagination.

"Ready?" Jasmine said to Blue.

"Ready."

Jasmine turned to everybody else and said: "All right, people. We're about to commence our fifth annual post-bonfire, spooky midnight walk. We'd like to salute the veterans, those of you who've walked the previous four, and we'd also like to welcome the virgins. We're so happy you could join us. Blue, will you do the honors?"

Blue laughed and pulled out a kid-sized cap gun and pointed it in the air and pulled the trigger. The gun made a dull popping sound and then a tiny puff of smoke lifted in the air and disappeared and everybody cracked up and said stuff about the toy gun and what Jasmine just said about virgins, and then we were walking.

When I looked around a few minutes later I realized I was right in the middle of everyone. And maybe it was only a lemonade funny mirror, but I felt like the middle was where I belonged. All of us moving north along the shore, the half moon glowing in the sky and glowing a second time blurry on top of the ocean. Sometimes the dark, foamy water would run up close to our feet and all of us would step away to avoid it, at the exact same time, like a pack of birds flying together. And the air was a mix of salt and seaweed and the sound of everyone talking around me.

I looked on both sides and thought about me, just some problem kid from Horizons, being with regular people. A smile went on my face that I couldn't wipe away.

A plane passed overhead, way up in the sky, and I pictured how we'd seem to some passenger in first class if he was staring down at us with binoculars. The surfer guys I was just sitting with and Blue and Jasmine and two other girls named Mary and Dorna. And me right in the middle, two people behind the prettiest girl you could ever meet. Olivia.

I waved at the plane and the two guys next to me laughed a little and I felt the chills that come whenever you make a joke people think is funny.

We walked for a long time and at some point Olivia drifted back from her friends and walked only a couple steps ahead.

She turned around and smiled at me and kept walking.

A few minutes later she looked at me a second time and said: "Hey."

I told her hey back without even thinking about it. Then my heart started going in my chest.

She glanced at the wet sand under her feet as she walked and looked at me and said: "You ever read *The Diving Bell and the Butterfly*?"

"The what?" I said.

"Not the movie, either. The book."

Even though I'd never even heard of what she was saying, I told her: "I think so."

"Trust me, you'd know."

She touched her ski-cap flap where it covered her cheek and then reached both her hands in her pockets. "It was written by some guy who was paralyzed except his left eye. He had a stroke. But then they came up with some code where he blinked for whatever letter he wanted to say, and this woman wrote everything down, one word at a time, and eventually he'd written an entire book like that and it's tragic and beautiful."

I looked at her.

She'd said everything so fast I lost track so I just nodded and kept walking.

Olivia took her hands out of her pockets again and said: "Do you believe the worst things that happen to people can end up being the best?"

I looked at her and squinted like I was really contemplating about that and said: "I guess I never thought about it."

"Some people believe that."

"They do?"

"Yeah. I don't know what world *they're* living in." She smiled and touched her flap again. Neither of us said anything else for a while, we just walked with everybody, but she was still next to me.

We passed another bonfire with a bunch of college-aged guys sitting around the flame and talking and drinking. A couple of them raised their beer bottles and some people from our group waved. Then one of the college kids yelled something I couldn't hear and his friends all laughed, and as soon as we were past them Blue said: "Assholes."

Jasmine shook her head and said: "Why are they always hanging around Moonlight?"

"And why are they always so trashed?" Blue said.

"It's disgusting."

"Right?"

As everybody said more stuff about the drunk college guys, Olivia tapped my arm and pointed at the lifeguard tower ahead of us and said: "That's my favorite thing about beaches."

"Lifeguard towers?"

"Abandoned ones. Ever since I was little."

The windows were all boarded up and covered with graffiti and part of the side wall was caved in. I was just about to tell her how much I liked them, too, when she said: "Anyway, the guy died right after his book came out. I think like five days or something. So it wasn't exactly the happy ending everybody says it was."

"The blinking writer?" I said.

She nodded. "Sad, right?"

"Yeah."

"A lot of people consider that some big triumph of the human spirit. It's more like a tragedy if you ask me."

Olivia kept walking and I thought she was done talking, but then she tapped me on the arm and said: "Hey."

I looked at her.

"Why were you watching me that day in the park?"

"I wasn't," I said, even though I was.

"I'm not mad." She smiled a little, with our eyes looking

at each other. It made my stomach ache. "Seriously," she said. "I was really depressed that day, and reading that book only made it worse. But you should've seen your face when I scared you. I don't know why, but it totally cheered me up."

I looked at the sand thinking how I cheered up Olivia.

"By the way," she said, pointing at my neck. "Is that a hickey?"

"No," I shot back. "It's a rash from a bush."

I covered it with my hand, wishing it would just disappear.

"Don't tell me you're one of *those* guys."

"What guys?"

"The ones who think it's hilarious to hook up with a new girl every weekend."

"I'm not like that," I said.

She patted my arm and then we both went quiet and kept walking. I wondered if my stupid neck mark made Olivia think less of me, even though it wasn't from kissing.

After a couple minutes she smiled at me and then sped up a little and walked with Blue and Jasmine again, and that was the last we talked all night.

But her smile.

It made everything feel okay.

After walking for over an hour Blue made us turn around and we started going back to the campsites, and people broke off from the group. Blue went with the long-blond-haired guy with green tips, Jackson, and they walked way ahead.

Mary went with Frankie.

Dorna went with the spiky-haired guy, Jeff.

Olivia went with Jasmine and Rob.

After a while I realized I was no longer walking in the middle of everyone, I was by myself. But I didn't care. For the first time in forever I felt like I was normal, like my mom always said I could be. Not a Horizons resident. Or a troubled teen. Or an at-risk case.

I was just Kidd Ellison.

A guy who went on a spooky midnight walk.

Someone who could talk to the girl he likes.

. . . After you told the doctor hi back he went to Mom's bed and read all her charts and asked her some questions and wrote things down on his clipboard, and then he smiled at you again and put his hand on top of your head and left.

Mom looked at you, said: "Come here."

You went to her and she touched your hair just like the doctor and smiled and said: "I know what has just happened seems so horrible right now, but it's not all bad. Believe it or not, I'm actually thankful. It lead to me having a moment of clarity. When I woke up in this room, in these bandages, with this ridiculous fear, I realized what I have to do."

"You did?"

She nodded and rubbed your hair again with her good hand. "I did, honey." She tried to seem really happy, even though there was a tear going down her right cheek, and she had to reach up with the back of her hand to wipe it away.

"We're going to be okay," she said, nodding her head up and down and biting her bottom lip. "You and me. We're a team." You told her okay and she laughed and rubbed your head some more and then let her arm go back next to her on the bed, and she looked up at the ceiling.

It went dead quiet and you looked all around the room. The glass jars of medicine and the health posters and the bars and levers of her bed and the muted TV up by the ceiling and magazines spread out on the table and the black-and-white tile. You looked back at Mom and her eyes were closing and you could tell by her breathing she was falling asleep.

But you should've thought about that hospital night when Olivia asked her question about bad things turning good. "Yes," you should've told her. "'Cause when bad things happen to people they can have a moment of clarity where they realize what they have to do, like my mom did."

And if you think about it, you had a moment of clarity, too. After Mom was gone. At first when they came to get you at school and told you what happened you thought you died right with her. But then Maria said you could think of it a different way, like how nobody could hurt your mom ever again and how there was still a piece of her inside you, everywhere you went, and about her going to a better place. And after thinking about it for a while you decided maybe Maria was right about that.

If Olivia ever asks that question again, you have to tell her, yes, sometimes a good thing can come out of a bad thing and how you should know.

What I Miss About Being Free

How I'd wake up on the beach sometimes, in the middle of the night, after sleepwalking. It always took me a while to think of who I was. And where I was. Not in Horizons or Fallbrook or my mom's apartment. But on the sand at the beach. I worked for Mr. Red. Then I'd smile, thinking how I could go anywhere or do anything and I was actually happy.

What the train sounds like when you see it coming from far away. The whistle sounding. The vibration of the tracks under your feet. The power it had going past, like a million car engines combined, the wind pressing your face and the roar and me thinking who was in there and if they were going where their family was.

Olivia telling me about the books she's read. Me listening and nodding but really just watching her. Getting excited 'cause she was.

Peanut waiting for me to wake up every morning, and waiting for me to get home from work, so I could put food in his bowl, and water, and pet him while I said whatever I was thinking. Peanut, who looked at me with his crooked face and messed-up teeth, and how once I'd known him long enough everything started seeming straight.

Mr. Red teaching me everything he knows about plumbing and landscaping and life. Girls. How he cared if I had friends and if I was okay. Mr. Red, who was always laughing and smiling and talking, but then sometimes he'd stare at the ground for a full minute, not moving, and I could tell in his eyes how sad he was and only now do I know why.

Olivia smiling at me when we'd pass at the campsites and she was with her friends. And how it felt like we had a secret.

The sound of waves breaking when you fall asleep in your tent. And birds in the morning. And people talking when they walk by on their way to get a coffee and paper. All of it blending into the sound of being free.

The hole at the top of my tent in the morning when I opened my eyes. How at a certain time of the day the sun went right inside it and the whole inside of my tent lit up and it felt like somebody was giving me special powers.

Going in the ocean every Sunday morning by myself, down from the campsites so nobody knows me. Coming out and laying on my towel. Letting the sun dry the ocean water off my skin. How it was cold at first, then tingled into warm. My face going into a smile 'cause of how good it felt. Then drifting into sleep.

Olivia touching her ski cap and sometimes turning to me, her eyes going on mine, and how my stomach feels like it's floating, like I don't weigh anything, and how I pretend like I'm not smiling and nothing's really happening, but really everything is.

"**Here's another thing about girls,**" Devon said as we walked back from the beach. "I don't like regular skinny ones, either. Yeah, they're all right to look at, and people give you props when they see you with one at the movies. But soon as you start hooking up, Special, trust me, it feels wrong."

I nodded, trying to think how skinny Olivia was.

"A dude's not supposed to graze bones when he's feeling on his girl. Or two little mosquito bites hiding inside a Victoria's Secret training bra. I like a girl who you can tell is a girl."

I shrugged as we went around the end of the campsites and up the side of the 101. It was late and the lifeguard tower was closed. The sun had just dropped under the ocean. I hadn't eaten anything since breakfast 'cause Devon made us stay on the beach the entire day so we could see every single girl that came and went to make it a complete study. If we left early he said we might miss the finest one of the day. So we sat there shirtless on our towels, the sun stuck on our skin, talking about every girl, arguing over ratings, pointing out features.

Whenever it got too hot we'd run down into the water and splash through the whitewash and duck under swells. We'd stay out there bodysurfing and spraying water at each other until Devon said we had to get back to our towels and scan for new talent.

We spent pretty much the entire day talking about girls, but somehow Devon had more to say.

"What I seriously don't get, though," he told me, "is your obsession with blondes." He was holding a long stick now, whacking rocks into the road. We watched each one skip into the traffic that raced past us on the 101.

"I just think some of them are pretty," I said.

"Pretty? What's pretty, though, Special? For real."

I shrugged.

"Pretty's stock, man. Pretty's like having bread and water for dinner. Yeah, maybe it's enough sustenance to make it to the next day, but it doesn't taste like anything. I'm talking about flavor, Special. I'm talking about herbs and spices."

"I *like* girls who are pretty," I said, but Devon wasn't listening.

"Dude, I know all those sayings they have like 'blondes have more fun,' but that was from, like, 1920. Our country didn't know any better. Since then all kinds of immigrants have come and settled here and made kids with white people and new combinations of girls have been born and it's woken people up to a whole new meaning of what's hot."

"I guess so."

"Look at *you*, Special. You're mixed."

I shrugged.

"When people first meet you, what do they think you are?"

I thought about it a sec, then told him: "Just regular, I guess."

"No, dude. I mean your race. What race do people think you are?"

"Sometimes they think I'm part Mexican," I said. "Or Puerto Rican or Spanish."

"See?" Devon said.

"One kid at Horizons said if I was from Iraq and if I was a terrorist. But he was joking."

"Oh, damn," Devon said, putting a fist to his mouth. "People are ignorant." He looked at me for a sec and said: "Actually, maybe I *would* have somebody take a wand to your ass at airport security."

"I don't look like a terrorist."

"I know, Special. I'm just messing with you. Dude, you take everything so personal."

I shrugged and kept walking.

"If anything you look like a white skater kid with a tan. Especially with those new threads I got you."

I looked down at my new shirt and surf trunks. I forgot I even had them on.

"Hey, Special."

I looked at Devon.

"But even if you can sort of blend in with these rich kids . . . really you're not."

"I know," I said.

"I don't think you do."

I looked at him, confused.

"You're not like them, man. You're different. Me too. And we have to understand that people are always gonna view us that way. As outsiders. Even if they seem nice to our faces. Behind closed doors it's something else."

"Maybe it's not like that here," I said.

"You honestly believe that?" Devon shot back. "If anything it's worse. Why do you think I can't hang out with these campsite kids? I can see it in their eyes, man. Deep down they think they're better than us. And you know why?"

"Why?"

"'Cause they're white. And 'cause they have money. And 'cause me and you, Special, we don't got nothing."

I kept walking.

It was quiet between us for a couple minutes, then Devon started smiling. "That's why I got one rule with the ladies," he said.

"What?"

"It's gotta be dark hair if it's gonna be Devon. And olive skin. And a little bit of booty. I mostly dig black girls and Mexican girls, but I'm flexible, you know? Some Asians are pretty sweet. Remember when I hooked up with that one Filipino girl, Tammy or whatever? At the community pool in Fallbrook?"

I nodded and looked up at him and then looked at the walkway again. That's about all you could do with Devon when he started going on like this about girls.

"I remember 'cause when they walked in I turned to you and said I'd probably end up marrying the Asian one. Of course, you were too busy staring at blond chicks to even notice."

"Oh yeah," I said.

I didn't actually remember, but Devon and me were always at that pool together, and he was always saying he was gonna marry somebody. The group home where he ended up was near Horizons, and both houses went to the same pool pretty much every day during the summer. I always hung out with Devon since I knew him from before.

"Anyways," Devon said, "we met up at the end of the day, after you guys left, and she told me she was Filipino and she asked what I was and I told her that was privileged information and she sat down with me and guessed like a hundred guesses. We hooked up a couple days later, when we were both back at the pool. And lemme tell you something, Special. The skin on that girl's legs was the softest I've ever felt in my life. If you ever get a chance to hook up with a Filipino girl, dude, make sure you feel her legs. You won't believe it."

We walked into the campsite through the front entrance, where the cars go, where Olivia jumped out from behind a tree to scare me. I looked up at the top of the tree and noticed all the dark clouds in the sky.

"Look how stormy it is," I told Devon.

Devon peeked, too, and told me: "Bet you it's gonna rain tonight."

"I know."

"I hate rain, dude. It's such a pain in the ass."

"But plants need it."

"Plants?" he said, looking at me. "Dude, Special. Sometimes you sound like some old lady tending her garden."

We turned onto the little street that led to my tent and then he smacked me on the shoulder again and stopped walking. "Hang on!" he said.

"What?"

"You see what you just did right there? I was talking about some girl's sweet legs and you totally changed the subject. Like you always do, Special. You started talking about *plants*."

"I didn't change the subject."

"Dude, trust me."

I looked at the ground for a sec, and then looked up at Devon.

He took a deep breath and let it out all slow. "Look, man, I've been meaning to ask you something."

"Me?"

He pulled his towel off one shoulder and draped it over his other one. "It's just, you never wanna talk about the ladies, man. And you don't have any experience. I know that for a fact."

"I have experience."

"Look, I'm just gonna come out and ask you, okay? Are you, like, gay?"

"What?" I threw my hands up and turned around and then turned back and punched him in the shoulder and said: "I'm not gay."

"You sure?"

"Of course I'm sure." I punched him again in the same spot.

"Okay, okay," he said, rubbing his arm. "Jesus. I was just asking a simple question."

My towel fell on the road.

He started laughing and holding down my fists. "Jesus, it's not even that big of a deal these days. People turn gay all the time. You can even get married, I think."

I stood there shaking my head, trying to figure out why somebody would ask if I was gay. I tried to think if I even understood what being gay meant. I knew it was when a guy liked other guys, but were there other things, too? Did it change how the person acted?

"I'm just messing with you, Special. I know you're hetero."

I reached down and picked up my towel and brushed off the dirt.

"I know everything about you, dude."

"You don't know everything."

"Oh, but I do."

"Okay, what am I thinking right this second?" I stared at him, trying to see if he'd change the subject.

"You're waiting to see if I'll change the subject and start talking about the weather."

"Not even close," I said.

But I couldn't believe it. Devon may have been depressed and he may have had a death drive, but he was one of the smartest people I knew when it came to reading people's minds.

"You sure?" he said.

"I wasn't thinking that at all."

He gave me a funny look and said: "Okay, Special, if you say so. Anyways, you're right, there is one thing I don't know about you."

"What?"

"Why you never wanna talk about girls."

"We talked about girls all day."

He shook his head and said: "There's nothing to be scared of, man. They don't bite."

"I know!"

He stood there for a sec like he was thinking and then he nodded and said: "Even when you were writing in your diary about that one, man. Who would pick the chick with the deformed face?"

I was just about to tell him how Olivia wasn't deformed, she was the prettiest girl ever. And how I even talked to her at the beach last week. But right then we got to my tent and Devon said: "Anyways, man, I gotta head across the highway."

"Good."

"Ah, come on, Special," he said. "Don't be like that. I'm sorry if I offended you."

I didn't say anything back.

"You take things way too personal, man. Friends are supposed to be able to talk and mess around with each other. Right?"

He held out his hand for me to slap, but I just looked at it.

"Come on, Kidd. At least acknowledge my existence."

I looked at him and shrugged. He reached his hand out closer to me and I slapped it away.

"Good enough," Devon said, laughing at me. Then he looked at Peanut, who was lying in front of my tent door again. "Jesus Christ!"

"What?"

He pointed at Peanut, whose middle section was going up and down with each breath. "Dude, that's like the ugliest dog I've ever seen."

"He's not *that* ugly," I said.

"It doesn't even look like a dog, man. It looks like an overgrown sewer rat. Look how far its teeth stick out."

Peanut must have known we were talking about him 'cause he lifted his head and looked at us. His eyes were yellow and his snout had a little mud stuck on the tip.

He growled at Devon.

"Anyways," Devon said. "I'll get up with you in a few days or something. Have fun cleaning toilets."

I watched him backpedal, looking at Peanut, then he said: "Hey, Special."

"What?"

"Remember what I just told you about spices, man. And Filipino girls' skin."

"I know."

"It's okay to talk about that stuff every once in a while. Maybe one day you'll even experience it for yourself."

"Maybe I already did," I said.

"Or maybe you didn't." He laughed and said: "Anyways, peace."

I watched Devon spin around and walk back down the road, out of sight. Then I stepped over Peanut and went in my tent and climbed in my sleeping bag and closed my eyes.

How I Still Couldn't Write About Olivia

I woke up in the middle of the night when I heard knocking. Soon as my eyes focused, though, I realized it wasn't somebody wanting to come in, it was rain hitting my tent roof.

I looked at my clock: two in the morning.

I sat up, happy I wasn't sleepwalking for once, and listened to the sound the rain made. For some reason it made me feel happy. Maybe 'cause of how I used to be locked up inside Horizons all day and now I was outside in a tent with rain and my new life seemed like an adventure.

I reached over and turned on my light and took out my philosophy of life book and tried to think what I could put. I thought about me and Devon bodysurfing in the shallow part. And looking at all the girls on the beach. And us talking about people's races. I thought of Mr. Red. In five hours he'd be teaching me how to operate the entire campsite sprinkler system.

But really I just wanted to write about me and Olivia walking together on the beach and how the week after she left a drawing on my tent door of an abandoned lifeguard tower and her signature.

I spent the next hour trying to write out our exact conversation so I could look at it whenever I wanted, even a long time from now. But everything I put didn't seem like what she said so I kept having to tear out pages.

Finally I gave up and put down my pen and looked at the tent wall. I wondered why my mind would never let me write about Olivia.

Outside the tent I could hear Peanut snoring in the rain. For two weeks he'd been sleeping right outside my tent, and every time I got up in the morning he'd get up, too, and as I zipped closed my door he'd lean against me and we'd look at each other and I'd tell him: "Nice to see you again, big guy."

I was starting to really like Peanut, even if he wasn't the kind of dog some animal magazine would pick out for a photo shoot. He was loyal to people like me and Mr. Red. And he hardly ever barked. And he seemed like my friend.

I put away my philosophy of life book and got out of my sleeping bag and unzipped my tent door. When I pushed it open Peanut raised his head and looked at me, the rain getting all on him. He sat up and opened his mouth and let his tongue fall all to the side and breathed that way.

I told him: "Come on, big guy. Let's get you outta the rain."

He didn't move, just stayed looking at me.

"Come on," I said again, holding open the tent door wider.

He got up and looked in my tent and then looked at me again.

"What's wrong?" I said.

He didn't say anything, obviously.

"Dogs shouldn't have to sleep in the rain, either, right? Think about it."

He looked at me and shook his fur and water went everywhere, then he stepped in my tent and sniffed around. He went around in two circles and laid down right by the door and put his head on his paws and looked up at me again.

"From now on when it rains," I told him, "you could just sleep in here, all right?"

One of his ears went up like he was listening, and I climbed back in my sleeping bag, flipped off my light and told him good night.

Dreams from Solitary Confinement

I suck in my stomach, slip through bars and again rise over the empty prison yard. I float above thin midnight clouds, above the familiar tops of buildings and street signs and lonely car headlights shining white or red into the dark pavement.

Like I'm Superman I hold my hands in front of me and watch the world move underneath. And what if I really *was* super in some way? If I could save all the people from their depression. Kids and parents stuck inside sad dreams, alone in their beds, wishing they were someone else, someone better.

Kidd Ellison, hero to America.

Protector from sadness.

I veer over the 101, drift over my old tent, Mr. Red's work shed, the cliff fence still cautioned off yellow where I shoved Devon. I think about my summer again.

The best time of my life.

Then the worst.

I make out two heads in the sand and lower toward them on the dark beach, across from their towel. It's Olivia again, this time with her friend Jasmine. They don't wave or say anything, just watch me land softly in my sitting position, like it's perfectly normal I can fly around the midnight sky.

I smile but they don't smile back, like I'm not just one towel away but an entire ocean.

Olivia glances down at her bare feet, curls her toes in the sand and sighs.

Jasmine sits behind her, braiding the blond hair under Olivia's ski cap. *I honestly think that,* she says.

Maybe, Olivia says, pulling her knees to her chest and wrapping around them with her arms.

Jasmine looks around Olivia's half-braided ponytail, still holding the ends of her hair in her fingers. *Not everything's in your control, you know.*

I keep running through the summer, though, Jaz. Every conversation we had. I should have seen it.

Jasmine shakes her head and goes back to braiding.

There were signs.

Of course there were signs, Jasmine says. *There are always signs when you look back after the fact.*

But you don't understand. The director of the place where he lived in Fallbrook was here this morning. I talked to him. Kidd had real problems, Jaz. Like, he was sick.

Olivia lowers her eyes.

What do you mean sick?

When Olivia looks up at me our eyes blend together and for three long seconds it feels like we're not in this dark beach dream but real life.

We both look away.

Even though I missed half their conversation I know what they're talking about, and I know what it means. They're discussing what I did to Devon and how I'm in prison now.

But more than that.

If the people from Horizons were here they probably told Olivia everything about me. And now she knows I'm not a normal kid, like the rest of her friends.

I used to be depressed.

And I used to be a danger to myself.

At least, that's what I know it says in my file.

I turn to the ocean, feeling so sad, like I'm holding everybody's depression in my arms while they sleep.

It's later than in my last dream. Past midnight. I can feel the darkness getting older. And I can see the dot of the distant ship a lot better this time. It's closer to shore.

I turn back to the girls and Olivia's crying, and Jasmine's no longer braiding her hair but rubbing her back and telling her: *It's been a long couple days, O. Maybe you should go home and get some sleep.*

I can't, Olivia says. She sits up and dries her eyes, looks at me again. Her eyes puffy wet and hurt and also the most perfect green you could imagine. *I don't want to abandon him, too. Like everybody else.*

But what about New York? Jasmine turns Olivia's face so they see each other's eyes. *You can't change everything that's happened to him by punishing yourself.*

I'm staying, Olivia says.

It's quiet for a minute and then she clears her throat and says: *I never told you about the time he protected me, did I?*

Jasmine shrugs.

We were at Moonlight, Olivia says. *On the abandoned lifeguard tower. And those college guys came up to us.*

Jasmine looks up at Olivia. *Why haven't you told me this?*

Olivia shakes her head and looks past me, to the ocean. *You know how my dad is.*

Like I'd go running to your dad.

Before Olivia says another word the night is already a movie in my head. Me and her sitting on the tower, looking at the ocean, talking for our second time.

I see the guys coming toward us.

Me standing up.

In my dream Olivia touches her fingers to the flap covering her cheek and says to Jasmine: *I went to his tent. I don't even remember what I said, but you should have seen his face. He was shocked to see me.*

That's because he was totally in love with you. He was from the first day. Me and Blue told you that.

Olivia looks at me. *Most guys play these stupid little games, you know? But he was always so honest.*

I turn red on my towel.

But I also realize something. Nothing in the whole world matters except what you truly think. Devon always said if you like a girl you should pretend you like someone else, or act like you don't care, but that's not right. 'Cause tomorrow you might get separated from everybody, and then you'd never have told the girl what you really meant, and I believe that's the worst thing possible.

He was so shy at first, Olivia says. She reaches for one of her sandals and plays with the strap. *He nodded a lot and smiled and repeated whatever I said. But once he got comfortable he started opening up. He asked me about all the traveling I'd done with my family. And what it was like to live in a big house with two parents.*

I can't believe he was in foster care.

Isn't that weird? Olivia says, touching the flap of her cap. *But like I told you, it wasn't even regular foster care. The director explained it to me this morning. It's a special program, where they rehabilitate kids who've experienced trauma.*

What was his trauma?

He wouldn't say.

Jasmine looks at me and says: *He definitely acted different, but me and Blue just figured it was 'cause he was from Fallbrook.*

Olivia nods, says: *Why would anybody ruin their life like that?*

I honestly don't know.

Look at him, Olivia says.

In my dream they're both staring at me.

And I feel so weird about it. Like a statue in a museum.

Olivia lowers her head for a while and then turns and puts her head on Jasmine's shoulder. *I don't care how many problems he had,* she says. *Or what trauma he experienced. He was always so happy. It's one of the reasons I liked hanging out with him.*

I stare at them, feeling shame for being in prison. And for making Olivia sad. And making her wait like this when who knows if I'll ever get out.

Jasmine pets Olivia's hair for a while. She tells her: *Finish your story, though. What happened with those college guys?*

Olivia sits up. *We were just sitting there, talking. I was telling him something about school, I think. And then we heard this loud popping sound of glass shattering behind us. Somebody had thrown a beer bottle. When I looked up I saw two of those college guys standing there, laughing. The shorter one yelled: Quit talking and get the bitch naked!*

Jasmine's face goes serious. *You swear he said that?*

I told them to just leave us alone, but they said it was a public beach and they'd do whatever they wanted. Next thing I know Kidd is hopping off the lifeguard tower and walking toward them. I jumped off after him, grabbed his arm and told him we should just forget them and go back to the campsites. But the way he looked at me, Jaz. There was something wild in his eyes. The only other time I saw it was on the cliff.

And what happened?

When he turned back around both guys were pulling off their backpacks and the smaller one started waving Kidd on and yelling how he was gonna kick his ass.

I sit across from Olivia and Jasmine in my dream. On my towel. Listening and remembering.

I grabbed for Kidd's arm again, Olivia says, *and he turned around, and this time you know what he said to me, Jaz?*

What?

He forced a little smile, even though his eyes were on fire, and he told me: I will save you.

You're kidding.

Swear to God. He said he'd save me.

And?

I let him go and he walked right up to the college guys and just stood there. Didn't say a word while they yelled at him and pushed him and threw sand in his face. Then the smaller guy punched Kidd right in the mouth, and Kidd went down. He reached up and touched his bloody lip, then turned and looked at them. He looked at me.

I yelled for the guys to leave us alone. Then I ran at the smaller one and pushed him.

Jasmine puts her hand over her mouth.

But his friend shoved me, and I fell to the sand, flat on my back. When I looked up, Kidd was grabbing the smaller guy by his shirt. He hit him twice in the face and threw him down. Then he went over to the guy who'd just shoved me and they grabbed each other and wrestled to the ground and Kidd head-butted him so hard, Jaz. It sounded like a plate shattering on the kitchen floor.

Jesus, Olivia.

Then Kidd pulled the guy up and punched him in the stomach and the guy went to his knees.

Tell me you got out of there.

We did. Kidd took my hand and we ran all the way back to the campsites.

Olivia sat there for a second, staring at the floor. *But you know what's weird?*

What?

The only thing I remember about getting home was that Kidd kept saying how sorry he was. Over and over. No matter how many times I told him he didn't have anything to be sorry about.

He was probably scared, Jasmine says. *I know when I got in my car accident sophomore year I kept apologizing to my parents. And it was totally the other guy's fault.*

Exactly, Olivia says. *Anyway, when we got to my tent I tried to talk to him some more, but he just hugged me and walked away and I stood there thinking about . . .*

In the middle of Olivia telling the last part of her story, the dream force pulls me back up into the sky. I try to fight, so I can hear the rest and picture it, but the force is too strong and I'm already back over the 101 and over all of Cardiff.

As I fly I think back to that night. Everything was so blurry, like a TV station that's blocked from kids. After I got her back to her tent I ducked around a tree and watched her until she finally went inside and was safe. Then I went to my own tent and let Peanut back in and zipped the door closed.

I felt on my forehead and looked at my fingers and there was blood.

Peanut watched me.

I tried to think if I needed stitches. But since I'd run away from Horizons I knew I shouldn't give my name out at a hospital so I just took out the duct tape Mr. Red had given me and tore off a piece and closed my cut together and taped it and then flipped off my light and concentrated on the throbbing, like my heart was in my cut.

At the exact second I picture myself closing my eyes that night, I open them in real life and find myself back in solitary confinement, in the dark, strapped down and alone.

And I can't even help it, tears instantly come from my eyes. But it's not 'cause I got hurt.

It's 'cause I wish I could still be in my dream, on the beach, listening to Olivia talk, even if it was about a bad time. 'Cause in real life, I don't know if I'll ever get to be near her beach towel again.

"**Follow me,**" Devon said, soon as I opened my tent door. He had a pissed-off look as he held my face and looked at the duct tape.

I had a sick feeling in my stomach before I even noticed the gun in his hand.

"What's that?" I said.

"A loaf of bread."

"It's not bread."

"Dude, what do you think it is?"

"A gun."

"Congratulations."

Peanut stood up behind me and started growling at Devon.

"But where'd you even get it?" I said.

"You know I got connects, Special." Devon looked down at Peanut, pointed the gun at him and said: "Pow."

"Put it down," I said, pushing the gun out of Peanut's face.

"Calm down," he said, tucking it in the back of his jeans. "I'm doing this for you."

I tried to think was this actually happening or was I sleep-walking again. 'Cause in all the time I'd known Devon, he'd never had a gun before.

I wondered if he was getting worse.

"Hurry up and throw a shirt on," Devon said. "We gotta do this now."

"Do what?" I said, pulling a shirt over my head.

He didn't answer.

He started walking and I followed, knowing whatever we

were gonna do would most likely be wrong and knowing I'd end up doing it anyway. My Horizons therapist would say I was in one of those moments of decision people have. The kind that can change your entire future.

I don't know why, but I always chose wrong.

"Basically, there are two kinds of people in this world," Devon said, walking along the dark ocean's edge. "People of privilege and everybody else."

I looked at the gun bulge in the back of his jeans, thinking how me and Olivia would be in different groups.

I stopped in my tracks, said: "I mean it. Why do you have a gun?"

Devon stopped, too. Smiled at me. "Look at Special trying to act all grown-up. Demanding information."

"Just say it."

"And here I thought the only role you played was Mr. Naïve Man. The token dummy."

I stared at Devon as hard as I could, tried to focus on his eyes. But they kept shifting 'cause it was so dark, and 'cause Devon was always looking away from people.

"You gotta start trusting your boy," he said. "Me and you got business to handle."

"What business?"

"Big-boy business."

"Is it something with Olivia?"

"Who's Olivia?" Devon said, and I could tell he really didn't know.

"Nothing," I said. "Just what business?"

He stared back at me for a few seconds and then a smile

slowly went on his face and he said: "You mean that deformed blond chick you're always stalking?"

"I'm not stalking."

He laughed and pulled his gun from the back of his jeans and looked at the side of it. His face went serious. "Look, this is bigger than some chick," he said. "And we don't have time to BS."

He started walking again and after a couple seconds I walked, too.

When I caught up to him he went on with what he was saying about the two groups: "What I seriously can't stand is the entitlement vibe I get from rich people. They think they rule the world, Special. And technically maybe they do. Maybe *that's* what pisses me off so much. I don't know. But I hate that their lives mean more than ours just because there's a higher number on their bank statements. Or because their cars are shinier or they have more bathrooms in their houses."

We both stepped away from the tide when it rolled up to our feet. "Some of them could be nice, though," I said.

"Of course some are nice," he said.

"So what about *that*?"

"Here's what you don't get, Special. When you choose to take a stand in this world, you have to accept the fact that a few innocent people will get hurt. Revolutions are bloody, dude."

"You're starting a revolution?"

"Figure of speech, man."

I thought about that as we kept walking. "It still doesn't seem right."

"It's not. At least not on a case-by-case. But if the overall benefit outweighs the individual harm, man . . . in the grand scheme of things you're good. Not that I really care about being good."

The tide came rushing up again, and this time Devon wasn't as quick as me to get out of the way. Both his shoes got soaked. But he was too wrapped up in his revolution talk to even care.

"It makes me sick how some people live, Special. Eating caviar and going out on their yachts. While the rest of us are just trying to survive. Take those rich punks that hassled you a few nights ago."

I looked at Devon and said: "Who?"

"Their parents pay all this money for college, give them spending cash, a fancy car to drive around campus. And look what happens?"

"You mean the guys by the lifeguard tower?"

"I can't let people think they're better than my boy, Special."

I looked ahead of us, trying to figure out how Devon could've already found out what happened.

"If you think about it," he said, "we're just doing what their parents failed to. Teaching respect."

He was waving the gun all around with his words now. And right then it hit me what was happening.

We were hunting those college guys with Devon's gun.

"You trust me, Special?"

I didn't say anything.

"Huh?" he said. "Do you?"

"My therapist told me people should try to make good decisions."

"Your therapist is one of *them*, man. Don't you get that? Do you know how many times I've seen her pull up to Horizons in that fancy Mercedes? Come on, dude."

I pictured us all staring out the window as she stepped out of her car, pushing her sunglasses onto the top of her head.

"Of course she tells you that crap about making good decisions. You know why?"

"Why?"

"'Cause rich people are smart. The last thing she wants is some disturbed kid like you coming after her Benz. So she scares you into submission. Same with the rest of the Horizons kids. The more she works that Jedi mind trick, the safer she can feel about her possessions."

That was the thing about Devon.

He was smart, too. Whenever he said stuff like that it always made me think. Even when it was stuff I didn't *wanna* think about.

Way ahead I could see the abandoned lifeguard tower, and I could see there were people standing near it. I peeked again at Devon's gun.

My stomach dropped.

"You know what she does after she tells you all this stuff about decision-making?"

I shook my head.

"She goes home to her corporate lawyer husband and they put on their fanciest rich-people clothes and they go to some expensive restaurant and order goddamn champagne, man."

He stared at me, holding his hands out like it was simple,

the gun pointing at the ocean. When he looked forward again he put his arm out for me to stop and said: "Those the guys?"

I looked at them.

I nodded.

Making People Pay

"I already fought them," I told Devon, pointing at the duct tape on my face.

"It's not enough. Just because they have money doesn't mean they can come up to my best friend like that. There are consequences."

"How'd you know?" I said again.

He turned and looked at me. "Because I know, man. I heard them talking. Or I heard you talking when you were sleepwalking."

"You know about that?"

"Or I heard your little girlfriend talking to her friends. Who cares. The point is, I know. And now, Special, it's time to make people pay."

He set off jogging toward them, holding the gun at his side, and when he got close enough he showed it and shouted: "Everybody down!"

I followed after Devon, watching all the college guys look up and watching their eyes grow big when they saw the gun.

"I said sit your ass down!"

All six of them quickly sat on the sand and looked at each other and back at Devon. The guy I head-butted had a big bandage on his nose.

Devon walked closer and aimed the gun at the head of the

smaller one, the guy who started the whole thing. "You. Come on over here. Now."

The guy pointed at himself like he was asking a question. He looked at his friends and then slowly rose, his hands shoulder high and trembling.

I grabbed Devon's arm, but he brushed me away.

"Let's go, rich boy," Devon said. "I want you to sit right here in front of me. That's it. Easy now."

The guy got up slowly and walked toward Devon, and Devon pointed with the gun where he wanted him to sit. The guy sat. "You think life is so easy," Devon said to all of them. "Sitting in your frat house, drinking your beer, laughing at everybody doing work-study jobs. But things aren't always funny, are they? Like tonight."

Devon looked at the guy in front of him and pressed the gun up to his cheek. "You messed with the wrong kid last weekend, didn't you, dude?"

The guy looked at the gun out of the corner of his eye and cowered and said: "I'm sorry."

"You wanted to order people around. Say stuff to their innocent girlfriends."

"I'm sorry," the guy said again, his whole body starting to tremble. "Please, just let me go."

"You wanted to hit somebody just 'cause he's poor and you're rich. You wanted him to know how much better you are. Isn't that right?"

"No, I swear. I was just drunk and acting stupid."

"You think you can do anything you want because you have money. But not tonight, huh?" Devon nudged the guy with the gun and cocked it and the guy closed his eyes.

A couple tears fell down his bright red face and he coughed. "I'm sorry," he said. "I swear to God."

Devon looked at the rest of the guys and said: "Look at your little punk friend. Crying like a baby. Mommy and Daddy can't buy his way out of this one, can they?"

"Let him go," I said, grabbing Devon's arm again. "They get it now."

Devon brushed me off and swung his foot into the guy's ribs. A retching sound coming from his mouth and him falling onto his stomach in the sand. Devon spit on his back. One of the other guys went to get up, but Devon pointed the gun at him and he sat back down.

Devon started laughing like a crazy person.

"Let's just go," I said.

He looked at me and pointed the gun at his own head and said: "You know what's the difference between us and these rich assholes?" He laughed some more and spit in front of his wet shoes.

I didn't say anything.

One of the guys sitting down said: "We'll leave. We'll never come back here."

Devon turned back to them. "The difference is you guys actually believe your lives are meaningful." He put the gun up to one of his eyeballs. "But it's all an illusion."

"You're right, man," one of the guys said.

"Me and Kidd here," Devon said. "We already know how meaningless we are. The world has already shown us. You could learn a lot from poor kids like me and him."

Devon pulled the gun from his own head with a big smile

and reached into his pocket for a knife. He flipped open the blade and held it up to the guys, said: "You see this?"

They all nodded.

"I wanna show you what it means when you know you're nothing."

"Please! We'll just leave!"

"Let's go," I told Devon.

He turned to me, smiling. There was nothing in his eyes. It made me feel sick to my stomach.

He looked back at the guys and ripped open his shirt sleeve with the knife and then stabbed himself in the shoulder, the blood flowing down his arm, into his dangling hand. He pulled the knife out and laughed.

"Jesus," one of the guys said.

I stared at the gushing blood.

"I know about myself," Devon said, wiping the blood on his face. "I'm nobody. One day you rich punks will learn the same thing about yourselves."

The guys were so scared. They wouldn't even look at Devon.

"By the way," Devon said. "If you go to the police about our little meeting tonight, I'll hunt you down. You hear me?"

They nodded.

"And I'll kill you."

He motioned for me to follow him, and we took off running down the beach together, Devon laughing and me watching the gun waving all around in front of me with his steps and his blood drips hitting the sand.

• • •

Devon Pulls the Trigger

When we got close to the campsite stairs Devon grabbed my arm and stopped running. We both bent over to catch our breath. Neither of us said anything for over a minute. The only sound was Devon laughing.

"How amazing was that?" he finally said.

"It wasn't," I said.

"What are you talking about? We put those punks in their place, man. We restored order."

I shook my head, still breathing hard. "I already fought them. Didn't you see his bandage?"

"That was just a superficial wound," Devon said. "We needed to hurt the guy on the inside. You see how he was crying like that? In front of his boys? That kind of wound doesn't go away."

Right then Devon stood upright and shoved the gun against his own head again.

"What are you doing?" I said.

"I'm proving what I said to them. How we have nothing. I'm living it."

"It's not true," I said. "*I* have something."

"Oh, yeah? What's that? Name one thing."

I thought of Olivia and her ski cap and our walk together. If I could see her even one more time, I thought. That would be something.

"I didn't think so," Devon said, cocking the gun.

"Don't," I said. I tried knocking it out of his hand, but he turned and kicked me away. Then he slashed me in the shoulder with his knife.

He put the gun back to his head, said: "I need you to see this, Special."

"What are you doing?" I yelled, grabbing my shoulder.

"Give me one good reason I shouldn't pull this trigger."

I tried to think what I could say. What would make him realize. But I didn't think fast enough.

"See?" Devon said. "Now I want you to watch. And I want you to remember this for the rest of your meaningless life."

He took a deep breath and closed his eyes.

He pulled the trigger.

I yelled as the gun went off.

A puff of dark smoke lifting in the air.

But nothing happened. Devon was still standing there. And when he opened his eyes he started laughing like a crazy person, like it was the funniest thing in the world.

"It's a fake gun," he said between laughs. "It's not even real."

"What?" I said.

"It's fake. I stole it from this prop shop on 101. Right next to a music store."

I kneeled in the sand 'cause my legs felt wobbly.

"We made that guy cry over a fake gun, Special. Isn't that amazing?"

I didn't say anything. Just looked at the sand and shook my head. I didn't know what to think or feel.

"What we told him, though," Devon said. "That part was real."

"What *you* told him," I said.

"We gave him something important to consider."

Devon tossed the fake gun and it landed in the sand right

in front of me. "Take it," he said. "Feel free to use it on any-one you think needs a dose of reality."

I looked up and watched him walking away, toward the steps. As he climbed them, two at a time, I could feel my heart pounding in my chest. I thought how Devon's death drive was way worse than before. When he escaped from his group home at the start of summer, to find me, the world became less safe. Not just for himself but everybody.

I knew right that second Devon would end up either dead or in jail. Those were the only possibilities.

After he got to the top stair and disappeared into the campsites, I looked down at the gun in front of me. I picked it up to feel how heavy it was. I'd never held a gun before, not even a fake one. I looked real close and saw Devon's bloody fingerprints all over it. And then I looked at my own hand, which was bloody, too.

When he slashed me in the shoulder he must've cut deeper than I thought. 'Cause blood was flowing down my arm.

I stood up and threw the fake gun into the ocean, as far as I could.

Then I sat in the sand, holding my bloody shoulder, my whole body trembling 'cause I was so mad and confused and fighting off the pain. I stared at the ocean, trying to think what I could do about Devon.

And thinking how I had to make sure I didn't end up dead right along with him.

They gave me and Mr. Red three days to fix the fence on the cliff, but it only took us two. First of all, they didn't supply us with enough material. And second, Mr. Red told me if we finished a day early he had a surprise trip we could do.

We worked as hard as possible, knocking out most of the old fence, hauling it to the dump, digging new ditches along the edge of the cliff, sinking wood posts, sealing everything with the cement Mr. Red mixed himself in his rusted wheelbarrow.

We barely talked.

My shoulder where Devon cut me hurt some, but it wasn't as bad as I thought. I just duct-taped it so no blood would show through my shirt. Mr. Red had told me that some police came through the campsites the night before, asking questions. He said somebody had pulled a gun on some college kids up the beach. They told Mr. Red to call the station if he heard anything.

He didn't seem like he suspected me or Devon or anything. He was just mentioning it. But I still decided to avoid Devon for a while.

I didn't even need to worry, though. In the week since the fake gun Devon hadn't come around even once.

During the second day Mr. Red was working so hard he took off his sombrero and hung it on a tree branch. I stared at it while I held one of the fence posts and Mr. Red poured cement. There were two holes in the front of the sombrero and the rim was partly rubbed off and you could tell it probably started out way lighter. It was the most beat-up hat I'd ever seen. I wanted to ask Mr. Red why he didn't just buy a new one, but I decided not to bother him.

At the end of that day I held up the last post we had and he secured it and taped everything off, and then we both stood back and looked at all the work we'd done.

"A shame, isn't it?" he said, shaking his head.

"What?" I said.

He pointed at the part where the old fence still stood, right at his favorite place to check out waves. "Only twenty more feet and we could've fixed the whole thing."

"Couldn't they get us more materials?"

"They could. But they won't. Management's cheap like that. Said the job was to replace the faulty parts and leave the rest as is. They didn't believe me when I said the whole thing was faulty."

I rubbed the cut on my shoulder.

Mr. Red shook his head. "Lucky I keep this part sort of hidden."

"I know."

"Only thing standing between some kid and falling forty feet down the cliff is whether or not he's stupid enough to test it."

I looked at the old part of the fence, and for the first time in my life I had that vertigo thing people talk about. Where your stomach hurts just imagining yourself falling.

Mr. Red shot me a look. "You all right, big guy?"

I nodded and went down on one knee and acted like I had to redo my shoelace.

Mr. Red grabbed his sombrero off the tree limb and stuck it back on his head. "Good news is we finished early."

"We're really not working tomorrow?"

He kicked at the old part of the fence and watched it sway back and forth. "Nope," he said. "I'm taking you on a field trip."

Mr. Red's Surprise

The next morning me and Mr. Red were driving in his truck, and he was explaining to me how many hours people work during their lifetime.

As he talked I looked out the window, at all the other cars. Everybody staring straight ahead, barely blinking. I thought how I was now a person who worked, too. And then I wondered if I'd ever considered myself like that before. An actual person. Like everybody else.

"That's why it's so important to like what you do, big guy. You're gonna spend a ton of hours doing it." Mr. Red sped up a little to pass a big rig, one of his hands on the steering wheel, the other flipping the radio dial to a sports station.

Maybe it was being outside of Horizons. Or maybe it was meeting Olivia. Or maybe it was Mr. Red's talk about jobs. But for the first time I found myself wondering what would happen with me in the future.

"Money should be the last thing people think about," Mr. Red went on. "I know dozens of folks who end up doing something they hate just because they like the numbers on their paycheck."

I nodded when he looked at me.

"A guy can buy a lot of stuff, Kidd, but he can't buy back all the hours he's spent doing a job he hates."

"Do you like our job, Mr. Red?"

"I like where our job *is*. We work at the beach, man. We breathe in the Pacific Ocean all day."

"The beach is the best smell," I said.

"People should work to live, not live to work. Know what I mean?"

I nodded. "I think so."

He changed the radio station back to music and kept driving.

Ten minutes later we went off the freeway and turned into a huge parking lot with a sign that said WORLD FAMOUS SAN DIEGO ZOO.

As Mr. Red looked for a spot he told me: "One day, Kidd, you're gonna do much better than a maintenance job at the campsites."

"I am?"

He nodded. "It's the reason I brought you down here today."

Mr. Red bought us tickets and we walked in together.

I wondered if anybody we passed thought he was the dad and I was the son. Then I thought what that would be like. And if I would've turned out different from how I am.

Mr. Red.

My dad.

The only problem was, his hair was shaggy and blond and mine was short and brown. And his skin was way lighter. So we didn't really look related.

Mr. Red handed me a zoo map and said: "Wherever you wanna go."

"Me?"

"You."

"What about what *you* wanna see?"

"Already seen it. This trip's about my partner."

I looked at him and then looked at the map. Then I looked at him again.

He laughed, said: "Look, you can either pick a place on the map and figure out how we get there, or we can just wander around. Totally up to you."

I looked on the map, then pointed to the center and said: "Maybe the monkeys?"

"Lead the way."

Over the next few hours I led us through almost the entire zoo. We watched the monkeys swing from one tree limb to another, sometimes whacking each other on the back of the head. We looked at the elephants and hippos and giraffes and zebras. We looked at polar bears, which seemed soft enough to be stuffed animals you could play with. We went in the reptile part and looked at alligators and giant turtles and coiled snakes and colorful lizards.

We bought sandwiches and Cokes and ate on a bench near the koalas. We went on the Skyfari, a ride the zoo has that takes people over the whole place, and when you look down, at all the heads of people walking by, they look like ants.

I asked Mr. Red a million questions, and for a while he tried to answer them. But eventually he told me it might be better to just take everything in and think about it later.

So I tried that.

I stared at all the animals and the people watching them through binoculars or taking pictures. I saw a kid tossing sticks into the baboon enclosure. A mom holding her little baby up to a flamingo, and the baby crying. I went by myself in the petting zoo, where baby sheep and goats ate food pellets right out of people's hands. I watched workers drive by in miniature zoo carts.

I saw a squirrel running up and down a tree, and I thought how it was free, even though it was just as much of an animal as the ones in cages. Which seemed weird. But I quickly put it out of my head like Mr. Red said and just watched.

That was when Mr. Red checked his watch and said there was someone he wanted me to meet.

Another Girl Mr. Red Knows

We walked into this part called the Tiger River Trail, down this narrow cement walkway where fog came up from the ground. The walls were made to look muddy with roots sticking out. And it was colder.

Mr. Red hopped off the walkway and waved for me to follow him up to this big wooden fence that said EMPLOYEES ONLY where he knocked.

We stood waiting.

"Are we supposed to be here?" I said.

"Doubt it," he said. "But you gotta trust me."

The fence stayed closed.

Mr. Red knocked again and called out: "Hey, Jess!"

"Who's Jess?" I said.

"Met her around six months ago at Seaside Market in Cardiff. We both reached for the same melon and our hands touched. One of those things, I guess."

I looked back at the fence, wondering why Mr. Red wanted

to know so many different women. Me and him were the opposite about that. He wanted to know a million, and I just wanted to know one.

"Do you like her?" I said.

He looked at me. "Who?"

"The woman in there."

He nodded a little, said: "She's great."

"Do you like her better than Maria?"

He got a frown on his face and just looked at me.

I remembered how Mr. Red and Maria would always be laughing when they were together, and how me and all the other kids at Horizons said they should get married.

He pulled off his sombrero and ran his fingers through his hair, said: "Look, Kidd. Maria's the best woman I know, all right? Out of all of them."

"She is?"

He nodded. "That's why we can't be together."

I looked at him, confused. "That doesn't make sense."

"Actually, it does," he said. "She deserves better than me."

I was about to say something else, but right then the gate swung open and a pretty Asian woman dressed in a zoo work outfit stepped toward us and said: "Hey, Red!"

She gave him a big hug.

He looked past the back of her head and winked at me.

After Mr. Red introduced us, Jessica took us behind the scenes and we saw two huge tigers in separate cages, pacing back and forth. Their heads were giant up close. Their paws, too.

Jessica pulled out some keys and jingled them and both tigers roared so loud me and Mr. Red jumped.

"Get a hold of yourself, big guy," Mr. Red said, straightening his shirt. "They're in cages. They can't get to you."

Jessica put away her keys and said: "Don't worry, Kidd. Red actually hid behind me."

We laughed and I pointed at Mr. Red and said: "See? You were scared, too, sir."

He frowned.

Jessica gave us a tour of the zookeeper offices and we met two other keepers, and they told us about the history of Tiger River and how it was the first to be its own section, but now almost the entire zoo was that way. And then the keeper with the beard, Al, gave me a tiger whisker and said it was good luck.

"You'll see," he said. "One day it'll change your life."

"He's right," Jessica said.

"Thanks," I told him.

I looked down at the whisker in my fingers, thinking how I wanted my life to change.

I pictured Olivia.

Jessica took us down this long hallway and pulled open a thick metal door and looked at me with a big smile. She rattled her keys and two little tiger cubs poked their heads out from behind a giant stuffed bear.

They were the cutest-looking animals I'd ever seen. They tried to hiss and growl at us, but their growls were so tiny it just sounded funny.

"Here," Jessica said, handing me a thick rope with a knot tied on both ends.

"What do I do?" I said.

"They love to play tug-o'-war. Max, the one with the light ears, will go at it for hours."

I took the rope and tossed half of it to the baby tigers. At first they backed off and growled at me more. But then Max darted at the rope and gripped it with his paws and bit it and tried to pull it out of my hands. The other one bit the rope, too, and suddenly I was pulling against two little tiger cubs. It was unbelievable.

I never thought I'd ever be so close to baby tigers.

We played together for over a half hour, while Mr. Red and Jessica stood behind and talked. Jessica gave me a glove for my right hand and I let the baby tigers bite into it. They grabbed and hissed and I batted them around, but we were just playing.

As we got up to go I realized I loved those baby tigers. I really did.

Like how I loved Peanut.

Back in the office part we got water and sat in chairs. Then Mr. Red stood up and looked at Jessica and she nodded and he said he had to go to the bathroom. When he was gone Jessica touched my arm and said: "You were really good with them."

"Thanks," I said. "I can't believe I got to do that."

She smiled. "Red tells me you might be interested in working with animals one day."

I set my water on the table next to me. "I never thought about it."

"It's a really great job. Every morning I look forward to coming in and seeing them. Even the big guys."

I picked up my cup again and looked in it, and then I looked at Jessica. "Do you like your job?"

"I love animals, that's for sure. And I like that I get to wear shorts to work and spend most of the day outside. Every job has its bad side. The crowds get on my nerves. And sometimes I think it's really wrong to keep animals in a zoo. They're better off in the wild, you know? But since we're here I try to make it the best it can be for them."

I picked up my cup again, even though there wasn't any water left, and pretended like I was drinking.

Mr. Red walked in. "You should see the way Kidd takes care of this old beat-up dog at the campsites," he said.

He poured himself some coffee. "Feeds him twice a day, makes sure he has water, picks up all his poop. Walks him on the sand."

"It comes naturally to some people," Jessica said.

Mr. Red sat next to her and pulled off his sombrero. "I promise you, Jess. He's turned that old dog's life around. It's amazing."

Jessica smiled. "I was that same way when I was young."

Mr. Red patted me on the back and said: "Guy works hard, too, Jess. Never complains."

"I'm going to ask you something," Jessica said to me. "Would you be interested in the zoo's summer intern program? It doesn't pay a lot, and you'd have to wait until next summer, but it's a great way to get your foot in the door."

I sat up, excited. "They'd really let me, ma'am?"

"I could write a letter of rec."

I looked at Mr. Red, who was smiling bigger than I'd ever seen him. "What do you think, big guy?"

"I'd love it," I said.

"I do have a little pull around here," Jessica said.

"Hey, Kidd," Mr. Red said, leaning forward in his chair.

I looked at him.

"I want you to listen, okay? 'Cause I'm only gonna say this once."

"Okay."

He pointed at me, said: "I believe you can do anything, Kidd Ellison. Anything you put your mind to."

"You do?"

"Anything." He turned to Jessica and smiled. "Guy's got a bright future."

"I have a good feeling about him," Jessica said, winking at me. She patted Mr. Red's arm and took his empty coffee cup and walked toward the trash to throw it away.

I knew Mr. Red was still looking at me so I looked at the ground and thought about what they'd just said about me.

At first I felt so good. 'Cause maybe I could do a job at the zoo. For the summer. And maybe I even had a future like they said. But then this heavy sadness went over me. Making it impossible to breathe right. It was exactly how I used to get at Horizons. When I'd stay in bed all day and sleep. When I couldn't eat. 'Cause I realized something.

It was actually really bad to have Mr. Red say I could do anything.

'Cause he was wrong.

And eventually he'd find out, and he'd be let down. Like when he tried to teach me how to surf. Only this would be ten times worse.

My stomach felt nauseous as I stared at the floor.

The backs of my eyes burned.

"All right," Mr. Red said, standing up, putting his sombrero back on. "Let's let Jess get back to work."

I couldn't look at him.

"Come on, big guy."

I stood up.

"Let's go get us a burrito," Mr. Red said. "That sound okay to you?"

I still couldn't look him in the eyes. Or tell him yes.

I had to just nod.

There were riptide warning signs posted all over the beach. Only strong swimmers were allowed to go in the water.

Devon didn't care.

He squeezed my wrists and pulled me in with him, talking the whole time about me needing a rebirth.

"And you hate those parts, don't you, Special?"

I let him drag me into the current water 'cause when I really thought about it, I *did* hate parts of me.

The exact ones he was saying.

Devon spit over his shoulder, said: "I watched you the other night, you know. With that rich chick."

"Where?"

He kept dragging me. "Does it matter? Maybe I was on the roof of that stupid coffee shop. Or under the steps. The point is, I saw how you were acting. And it made me sick."

The water was up to my waist now. Up to my belly button. The current pulled at my legs. I tried to think how I acted with Olivia as Devon kept pulling me out farther and farther.

I went to pull my wrist away, but Devon gripped harder and said: "Why are you like that?"

I shook my head.

"Answer me," he said.

"I don't know."

"It was pathetic. *You* were pathetic."

"I didn't do anything to you," I said in a soft voice.

"Actually you did," he said. "You embarrassed me. And you know what, Special?"

I didn't say anything.

"You embarrassed yourself, too. Isn't that right?"

My stomach started hurting, and I couldn't look at Devon. My eyes burned. The water was up to my chest.

"Special. Look at me."

I looked at him.

"She doesn't like you for you, man."

"What are you talking about?"

Devon spit in the water behind him. "She's doing charity work, dumbass. She's slumming it for the summer."

"That's not true."

"She doesn't wanna *be* with you, man. Soon as school starts back up it'll be game over. You'll never cross her rich-chick mind again."

"Olivia's not like that."

"And you know what the worst part is?"

I tried to pull my wrists away, but he kept ahold of them.

"The worst part is you wish you could abandon yourself, too."

"No, I don't," I said. My eyes stinging, the current pulling.

"I want you to be honest," Devon said. "Can you do that for once in your life, Special?"

I stayed looking at him as a small swell broke in front of us. We had to jump to keep our heads above water.

"You hate yourself, don't you?"

A lump went in my throat, and I looked away.

"Say it, Special! Say you hate yourself!"

"I hate myself," I whispered, and I instantly felt so broken tears came down my cheeks and blended with the ocean water.

"I know you do," Devon said. "I can see it in your eyes. You're so tired of pretending."

I thought of Mr. Red saying I could do anything.

And be anything.

Him saying I had a bright future.

"I'm tired," I said, feeling like I was gonna throw up. 'Cause Mr. Red just didn't know me yet. Soon he'd figure out how wrong he was.

Devon's head went slightly under as the current sucked us out. He came up and spit water and said: "Today we change you. We make you real again."

I went under, too.

The pull of the water was so strong it swept us both off our feet. We couldn't touch anymore. I started hyperventilating 'cause I couldn't swim.

But Devon didn't care. He grabbed my face and said: "When your mom pulled the trigger that day, and her body fell, your body fell, too, Special."

I closed my eyes and sucked for breaths.

"When those ambulance people came and scraped her off that woman's rug, they scraped you off, too." Devon splashed me in the face and said: "Open your eyes, Special."

I opened my eyes.

He slapped me.

Hard.

The pain a total shock. The loud ringing in my ear. I touched my fingers to my tingling skin and looked at him, barely keeping my mouth and nose above water 'cause of the current.

He grabbed me by the hair and looked me in the eyes. "Do you even know what it feels like when a girl says she doesn't like you anymore?"

"We have to go back," I shouted. "I can't swim."

He yanked my hair, said: "It feels like somebody shot you in the chest. It feels like you can't breathe. Like right now. You want this the rest of your life?"

I splashed my hands all around to keep my head above water. I was crying. But in the ocean you couldn't tell.

"That's what this rich chick is gonna do to you. Soon as she finds out how you really are."

He took my wrists again, said: "Look at me."

I looked at him through blurry eyes.

"That dude you work for, too. When he realizes how fake you are he's gonna walk away, too. He'll never talk to you again."

I squeezed my eyes shut and kicked and tried to imagine I was something else. Seaweed or a bird or a blowing leaf. I wanted to be anything but Kidd Ellison from Horizons.

"If you trust me, though," Devon said. "I'll make it so you can never be hurt again."

He shoved my head under.

I thrashed around under the soundless ocean.

I kicked and bit and dug into his skin with my fingernails.

Devon yanked me up and I gasped for breath.

"Don't you get it?" Devon shouted. "I'm trying to save you!"

He shoved me under again.

Water went in my mouth and burned down my nose and I thrashed more. My lungs burning. Mind racing.

He held me under by my hair.

I reached up for his face and pushed him away and got my mouth above water and sucked in a huge breath.

I coughed salt water.

I couldn't see.

Devon shouted: "For the past seven years you've been putting on this act! Pretending you're a dummy!"

"I'm not pretending!"

"You are!" He shoved me back underwater, and when he let me up this time he slapped me in the face and shouted: "We have to kill that part of you!"

He pushed me under again, and this time I just wanted to give up.

Not try.

Suck in water.

Be done.

He let me go. Let the current take me deeper. Take me under. He started swimming away. Fast as he could. Never looking back.

Left me to drown.

I got pulled under again. And this time I opened my mouth to suck in water.

Breathe water.

Die.

But something in me didn't wanna die. Not yet. It wanted me to live. 'Cause when I sucked in water my lungs stopped it, made me spit it out, made me throw it up, suck in air instead.

I couldn't see 'cause my eyes were stinging from the salt. From the crying. I couldn't think. My arms just thrashed and thrashed to keep my head up. To fight the current.

And then I felt someone.

Lifting me.

I pictured Devon.

But he was still swimming away.

I pictured God.

I woke up on the beach with the lifeguard, Christian, kneeling over me and pushing on my chest. I coughed and water came from my lungs.

I sucked in a huge, frantic breath.

Then I tried to talk, to see what happened, but I couldn't.

My throat burned.

I didn't know if I was okay.

Somebody was holding my right hand, telling me to keep still. An adult with no shirt on. He said an ambulance was coming.

My eyes too blurry to see if I knew him.

But it felt like Mr. Red.

I tried to feel if I was different, if Devon killed the bad part of me, but I felt the same.

I turned my head and threw up again.

There were a bunch of people around me now, looking down, saying things. I tried to get up, but the man held me there.

I looked up at the sky, saw birds flying around me. Everything felt so confused. My mind wasn't working.

All I knew was about Devon.

And how for the first time he'd tried to hurt me.

His own best friend.

Philosophy 4:
About How Some Things
Are Meant to Be

Dear Kidd:

Some people don't believe in fate, even people who seem like they would, but you know it's true from firsthand experience. You should always remember that. Like what happened with the letter mom left under your pillow. She knew exactly what was gonna happen before it happened and thought to leave a letter so you'd understand, too. But it's not the letter itself you should think about, it's how you finally learned what it said.

Remember when you came home from school early that day? With the police and the social-worker lady? I know you try not to think about that, but you shouldn't just forget, either.

They wanted you to pack a bag and that's what you were doing when you saw the letter peeking out from under your pillow. The police were walking around the living room, picking things up and putting them down, but the social worker came in the room with you and kept saying how it was okay to be upset and it was okay to feel angry and confused, but you could barely think about her words. You were too busy slipping that letter in your pocket so she wouldn't see. And thinking what it might say. And as you packed the lady said how it wasn't your fault and you shouldn't blame yourself, and it was okay to cry, to let it all out, even the strongest people got emotional sometimes. But your mind kept picturing the way Mom's writing might look in the last thing she ever wrote.

Before leaving you said you had to go to the bathroom and the police looked at the social worker and she nodded and led you to your own bathroom door and you went in and shut it and did the lock, not even thinking how this would be the last time you'd ever be in there. You didn't go to the bathroom, though, remember? You sat on the side of the tub and pulled out Mom's letter and looked at it. The writing on the front said: "To My Son."

But you couldn't open it. All you could do was stare at her handwriting. And the lady said through the door: "Everything okay in there, sweetie?" And you sat there, staring at the envelope, thinking how Mom would never say sweetie. The woman rattled the door and said your name again, your old one. She said it over and over. But you just sat there. You didn't go out until you heard one of the police people talking to the lady.

In the backseat of the van, as the lady drove you to the county intake home, you pulled out the letter and looked at it again, but you still couldn't open it. And in the waiting room outside the woman's office. And the next day when she was driving you to Horizons, and talking about the kids there and the counselors and therapists, and explaining how it could be a fresh start . . . that whole time you fingered the letter in your pocket but never opened it. And even in your new room, after Maria gave you her talk about how nobody could hurt your mom anymore, and she showed you where everything went. After she left you sat on your new bed, up by your new pillow, and pulled the letter from your pocket and just looked at it, felt it in your hands, thinking how less than a day ago it was in *her* hands.

But you couldn't open it.

Even back then, when you were still in complete shock about what happened, when you hadn't cried or said a word. Still. You knew. Whatever was inside that envelope would change the whole world, even more than it was already changed. And once you read those words there'd be nothing left from her.

It made you think about before the first day of fourth grade, when Mom took you to get new sneakers at the mall. You picked out the whitest pair and Mom paid and you took them home and set them on the bed and stared at them. But you didn't wear them to school the next day. Or the day after. You didn't wear them for over three months. Mom asked if you picked ones you didn't like, but it was actually the exact opposite. You liked them so much you didn't wanna mess them up. Every day you'd come home from school and pull them out of the box and set them on the bed and look at them. Or you'd try them on in the mirror. But you couldn't wear them outside. 'Cause the second you walked out the apartment door they wouldn't be new anymore.

Right when you were thinking about that, the box with your new shoes, and the letter, and Mom, another kid walked in the room and said: "They got you rooming with Jimmy, eh?"

You shrugged and quickly slipped Mom's letter back in your bag.

"Sleeps in that bed." He pointed at the bed across from yours. "Dude masturbates like sixteen times a day. Just so you know."

You looked at him. He was dark-skinned, and his hair was short and messy and he kept smiling this devious smile, like he was about to play a trick on you.

He reached out his hand and told you: "By the way, I'm Devon. . . ."

I spent two straight days in my tent, trying to figure out what really happened after Devon let me go in the current. I didn't unzip the door no matter who came by, not Mr. Red or Olivia or Devon or even Peanut. I think I was depressed again 'cause all I did was lay on my back and stare up at the hole in my tent roof, thinking about how I could have died.

I wrote stuff in my philosophy of life book but most of it wasn't what I meant so I tore it out and crumpled it and threw it away. I left the last few paragraphs I wrote but that was only 'cause I was too depressed to rip out any more pages.

On Monday I went to work, but after listening to Mr. Red go on and on about me almost drowning, asking a hundred different questions, I told him if I could please not say anything about it for now.

"Got it, big guy," he said, passing me a shovel. "You won't hear another peep out of me, either. We'll just sweep it right under the rug, all right?"

We started digging a big hole where he'd chalked it off near the restroom. We had to put in new pipes because one of the old ones had a leak, and all the water in the campsites was shut off. Mr. Red said we had to do the job as fast as possible so we wouldn't inconvenience people.

We dug across from each other for a few minutes and then he said: "So, you just didn't see the signs about the riptide?"

I stopped shoveling and looked at him.

He nodded and kept digging and it was quiet for a few more minutes, except the sound of our shovels going in the dirt, and then Mr. Red cleared his throat and told me: "It's just, you know, you're not the strongest swimmer." He tossed a shovelful on the pile to his left. "And there were signs posted all over the beach. I just wondered if somebody talked you into it or something."

I kept digging and didn't look up.

"Okay, okay," he said. "I'll shut up."

He dug for a while longer and then held a hand up for me to stop. He stepped into the hole and reached into the dirt and dug his fingers around a big rock. "Hand me the pick," he said. I gave it to him and he broke up the ground around the rock and said from inside the hole: "Look, I'm just glad you're okay. You scared me, big guy. I thought I lost you."

I was surprised Mr. Red cared so much. I was about to tell him thank you, but the words wouldn't come out of my mouth.

When I got off work I'd go right back to my tent and lay down and stare at the dust particles spinning in the tiny line of light coming through the hole in my tent roof.

On Friday I finally let Peanut back in, and I pet him some, realizing how petting an animal can make you think less about being depressed. It's probably why they have pets at old people's homes.

On Saturday Devon knocked for the third time since what happened, but I didn't say anything.

"Come on, Special," he said through my tent.

I stared at his shadow moving on my wall.

"Why you so pissed?" his voice said. "You know I was just trying to help you."

Peanut made a low growl and looked at me.

"Poor people gotta stay together, man. How else do you think our revolution is gonna work?"

I didn't answer.

Devon stood out there for the longest time, talking about poor people versus rich people and how nobody was gonna come along and change things for us, we had to do it ourselves. I stared at his shadow and listened to him talk.

When he went quiet I listened to his breathing.

Then he left.

On Sunday Olivia came to my tent again. But this time she didn't say she wanted to talk. She said she wanted to take me somewhere.

I told her through the tent wall that I was sleeping.

"Um, if that was true," she said, "you probably wouldn't be talking to me right now."

"I'm not."

"What do you call that?"

I didn't say anything.

"Kidd, you have to come out," she said.

I felt so bad acting depressed in front of Olivia, but I was honestly stuck. "I'm sorry," I told her. "I just can't."

It was quiet for a minute and then I heard her walk around the tent, and I saw my zipper moving up the door. She peeked her head in and said: "What do you mean you can't?"

Peanut looked up at her.

"I can't move," I told her. "I think something's wrong with me."

"Wanna talk about it?"

I shook my head and looked at my hands.

She crawled the rest of the way into my tent and looked at Peanut. "Hey, dog."

Peanut inched his way closer to her and she pet his head.

"You know what I think?" Olivia said.

I shook my head.

"I think you could use a nice sunset walk with the most interesting girl you've ever met."

I didn't say anything, just looked at her.

She was wearing her ski cap like usual and a white collared shirt and a short brown corduroy skirt and she looked so pretty it hurt my stomach. I thought how Devon said she'd forget all about me soon as the summer ended.

"If you come with," Olivia said, "I'll make you a deal."

"Like what?"

"I'll take you to the most secret place I know. I haven't been there with another person since I was ten years old."

I peeked at Peanut, who was arching his back and closing his eyes as Olivia pet him. My stomach still ached when I looked at her, and I realized why.

I liked her *too* much.

I could feel it through my whole body.

And even though it seemed like she liked me back, I knew it'd never be as much. And probably not in the same way.

And I didn't know what I should think about that.

"So are you coming or what?" she said.

I looked at my hands again. "I can't."

"Oh, really? And that's because . . . ?"

"I don't know." I tried to lift my arm to test it, but it felt like lifting a car. Then I remembered how Devon said everything

I did was an act. I wondered if I was acting right then, with the heaviness of my arm, in front of Olivia.

"You don't know?" she said.

I shook my head.

"You don't know what?"

"Something's wrong with me."

Olivia crawled closer to me and sat on the edge of my sleeping bag. "I think what's wrong with you might be in here"–she pointed at my head–"not here." She pointed at my body.

I lowered my eyes.

She took a deep breath and let out a sigh. "You might not know this about me," she said. "But I've felt exactly the way you're feeling right now."

"You have?"

She nodded. "But you wanna hear my new theory about it?"

I nodded.

"I think there's something wrong with each and every one of us. Even famous people. And the president. Because when you break it all down we're all just human beings and human beings are flawed."

"Nothing's wrong with you," I said.

She acted like she was choking. "Are you kidding me? I'm a mess."

"No, you're not."

She laughed and slapped my knee. "Oh, my God, Kidd. You're like a comedian."

Peanut licked her hand so she'd keep petting him and she

did. "I think the only time any of us are flawless is the day we're born. When we come out of the womb. After that we keep getting scarred by every little thing you can think of: ear infections, the chicken pox, overhearing our parents argue, friends spreading rumors behind our backs, being the last one picked for soccer in PE."

She pulled my shoelace undone, said: "The worst scars aren't even physical. They're emotional or psychological. But you know what?"

"What?"

"We keep going."

I reached down and redid my shoelace.

"And some people are so smart they don't even think of their scars as flaws. They think of them as character."

"I guess so."

"I'm not saying I'm one of them." She pointed to her flap-covered cheek and said: "Did you know I almost didn't come to the campsites this summer?"

"Why not?"

"I was too embarrassed. My friends had to talk me into it." She reached out and untied my shoelace again.

I watched her pet Peanut for a while and then decided to ask it. "What happened?"

"Under my camouflage here?"

"Yeah."

She smiled, said: "Let's make a pact. Neither one of us is allowed to ask about each other's scars. Not tonight."

"Okay."

"Tonight's not a scar night. Tonight we just go for a nice sunset walk."

I looked at her and then looked at Peanut. His head was laying back on his paws now, and his eyes were drooping. I thought how Devon said Olivia would forget about me after the summer. I knew that would leave one of the emotional scars Olivia just talked about.

But then I thought, maybe a scar from Olivia could at least make me remember how I once knew her, and how she was once sitting inside my tent like this, petting Peanut and talking about subjects like human flaws.

"What do you think?" Olivia said.

"Okay."

"Okay, what?"

"I'll go with you."

"Good," she said, and she turned to Peanut. "All right, dog. Keep an eye on Kidd's tent while he's gone, okay?"

"His name's Peanut," I said, getting up.

"Peanut," she said, reaching down to pet him one last time. Then she looked at me and said: "I'd tie my shoe if I was you."

The 100% Perfect Girl

Olivia did all the talking as we walked out of the campsites and down the 101, into Encinitas. She told me about this book of short stories she was reading called *The Elephant Vanishes,* and how she was obsessed with one called "On Seeing the 100% Perfect Girl One Beautiful April Morning."

"Really it's a story within a story," she said as we passed this self-realization place with big white walls. Mr. Red once told me people go there to do regular work like planting trees and mowing lawns and it's supposed to make them feel better about their lives, which he said is an example of how stupid people are.

I looked at the sign and then looked forward again, realizing how me and Olivia were walking so close sometimes the backs of our hands were accidentally touching, but it didn't even seem that weird. It seemed like it happened all the time.

"Are you even listening?" Olivia said.

I looked up from our hands and told her: "I'm listening."

She rolled her eyes.

Then smiled.

"So basically," she said, "two people around our age meet and fall in love. They're each other's one-hundred-percent perfect match. Like a miracle. For months and months they do everything together and they're unbelievably happy. Then one day the smallest hint of doubt comes into the boy's head. How do they really know they're meant to be, right? So they agree to test it one time. Then they'll know for sure whether or not they're each other's one-hundred-percent perfect match."

Olivia was so excited telling her story her eyes got wider than usual and she kept making all these gestures with her hands. Sometimes she'd even grab my arm. Every time she looked at me I'd nod so she knew I was paying attention.

"So they decide to split up, go their separate ways. If their paths cross again in the future then they'll know it was meant to be. But a few months later both of them come down with this horrible case of influenza, which is another word for the flu. They're bedridden. It's so bad they almost die. Both of them. And even when they recover, much of their memories have been erased. They basically have to start their lives over, relearn basic things like math and history. And neither of them remembers the pact they made with their one-hundred-percent perfect other. Years later, when they're much older, I think thirty or something, and they're both still single, they pass each other on a street in Japan, and they both get a weird feeling in their stomachs. They turn around and stare at each other. There's a twinkle of something familiar for both of them, something important, but they're not sure what it is. Not wanting to seem rude they both turn back around and keep going. They return to their busy and empty lives and never cross paths again."

She shoved me and said: "Is that, like, the craziest story you've ever heard or what?"

"It's sad," I said.

We crossed the 101 and passed some clothing stores, and Olivia pointed to the sky over the ocean. "You're missing a pretty awesome sunset, by the way."

I looked at the sky and it was so colorful it didn't even look real. It looked like what some painter would do. Or a postcard. And then I thought, How could I let Devon pull me out in a riptide? If I had drowned I never would've seen the sunset sky again or heard about one of Olivia's books.

"Anyway," she said, stopping in front of a store sign that said MOONLIGHT MUSIC, "this is where I'm taking you."

I looked in the store window and saw a big row of guitars.

"Before we go in, though, I have to finish what I was saying."

"Okay," I said.

"The first time I read the story I thought the two young people were total idiots. They had true love, right? They were each other's one-hundred-percent perfect match. Why the hell would anybody test something like that? I was so mad at the author I threw the book against the wall and swore I'd never read anything by him again. But later that night I kept thinking about it. And I picked it up and looked at it again. Then I reread the entire story and saw it a different way."

She grabbed my arm again, said: "What if the couple was right to test their love like that? And even though they got really sick and lost their memory of each other and never came together again, maybe it was still a happier story than if they'd gotten married and moved to the suburbs and had two point five kids. It's kind of like *Romeo and Juliet* in a way."

I looked at the ground thinking about which ending would be happier, them staying together or them splitting up. I put me and Olivia as the characters.

Olivia pushed up my chin so our eyes looked at each other. "What do you think?" she said.

"But they could've just stayed together."

"I know," she said. "But maybe *that* would've been the truly sad part. You know what I mean?"

I shook my head and told her the sad part was how they were meant to be. And they didn't believe it.

"Here's what I mean," she said. "Say Romeo and Juliet had stayed together, right? Their love would've eventually faded like all love fades and they'd have had kids and jobs and errands just like everybody else. Eventually their lives would become amazingly ordinary. The only reason *Romeo and Juliet* is such a famous love story is because their relationship was cut off at its most intense moment."

I thought about me and Olivia having an ordinary life. Sitting on the couch, eating pizza.

It sounded like the best life ever.

"Same thing with the young Japanese couple in the story. Sure, technically it's a sad ending because they don't recognize each other later on, when they're both single. But I think the author is saying that even though they don't end up together they also never have to see their perfect love fade and become ordinary like everybody's parents. You see what I mean?"

"I guess so." I looked at the ground and then looked back at her. I knew Olivia was smarter than me, but her opinion didn't seem right.

"What?" she said.

"I still think they should've stayed together, though. I bet they're more sad being alone than being ordinary together."

She nodded and looked at me like she was thinking.

"I don't know, though," I said.

"Me either," she said. "But I love stories like that. Ones that make you really think."

"Me too."

"Hey," she said. "I have an idea. Maybe I could give you the book, and you could read the story for yourself, and when you're done we can discuss. Like our own book club."

"Okay," I said, even though I was nervous about reading the same story as her.

"Nice. Now come on." She grabbed my arm and pulled me into Moonlight Music.

She waved at the old man behind the counter and we went right up to him. "There she is," he said, and he slid a key across the counter.

"Bobby's not doing lessons today, right?" Olivia said.

He shook his head. "Bobby's fishing in Mexico with his kid."

"They're talking again?"

The old guy nodded and looked at me.

"Oh, this is my friend Kidd," Olivia said, picking up the key. She turned to me. "And this is DJ. He's owned this place for eighty-something years."

"Thirty-seven," DJ said.

"This is where my dad bought my piano."

"And where Olivia comes to practice when her folks are home. You know she's a virtuoso, right?"

I looked at Olivia.

She was blushing.

DJ waved us off and said: "Well, you didn't come here to talk to me. Go on."

Olivia led me through this solid door, into a room with a piano, and turned around a folding chair. "Okay, you can sit here," she said. "I'm gonna play this song I wrote about you, okay?"

"You made a song about me?" I couldn't believe she'd just said that. It didn't seem possible.

She laughed. "It's just a silly one, but I promised myself I'd play it for you someday."

Nobody'd ever done anything like that for me before. My own song. From Olivia. It proved she thought about me sometimes. Even when I wasn't there. Which made me think maybe Devon was wrong.

I had to tell myself to stop smiling.

"Okay, sit," she said, pointing to the chair.

"It's facing the wrong way."

"Exactly."

I sat down facing the wall and looked over my shoulder as Olivia went and turned off the overhead light and sat at the piano bench. She turned on this dull night-light on the piano.

"Here are the rules," she said. "You have to face the other way the whole time, no peeking, and when I'm done you can't say anything about what I've just played. You have to act like it never even happened. Deal?"

"Okay."

"Good." She looked at me, said: "Well?"

"Oh," I said, turning to face the wall.

It was quiet and dark for a few minutes. Three different times Olivia said "okay," but she still didn't play. I never thought she'd be so shy.

Then a few low notes came out of the piano.

It was a happy-sounding piano and she hummed with the chords a few times through, and then she started singing. I closed my eyes and listened to her tell the story of me and Mr. Red fixing everything around the campsites and how before we met she considered breaking things on purpose, close to her tent, so we'd have to work next to her, but she didn't want to make us do more than we had to.

She sang how she'd actually followed *me* into the park the day I saw her on the swing. She'd been waiting for me to notice her. I was shocked.

It was mostly a funny song, and I was smiling the whole time. But I also had chills, 'cause I kept thinking how Olivia had followed me. And how she'd sat there, writing these lyrics about me. I never would've considered that.

After a while I started daydreaming.

I pictured me and her walking to the music store, how the backs of our hands sometimes touched. I pictured her undoing my shoelace and petting Peanut. I pictured Devon holding my arms in the riptide ocean.

Olivia played and sang and I thought about everything, the summer so far, even before the summer, at Horizons, in my therapist's office, and then my mind went to the craziest thing ever. I pictured me and Olivia facing each other on a stage somewhere, holding each others' hands, as a priest person said: "You may now kiss the bride." I saw our faces slowly leaning together and us kissing and everybody cheering and the band playing this exact song.

We just kept kissing.

And the priest said: "I now pronounce you man and wife."

And right then, at the exact second I was picturing me and Olivia walking off the stage together, going toward our honeymoon, her telling me on the plane how wrong she was about the story of the boy and girl who tested their love, they should've just stayed together, like us. Right that second Olivia's last note faded out.

I opened my eyes and stared at the dark wall in front of me and all my insides felt tight and my head felt dizzy.

I wondered if that's what love was like.

Becoming unsteady.

Olivia got up and flipped on the lights.

I turned around and went to say something, but she put a finger to my lips and said: "Remember the rules."

"Okay," I said, smiling. "But I loved your song."

"That's a clear violation."

"Sorry."

We were both quiet for a sec, while she turned off the night-light on the piano and fixed my chair. Then she looked up at me and said: "But you see what happened here, right?"

"What?"

"I got you to leave your tent."

I smiled.

When I took my next breath it seemed like I was breathing in the world.

As we walked out of the piano room I told her: "Hey, Olivia."

"Yeah?"

I shoved my hands in my pockets. "I think that couple in the story should've stayed together."

"I've been picking up on that."

"I believe some things are meant to be."

She smiled and touched my arm. "I know you do, Kidd." She flipped off the lights and told me: "And you wanna know something weird?"

"What?"

"That's one of the reasons I like hanging out with you. I'm secretly hoping you'll rub off on me."

. . . After Devon said his name, he didn't wait for you to say yours back, he just came in your room and sat on the other end of the bed and looked all around. "Worst thing you can do in here, by the way, is act shy. No foster parent will ever pick you. Especially from a freak show like Horizons. It's the same as when people go to pick out a puppy from the pound. First one who runs over and licks their stupid hand, man. That's who they pick. It's all psychological."

You just stared at him. You'd never met somebody who'd just come up and start talking like that, like you were supposed to instantly know each other.

"Wanna know why I call Horizons a freak show? It's 'cause we get the most messed-up kids in San Diego who don't have parents. Like, I'm guessing something pretty messed up happened with your family for them to ship you out here. Am I right?"

You didn't answer.

"Maybe your dad's a serial killer. Or your mom's a porn star. Or maybe they sold you into child slavery and got thrown in a max-security prison. Or you're all part of a cult."

Devon reached across the bed and into your bag, pulled out Mom's letter and looked at the writing. He flipped it over a couple times, said: "And what do we have here?"

"Nothing," you told him and reached for it, but he turned to shield you with his back and tore open the envelope and started reading: " 'To My Son . . .' " He turned to look at you. "Wait, you haven't read this yet?"

You shook your head.

"Oh, damn. So this is, like, a pretty big moment, then. It's the part of the movie where super-dramatic music starts playing."

You reached for the letter again, but he held it out of reach.

"You really want me to stop? Or do you want me to keep reading?"

You didn't answer.

"That's what I thought," he said. "Let's be honest—you're too scared to read it on your own. You've been sitting here waiting for someone like me to walk through that door." He smiled. "I know how it is, dude. Life's a bitch." He looked at the letter and started again.

And it was through this kid you'd just met, Devon, that you heard the last thing your Mom ever wrote. How if you were reading this then she had some explaining to do. She'd been dealing with abuse from your father for as long as she could remember. He wasn't evil, but something had happened to him when he was young. His own father, a construction worker and a drunk, had almost beaten him to death. He was twelve. He'd left his bike in the front yard overnight, and it was stolen. His father had always beaten him and his mom, but this time he put his own son in the hospital. And though he recovered physically, something in his heart died. When she first heard his story she wanted to save him, she wanted to fix him, teach him about love and show him another way to live. And for a while it worked. Their relationship was beautiful. But eventually, she realized, people who've been hurt that bad revert back to what they know.

He panicked about the sudden responsibility of having a family. He took it out on her. Eventually he started taking it out on you, too. She kicked him out of the apartment. Things got better. But he'd still come knocking. Mostly when he was using. Or when he needed something. He'd break in, middle of the night. She had bars put on all the windows. But then she'd trust that he was trying to turn his life around and she'd let him in for a few days. Only to have him raise his hand again. She went to the police, got restraining orders, moved to an unlisted address, but he always came back.

The last time he beat her, in the living room, with you standing there watching, it was so bad he knocked her unconscious, broke her arm and her orbital bone and detached her left retina. Laying in the hospital bed, she finally realized what she had to do.

Devon looked up at you with a frowning face and said: "Jesus, dude, is this all true?"

You stared at him.

You could barely breathe.

"Your family's, like, seriously screwed up." He shook his head and turned back to the letter. He read on: "'I realized the only thing that matters to me is your safety. Your chance at a real life. So, this time, I'm going to your father. And I'm going to deal with him once and for all. Please understand and forgive me. Please know my only motivation is to set us free.

"'And I want you to promise me something, baby. The Ellison abuse stops with your father. His evil may lurk somewhere inside of you, too. But you don't have to let it come out. You don't have to be like him. Or his father. You're your own person, baby. I want to look down from heaven one day and see you happily married and raising a family. Please. You have to always remember, you're your very own unique and wonderful kid. And nobody can take that away. Mommy loves you, baby. And she's so sorry for what she has to do.'"

You were staring at the floor, not crying, but your heart racing and your mind thinking everything at once. And Devon snapped for you to look at him, and he said: "Dude, did your mom kill your dad?"

You looked at him. Your breaths going faster and faster.

"She shot him, didn't she? Because he was a wife beater and a child abuser. Holy shit, dude. That's right out of a movie!"

You watched Devon fold the letter and put it back in the envelope and flip it toward your bag. Then he stood up, shaking his head. "Look, man, I'm guessing you might need a little solo time. You know, to think about what you just heard."

You looked at the rug. And his shoes.

"What's your name, anyway?" he said. "You never told me."

You looked up, thinking about that question. You knew whatever you said could be the new version of you, the one your mom wanted to look down at from heaven.

"Hello?" Devon said.

"Kidd," you told him.

"Kidd?"

You nodded.

He smiled. "Look, I know you just heard some pretty heavy news, man. So I'm not gonna bust your balls. But 'Kidd'? Really? That's pretty generic brand. What are you gonna do when you turn eighteen, switch your name to 'Adult'?"

He laughed, then walked out the door.

And you were alone.

You looked at the letter. You opened the envelope and pulled it out and read it, over and over, pausing between every sentence to think what it meant. Between every paragraph. You spent the rest of the night reading it. The rest of the week. The rest of the month and year. You read it so many times the paper turned soft and brown in your hands. It ripped at the creases. You read it until you had every word memorized. Until you could picture the letters floating in the clouds when you closed your eyes at night.

But here's why you have to remember that

night when Devon came in. Because fate brought him when you couldn't read the letter for yourself. Just like he said. If Devon never walked in that night maybe you never would've been able to open it. Maybe it would've stayed sealed and stuck inside your bag forever. Buried in your Horizons closet like a pair of new shoes still in the box.

And maybe you never would've known what your mom did for you. Or about the evil in your genes. Or the new person you had to become. Kidd Ellison.

What I Remember About My Dad

How he played on a work softball team with the guys from his construction crew, and how one time when I was little he made the game-winning hit and everybody jumped on him at home plate and patted him on the back. And when he came off the field his whole face was a smile and he picked me up and spun me around and everybody was looking.

His skin was dark and hair long and brown and how Mom said all the girls wanted him in high school. How he always wore Dickies pants and a white wifebeater and his scraggly beard only on his chin. His arms with tattoos of names and places, the biggest one of an old man in a rocking chair holding up a beer. Him explaining how he dreamed of that man one night and as soon as he woke up he went to the tattoo parlor and had it done so he'd never forget. "Who is it?" I asked him, but he just looked at me.

How he always had a cigarette behind his right ear. Even when he was smoking another one.

Me coming home wearing the Superman cape, telling him about the man in the suit who bought it 'cause he saw me looking at it in the store window. Dad staring at Mom, then shouting: "Take it off!" Him pulling his switchblade and stabbing through it, ripping the costume right down the middle, throwing it in the trash. Saying how he better never hear of me taking something from some rich person ever again. We didn't need no charity.

Him breaking my nose when he hit me with the back of his hand. Then hugging me and saying he didn't mean it. And how we both told my mom I fell.

Him riding me on his motorcycle to school that time when I missed the bus and all the kids turning to watch.

The look in his eyes when he got mad. How it didn't even look like my dad anymore. The veins in his neck as he swung his open hand. The things he'd yell. Spit going from his mouth. "See what you made me do! Do you even understand?"

Him being gone so long and then coming to my bedroom window and knocking and me opening the curtains and how he'd always be smiling, but not his regular one.

But mostly I remember a night when he went in my room with his CD player and made me listen to this old song, over and over. How he said to pay attention to the lyrics. Me listening as hard as I could, and him staring at me and then playing it again. His face so serious. Tiny red lines in the white parts of his eyes. "You hear what he's singing?" Me nodding. Him pointing at the CD player and then starting it over. "It's Nick Drake. He's singing that he loves the person, but at the same time he doesn't care. And that last line: 'Know that I see you / Know I'm not there.'"

· · ·

How when he finally shut the stereo off he looked down at his hands for the longest time and then he said the song made him think of his old man, and how last night his old man died. Him looking at me and nodding and crying. "You should only believe in animals, little man." Me nodding. "You understand me?" "Yes, sir." "Animals are better than people. They're the only thing that won't hurt you." Me nodding, trying not to seem like I knew he was crying. "They're the only thing you can trust."

Him crying so hard his whole body was twitching. Me staring at the bedspread and nodding and promising him, over and over, and then him taking his CD player and going out of my room.

"Come on, Special," Devon said from outside my tent. "How long we gonna play this stupid game?"

I didn't say anything.

"What, you're just going radio silent for the rest of your life? You'll never be able to do it."

It was a week after Olivia played me her song, and I was laying in my sleeping bag, with all my clothes on, looking at the book Olivia had given me earlier in the day. The one with the story she'd told me about, "The 100% Perfect Girl."

But I was also ready to do my plan.

Devon had knocked on my tent door like this every single day, at this exact time, and I never answered. He'd stand out there telling me I had to trust him and how I was his best friend and if I kept holding a grudge maybe one day he'd decide to quit coming around altogether. And I'd be totally alone. I'd have no one.

But I didn't care anymore.

"Special, man," he said, smacking my tent wall. "Dude, when you gonna grow up and deal with your problems?" He paused for a few seconds. "Maybe you're getting corrupted by all these rich people around here. Is that what's happening? You crossing the picket line on your boy?"

I never said anything back, though, no matter what he asked. 'Cause over the past week I'd been thinking a lot about Devon. And what happened in the ocean. What he said. Maybe he was *never* my real friend. Maybe my therapist had it right all along when she said the only way I could get better was to cut Devon out of my life.

"It's not that hard to answer a simple question, dude. I know you aren't exactly valedictorian material, but you can talk, right?"

I didn't say anything.

"So now you're a deaf-mute?"

I thought up questions about Devon. Like, he'd found me at the campsites almost two months ago, but I still didn't know where he was staying. Or who he was with. Or what kind of stuff he did. Or where he got his money. When I really thought about it, I barely knew anything about Devon since he was at Horizons with me. When he took all those pills.

That's why I decided to follow him.

He was quiet for a few minutes, me just watching his shadow move along my tent wall. Then he cleared his throat and said: "Watch, one day I'm gonna say screw it and never come back. And you'll be all alone, Special, with your ugly old dog. You'll be like some woman who has thirty cats and her whole house smells like piss."

He kicked my tent wall and stormed off.

I sat up and listened to his steps.

When I could barely hear them anymore I stuck my head out of my tent door and saw him turn out of the campsites.

I jumped through my door and Peanut came out, too. He rubbed his head on my leg, and I reached down to pet him, said: "I gotta go, big guy. You stay here."

He looked up to my eyes.

"Trust me," I said, backing up. "Stay."

He sat down and watched me and wagged his tail.

I turned and jogged to the campsite exit and watched

Devon crossing the street toward the train tracks. When he slid down the dirt hill, I crossed, too, spied him walking along the tracks.

I stayed up on the cliff, by the cars, watching.

For a while Devon just stood there, throwing rocks at a yellow crossing sign. Then when a train came he dropped his rocks and turned around and faced it.

He stood right in the middle of the tracks and closed his eyes and held out his hands, and as the train came barreling down the tracks it blew its low whistle, over and over, so Devon would get out of the way, but he just stood there.

Waiting for it to crush him.

I closed my eyes and turned away, plugged my ears. I could almost feel it myself, the wind going past his face and the ground rumbling and his teeth clenching down and then the huge train exploding into his body, his death-drive soul rising above the wreckage, finally free from its misery.

But when I opened my eyes again, the train was past.

And Devon wasn't crushed.

He was laying on the rocks to the side of the tracks, watching it speed away.

He hopped up and brushed off his shirt and jeans and laughed. And for the first time ever I saw Devon in a different way. He was truly crazy. Somebody who needed therapy more than anyone we had at Horizons.

I imagined him turning into one of those homeless people who stands outside the store all day talking to themselves and asking if you could spare change.

• • •

Devon moved on to the park.

He sat on the same swing where I first saw Olivia and watched the guys playing basketball. I was surprised. The old Devon would've hopped right in the game, made friends with everybody. But this Devon just sat there for over two hours, watching, not even swinging.

When the guys finished playing and gathered their stuff and drove off, he stayed sitting on his swing, staring at the court.

It was dark when he finally left.

He went out of the park and walked up a steep street called Birmingham and went into the gas station at the top of the hill. I stayed outside and tried to look through the streaked glass doors. Devon was talking to the woman behind the counter. I saw her laugh and point at something. Devon came out a couple minutes later with a big bag of chips. He opened the bag and started eating them as he walked toward the freeway.

I followed.

He stopped at the on-ramp, stood there eating his chips and watching cars merge onto the freeway. I ducked behind the freeway sign and watched, listening to the crunching sound of him chewing.

For a second I thought he was getting ready to jump off the bridge. And maybe the chips were his last meal. But when he was done with the bag all he did was throw it in a garbage can, jog across the on-ramp and duck *under* the bridge.

Devon's Secret Life

I waited a couple minutes, then came out from behind the sign and darted across the on-ramp, too. And when I peeked under the bridge I was in complete shock.

There were three mattresses and five sleeping bags and two grocery carts full of cans and bottles and layers of cardboard. Litter all over. Devon sat with a girl and a woman, and both of them looked homeless. He was leaning against the concrete wall of the bridge and the girl was trying to kiss him, but Devon kept pushing her away.

"Come on," she said. "Just one little one."

"I already told you, June. Not now."

"One kiss isn't gonna kill anybody. I promise I won't go by your neck."

The woman sat up, said: "He knows you won't, honey, 'cause he isn't letting anybody kiss him."

The girl turned her head and pouted. She was a light-skinned black girl with hair down to her shoulders. She had a star tattoo on the side of her neck and she was burned on one of her arms and she seemed familiar. Like I'd seen her at the beach or in a store at some point.

The woman stared at Devon for a while, then she opened the big green trash bag by her feet and dug around, pulled out some clippers and started doing her fingernails. She was skinny and white and her face seemed leathery, like pictures you see of old farmer people sitting on their tractors.

Without looking up she said: "What do you expect, though, Devon? The poor girl never knows when she's gonna see you."

He shook his head, looked at the bridge above him.

"What?" the woman said.

"I don't even know."

The woman cackled. "I've met a lot of people in my day. But you're easily the biggest enigma."

Devon looked at her. "Who? Me?"

"You," she said, clipping another nail.

"What's an enigma?" the girl said.

"Somebody who's like a puzzle," the woman said.

"Now I'm a puzzle."

"And the pieces are scattered all around. Nobody knows where they go."

I sat perfectly still, hanging on every word of their conversation, watching their every move. This was such a different Devon. When he was with me he was laughing or telling me his theories about rich people or acting like he was helping me.

The Devon under the bridge seemed like somebody I'd never met before.

"Whatever," Devon said. He sat there for a while and then said: "So, you know that thing I told you last week? How I have this feeling I'm gonna hurt somebody?"

My whole body froze.

I pictured him shoving my head underwater.

Him looking at Olivia.

"How could we forget?" the woman said.

The girl sat up. "You don't have to, though. It's in your control."

"That's what it *seems* like. To people on the outside."

"No, June's right," the woman said. "You have a choice."

Devon shook his head and looked at the ground. "Nah, it's already been decided in my DNA. You can only pretend for so long."

The woman shook her head. "You really believe in that?"

Devon shrugged.

"I sure as hell don't. It wasn't decided that I'd end up under this stupid bridge. With runaways half my age. My dad was an electrician."

"He was?" the girl said.

"Until the day he died. My mom took care of me and my brothers. They had nothing to do with where I am right now."

"It's not the same with everybody," Devon said.

The black girl played with her hair and stared at Devon.

The woman tossed her nail clipper back in her bag. "I used to promote comedians in L.A. Did you know that?"

Devon just sat there.

"I'd come back from lunch and there'd be thirty e-mails in my in-box. People needed to reach me."

Devon picked up a stick, stuck it into one of his shoelace holes.

"It's not all about your DNA. You can be anybody you wanna be."

"I believe that, too," the girl said.

Devon shook his head. "Well, that's your fairy tale," he said. "I believe it's already determined what we're gonna do. No matter what choices we make, it still leads back to how it's supposed to happen."

"That's depressing," the girl said.

The woman scoffed. "And what if somebody just jumped off a bridge? What then? That wouldn't change a thing?"

Devon tossed the stick and looked at the woman. He opened his mouth to talk, but nothing came out and he looked at his hands instead.

The girl started rubbing Devon's back, but when he looked at her she stopped: "Jesus, sorry. I don't understand how you can hate being touched."

"He'll always hate it," the woman said. "It's written in his DNA."

She laughed, but nobody else did.

They were all quiet for a few minutes and then Devon stood up.

"What?" the girl said.

Devon started looking all around so I ducked behind the concrete wall.

"What now?" I heard the woman say.

"Somebody's watching us," Devon said.

I peeked around the wall, saw the woman stand up, too. "It's probably just Texas or Sean," she said.

"Probably," Devon said.

I slipped back out of sight and climbed out from under the bridge. When there weren't any cars coming I ran across the on-ramp, past the gas station.

I looked back, saw Devon come up from under the bridge, too. Then the woman and the girl. But they weren't looking in my direction.

I turned around and jogged past the gas station, back down Birmingham and through the park.

I didn't stop running until I got back to the campsites and went in my tent with Peanut. Then I just sat there, petting him, trying to catch my breath.

I looked everywhere for the book Olivia had given me, but it was gone. I tried to think how I could lose it in one day. I looked at Peanut, wondering if he carried it somewhere.

But mostly I kept thinking over and over about what I just saw and heard. And how Devon was actually a homeless person. He lived under a freeway. I knew even less about him than I thought.

My stomach felt sick for some reason.

And unbalanced.

But at the same time, I couldn't wait to follow him again.

I became obsessed with finding out about Devon. For the next week I couldn't get it out of my head. I'd go to work with Mr. Red and daydream about what Devon might be doing. I'd be with Olivia at the beach, at night, listening to her talk and I'd start wondering about Devon.

I was no longer depressed, either. I was too busy looking for clues. Some nights I'd spy him under the freeway bridge or hanging out along the train tracks or in the park. Sometimes I'd see him wandering the streets by himself in the middle of the night.

One time I followed him into a grocery store. Watched him go up and down every aisle with his empty cart, picking things up and reading the labels and putting them back down, then wheeling his cart to the next item. He didn't buy or steal anything. He just seemed lonely, like he didn't have anything else to do. I actually felt sorry for him.

Another night I followed Devon out from under the bridge with his girlfriend. They walked along the side of the freeway together, barely talking, and disappeared into the mouth of this big drainage pipe. When I got up to them I waited. I figured they'd probably come right back out, and I didn't want them to see me.

Ten minutes went by.

Twenty minutes.

Finally I climbed down near the pipe and peeked in. My eyes went wide with what I saw.

Devon and his homeless girlfriend half naked and kissing

and him laying on her and her hands wrapped around his neck. She was making little noises and her eyes were shut tight.

I felt instantly ashamed and went away from the pipe and climbed up the hill and sat there behind the bushes, trying not to picture it.

I watched night cars whizz by on the freeway. All different colors and sizes holding all different kinds of people. I wondered if Devon liked the homeless girl as much as I liked Olivia. And why didn't he ever talk about her? And would me and Olivia ever kiss like that? Or were we just friends?

I wondered if I'd ever be undressed like that with *any* girl. And if I'd know what to do. And would that mean the girl loved me? And we were together?

All kinds of strange thoughts on love were running through my head, and then I heard Devon and his girlfriend start to come out. I hid behind the bushes, watched them walk along the freeway back toward the bridge, still not holding hands or talking.

I decided not to follow them anymore that night.

Another time I followed Devon as he walked the beach by himself, in the same direction as Olivia's favorite boarded-up lifeguard tower. He went slow and kept looking at the ocean, like something was happening out there. But the water was calm like any other night. He walked all the way to where we confronted the college guys, and then he stopped. Like he was looking for them. But there was nobody.

He sat in the sand and pulled a banana out of his bag and started eating it.

Here's the weirdest thing, though. During all the times I followed Devon, I kept thinking he knew someone was behind him. He'd sometimes peek over his shoulder. Or he'd stop in his tracks and just stand there, listening. But he never looked at me.

Maybe it was too dark and I was just being paranoid.

As I watched Devon with his banana, I started wondering even more about him. I knew he had no family, and he had a death drive, and he was depressed. I knew he wanted to have a revolution against rich people, and he didn't think blond girls had spices, and he stole everything he owned.

But what else?

Like, what'd he think about when he walked the beach all alone? And why'd he always go to the train tracks? And did he ever think about his future? Like how I thought about doing the summer intern thing with the zoo?

I wondered what would happen to him.

The Scariest Place I Followed Devon

One night Devon came by later than usual and stood on the other side of my tent, just breathing.

"Special, man," he finally said. "I've been thinking."

I didn't say anything back.

Peanut made a growling face at me until I pet him.

"Maybe I've been wrong about you all these years," Devon said.

There was another long pause, and then he cleared his throat and turned his shadow face to the ground. "Maybe you're better off here. With these rich people you hang with. Maybe this is where you belong."

I sat there in shock.

As long as I'd known Devon he never said anything like that. I even thought about unzipping my tent to make sure it was really him.

"I've decided to leave you alone," he said.

I stared at Peanut.

Peanut stared back.

"But you're no longer part of my revolution," he said. "And just so we're clear. If you're not with me, Special, you're against me. You understand?"

I didn't answer.

He ran a finger down my tent wall and said: "Anyways, this is it, dude. This is goodbye."

I listened to Devon's footsteps going away from my tent. I waited a few seconds, then unzipped my tent and saw him walking down the campsite path toward Mr. Red's work shed.

I slipped out and followed him.

Devon jimmied Mr. Red's lock and went in and pulled the door partly closed behind him. I stared at the outside of the shed, wondering why anybody'd wanna break into a work shed. All that was in there was Mr. Red's tools and materials like paint and water hoses and bags of fertilizer and work gloves. And it wasn't big. You had to duck your head to walk around.

I slipped behind a bush and stared at the shed door. For a while I thought he must be sleeping, and I wondered what Mr. Red would say when he found Devon in the morning. But then Devon came out and redid the lock and looked all around. He didn't have any tools in his hands.

He walked right past my bush but didn't see me.

When he was far enough ahead I followed again.

He went to Olivia and her friends' campsite and hid behind a tree. I watched Devon watch them and I instantly realized what was happening. The girls were just sitting around their campfire, talking, and eating s'mores, but Devon's eyes were stuck on only one of the girls.

Olivia.

He was staring at her the whole time. Even when she walked to the bathroom a couple campsites up the path, Devon's eyes never left her.

Everything he'd just said at my tent was a fake. He wasn't leaving me alone, letting me be on another side. He was just trying a different way to get back at me.

Through Olivia.

I remembered all the times Devon said Olivia wasn't pretty and why would I waste my time on a blonde, especially one who hid part of her face under a ski cap. I didn't think he could actually *like* her.

So I decided something.

He must wanna *hurt* her.

Which would hurt me.

As I watched Devon watch Olivia I felt like I was gonna throw up. I thought about my mom's letter, telling me how sometimes people have to do things to protect the people they love. How she hoped one day I'd forgive her.

And then I realized something.

All these years I'd had every word in her letter memorized. I could say them by heart. But I never truly understood what those words *meant*.

Until now.

An hour later all the girls, including Olivia, went in their tents for the night and shut off their lights. I watched Devon go out from behind his tree and walk toward the campsite exit.

As he faded from my view I made myself a promise.

Next time Devon came knocking on my tent I was gonna answer it.

Dreams from Solitary Confinement

I suck in my breath and slip through cell bars. Again. Float into the nighttime sky, up near comb-over clouds.

I move past freeway cars and empty mini-mall parking lots, crisscrossing phone wires that frame deserted neighborhood streets. Cars are pulled into driveways where people are locked safely inside, in their beds, asleep, dreaming like I'm dreaming but more innocent and free.

I drift over Devon's train tracks, past Olivia's quiet tent, past Campsite Coffee and the never-ending stairs going down to the sand. And this time when I lower onto my beach towel across from Olivia she's with Mr. Red, who has Peanut on a leash.

When I land Mr. Red and Olivia stay facing each other and talking. They don't look at me.

But Peanut lifts his head.

Peanut stares, his tongue paused out the side of his mouth how dogs think.

Hey, big guy, I say in my head.

It's me.

Kidd.

But I already know my dreams are wordless.

Peanut barks.

Mr. Red reaches down and rubs Peanut's scraggly head, says: *You wanna get us kicked out of here, man?*

Olivia looks down at Peanut. *You think dogs can really miss people?*

Mr. Red pets Peanut until Peanut lays his head back down. *I think this one misses Kidd.*

Olivia looks at Peanut. *Me too.*

She smoothes her ski-cap flap over her cheek and sighs. *Anyway, go on with what you were saying.*

Mr. Red shrugs. *It's nothing. I just . . . You know, I made up all these rules. When he stayed with me he couldn't eat sugar cereals. Or drink soda.*

All parents make up rules like that. It's in the handbook or something.

Those handbooks should be burned. Mr. Red switches Peanut's leash to his other hand and coughs into the back of his wrist, says: *Think about it. What's so wrong about an occasional bowl of Frosted Flakes?*

Olivia looks at the sand in front of her flip-flop feet, her red toenail polish chipped and worn.

In my dream I look into the beach sky. It's lighter than in my last dreams. I wonder why in every one it gets closer and closer to morning.

I can now see the tiny swells moving toward shore, breaking gently on the sand. The muted beach sound like the inside of an unbroken shell.

Mr. Red looks at me and shakes his head. *He always reminded me of Ben, you know. From the first day I saw him.*

Olivia looks at Mr. Red.

Not physically. Kidd's taller and darker. But his way. How quiet he is.

Olivia reaches down and pats Peanut's head. *Was your son handsome like Kidd?*

A smile goes on Mr. Red's face, but he doesn't say anything.

It's quiet for a long time, and I wonder why I keep dreaming this every time I sleep. About me being on the beach with Olivia. Not being able to talk. Her barely noticing me.

The worst part of being in prison, I decide, is the first few seconds after you wake up from your dream. When you still think you're on the beach. With Olivia.

'Cause then you realize.

Sometimes I'd ride us along the beach, Mr. Red says. *Just me and Ben. On my old beach cruiser. And I'd just look at him. Sitting there on the handlebars, right in front of me. Taking everything in. And I'd get this crazy feeling in my stomach. It was just so unbelievable, you know? This skinny, floppy-haired ten-year-old. This beautiful boy. These innocent blue eyes. And I was his dad.*

Olivia smiles.

Peanut stares at me.

I look at the ocean again. The ship's so much closer to shore. It's just outside the breakers now. And I wonder why I always have a ship in my dream. And why it's always coming closer. And who's on it. My Horizons therapist always said dreams have symbols, objects that really mean something else.

I wonder what my dream ship could mean.

Mr. Red lifts his head and says to Olivia: *Can I give you some advice?*

I'd love some advice.

Don't expect to feel like an adult when you become an adult. Even when you become my age. Even when you have a job and a marriage and two little kids running around the backyard.

What do you mean?

If you expect to feel different, you'll be disappointed.

I heard it's like that when you first go to college, too. You expect to immediately feel more mature, but you're still the same person.

I used to lay awake some nights thinking of all the ways I might screw up Ben because I still wasn't a real adult.

Do you miss him as much as when it first happened?

More, Mr. Red said.

Really? It doesn't get better?

Mr. Red takes off his new sombrero and shakes his head. *You never forget. Doesn't matter how many days pass. Or months. Or years . . . And now this thing with Kidd.*

Mr. Red looks toward the ocean.

Olivia looks at me.

What about you? Mr. Red says, motioning toward Olivia with his chin. *Aren't you supposed to be in New York right now?*

Olivia nods. *I decided to wait here.*

Long as it takes?

Long as it takes.

Even after everything you heard yesterday from the Horizons people?

Olivia nods.

Mr. Red smiles. *What is it with you two, anyway? Sort of an odd match, don't you think?*

Olivia shrugs. *At first I was just curious, I guess. We all thought he was cute. And he seemed so much different than the kids at my school.*

You were curious about the other side of the tracks.

Olivia looks at me. *I guess that's true.*

It's not a bad thing.

But there was something else, too. He was always so alone. I think I felt sorry for him. Does that sound bad?

Sounds honest.

I've always been drawn to people with fewer opportunities. I know it's not the same, but I think there's a part of me that identifies. She points to her face.

Mr. Red nods.

Olivia motions toward the ship on the ocean and says: *I remember the day I took that picture. I could tell he was alone, too. And when I talked to him for the first time. And he told me about being in foster care. I don't know. I just wanted to put him in my pocket. Make sure nobody else hurt him.*

I stare at the sand the whole time Olivia talks, ashamed.

I'm not supposed to be hearing this.

Then things changed, she says. *I don't even know when or how or why. But I started to see him differently.*

Olivia touches the back of both hands to her eyes like she might start crying. *I can't believe he did that.*

None of us can, Mr. Red says and he puts his hand on Olivia's shoulder.

I feel myself about to cry, too, since I can see how bad I hurt them when I pushed Devon. In my dream my eyes start burning. A lump goes in my throat.

Mr. Red holds out his new sombrero and says: *He got this for me.*

I know.

He said it was time.

Olivia smiles through her sad eyes.

Ben got me the old one. For my birthday. He was six. Wrapped the box himself and put it on my spot on the couch. I came out from the bathroom and said, Well, what do we got here, big guy? I tore off the paper and told him it was the sweetest-looking sombrero I'd ever seen.

Mr. Red runs his fingers through his hair and puts his new one back on his head. *I put it in a closet that night. I had another one that was still in decent shape. Ben asked me about it the next day and I told him: Relax, buddy. I'll break it out when the time's right.*

Did you?

Mr. Red looks at her, shaking his head. *About five years later. The day after Ben passed I found it buried in the back of a closet. Wore it for the first time at his funeral. And I wore it every single day after. Until Kidd got me this one.*

Olivia lowers her eyes to Peanut and rubs the top of his head.

Mr. Red stares at me for a few minutes. Then he looks back at Olivia and tells her: *All I'm saying is I should've brought home a box of Lucky Charms every once in a while. Wouldn't have killed anybody.*

Olivia smiles through glassy eyes.

Mr. Red points at me and says: *I love this guy, you know that?*

Olivia nods.

First time I felt like that about anybody since Ben. If he doesn't come back, Olivia . . . I don't know what I'm gonna do.

Tears go down Olivia's face and my breath catches. 'Cause I realize they're all I care about in this entire life. Just Olivia and Mr. Red.

And Maria.

A lot of these surf rats around here asked me if Kidd was slow, Mr. Red says. *And maybe in some ways he is. But at the same time he's smart, too. In other ways. You have to hang around him awhile to understand.*

That's exactly what I was telling Jasmine last night.

They both go quiet for a couple minutes. Then Mr. Red clears his throat and says: *None of us knew what was really going on. His people explained it to me yesterday, and I still haven't wrapped my head around it.*

Kidd tried to tell me, Olivia says.

He did?

I feel my face getting red and when I look down at Peanut he raises his head again and barks.

Quiet, Mr. Red says, and he looks all around the beach like somebody might be listening.

But there's nobody.

Olivia pets Peanut.

She starts saying how I warned her about Devon, only at the time she didn't understand what I meant, and how she never could've imagined it would end up like this.

She starts saying more about Devon, things I really wanna hear, but in the middle of her talking a powerful wind comes and I'm instantly lifted back into my dream sky.

Above Olivia.

And above Mr. Red and Peanut, who's now barking.

I rise up into the clouds.

High above the campsite tents and the train tracks and the freeway lanes.

I drift above the ugly prison yard with its two-story chainlink fence and barbed wire and armed guards.

I slip back through the bars of my cell and go under my sheets and when I open my eyes everything is blurry and lost and claustrophobic and I realize if I had the choice I'd never dream again.

For the rest of my life.

'Cause it only makes you feel the worst possible sadness the second your dream ends.

I heard something outside my tent in the middle of the night and thought for sure it was Devon. I sat up and listened.

A bunch of people walking and voices.

I peeked outside my tent door but instead of seeing Devon I found all the campsite surfers passing in just trunks with their boards tucked under their arms, the campsite girls behind them bundled in hoodie sweatshirts and Uggs.

Olivia was the only girl carrying a surfboard. She came right up to my tent and set it down.

Her friends smiled and kept walking.

"Where's everybody going?" I said, stepping the rest of the way out of my tent.

"The guys are paddling to the kelp beds," she said.

"The kelp beds?"

"You know those dark patches of seaweed way out there, past the waves?" She looked down at my hand and said: "Uh, why are you holding a wrench?"

I looked at the wrench in my hand and shrugged, tossed it back in the tent. "I didn't know who it was," I said.

She gave me a strange look.

There was a rustling sound in my tent, and when me and Olivia turned around Peanut's head was poking through the door and his tongue was going. She reached down to pet him. "Who needs a wrench," she said, "when you have such a high-quality guard dog?"

I smiled and asked her if she was going to the kelp beds, too.

"Nope," she said. "But I thought you might want to."

"Me?"

"You."

"How?"

"On my dad's board." We both looked at the foam board by my feet. "He brings it every summer but he never goes out. I had to wipe down all the dust."

I thought about going back in the ocean. I hadn't been out there since Devon pulled me into the riptide. "How can you see the waves in the dark?"

"I guess that's the point," Olivia said. "You don't have to go. You're welcome to sit in the sand with us."

"I wanna go," I said, even though I didn't.

"You sure?" she said.

"I'm sure."

"Okay, grab the board," she said, "and follow me."

Waves You Can't See

Me and the surfer guys stood next to our boards in the wet sand, strapping leashes around our ankles, me doing it exactly like them. They made small talk about how the summer had flown by and what their senior year might be like and who was entering what surf contests in the winter. Behind us, the girls sat together in the sand, talking.

Olivia saw me looking and gave me a tiny smile.

I smiled back.

I felt overwhelming butterflies in my stomach about going in the ocean again, especially in the middle of the night. But I knew I had to. Olivia had brought me her dad's board. And she was watching. And I knew secretly she wanted me to be more like everybody else.

I wanted that, too.

The guys picked up their boards and tucked them under their arms. I followed. All of us moving toward the dark ocean, shivering in our surf trunks. I stared at the line of moonlight going down the middle of the water. It was like a pathway into my fear of the ocean currents and drowning.

I knew I had to walk it.

As we stood at the water's edge, looking out, I asked the guy with green tips in his hair, Jackson: "What do we do?"

"Just paddle out," he said.

"All the way past the break," Rob said. "To the kelp beds."

"Water's cold, too," Jeff said. "I'm warning you."

Jackson laughed, told me: "Wait till it hits your nut sack."

"Shit hurts, dude," Rob said.

A couple of the other guys laughed and Frankie said: "We're like that group that goes swimming in the snow."

"The Polar Bear Club."

"Exactly. The Polar Bear Club."

"We're the surfing version. I think we made it up."

Everybody howled and laughed as we stepped in. Some of the guys splashed water at each other. Jeff even tackled Frankie and they both came up laughing and cursing. The girls stood along the shore, pointing at us.

The water was ice cold on my bare feet, then my ankles and calves. My knees.

I howled like everybody else.

When the water got up to their waists they all dove under

and came up yelling and hopped on their boards and started paddling. I watched their horizontal shapes rise and fall over swells, their arms plunging into the water over and over, feet kicked up.

I was behind them, still walking my board.

When the cold water hit my stuff it felt like someone squeezing with their bare hand. I opened my mouth to yell but no sound came out. It hurt worse than a football pass hitting there, and I bent over picturing my warm sleeping bag.

But at the same time I knew Olivia was watching.

I looked back at the girls who were all sitting in a line on the sand now, huddled together. Then I turned around and forced myself to dive under. I came up freezing in the cold air and hopped on my board and paddled after everybody.

Soon I could see the shadow of waves before they hit me, and I'd duck-dive under like Mr. Red taught me—which is where you push the nose of your board down and purposely go under and let the wave break over you.

I stayed on the same part of the moon path as the guys paddling ahead of me. All of us in the same splashing rhythm. One hand in the water and pulling, then the other hand in and pulling, over and over, my arms and shoulders burning, my neck sore from looking up. Foam board gliding along the water's surface, taking me out farther and farther.

After a while I got sort of used to the cold water, and when I got past where the waves broke everything got flatter and it was easier to paddle.

The guys all stopped and sat up on their boards.

Nobody said a word.

When I caught up, I sat just like them.

The beach was now just a line of land behind us, seaweed floating in giant knots under our boards: baseball-sized bulbs and long, ropey tentacles and slimy-looking leaves swaying in the current. Everything out there quiet and a million times bigger than humans. The moon peeking through the puffy gray clouds that sat in the sky.

I thought how different my life was from Fallbrook. Sitting on a surfboard in the ocean with a bunch of surfers, our feet dangling in seaweed.

But just when I was feeling part of everything, the guys and the campsites and Cardiff by the Sea, I heard a quiet splashing behind me.

I turned around to look and my stomach dropped.

Devon.

He was paddling toward us on a beat-up surfboard, one that looked like he'd pulled it right out of a trash Dumpster. He gave me a devious smile and went on the other side of the guys.

I saw Frankie look at him.

Devon sat up like the rest of us, put a finger to his lips for me to keep quiet.

I looked back at the ocean and felt more frustrated than I'd ever felt in my life. It was such an important night. Just me and the surfer guys and the dark ocean. And then Devon had to show up. Like he always showed up.

But at the same time I felt worried, too.

I didn't know what Devon would do.

I looked at him again, just sitting there, smiling, sifting his fingers through the ocean water.

• • •

Eventually, without even saying anything, the guys all turned around, one by one, including me, and started paddling back to shore.

Devon stayed.

Jeff looked at him and sort of nodded for him to follow us, but Devon just stayed floating in the kelp beds, on his beat-up board, staring into the black night.

The rest of us got off our boards near the shore and walked out of the water, onto wet sand. The wind was freezing. We wrapped our leashes back around our boards, down by the fins, then we hurried up to the girls who were standing in a circle holding out towels for us.

Jackson went to hug Jasmine to get her wet, but she backed away squealing.

"So?" Blue said, pulling her hood off her head. "How was it?"

"Cold," Jeff said.

I looked at the ocean.

Devon was still sitting in the kelp beds.

"You guys were out there long enough," Jasmine said.

We dried off and left our towels draped over our backs for warmth, picked up our boards and started toward the stairs.

Olivia touched my arm, said: "What'd you think?"

"I loved it," I told her.

"I'm so glad," she said.

We both smiled, but inside I was still worried about Devon. The look in his eyes when he paddled up to us was different. And he barely glanced at me. Like he was trying to prove we weren't friends anymore. Which made me think of his revolution.

"I can't believe you guys won't even wear wet suits," Jasmine said.

"It's all good," Jackson said.

Blue laughed out loud, and Rob said: "What's so funny?"

"Nothing."

"Come on, what?"

"I was just thinking of everybody's shrinkage."

The girls laughed.

"Shrinkage?" Frankie said.

"You know," Blue said. "When your little wee-wees get cold and try to suck back into their little homes."

The guys all frowned and said that never happened to them, and the girls kept laughing. Then Jackson said: "Why don't you join me in my tent, Blue. See for yourself."

"In your dreams," she said, and everybody laughed some more.

When we got to the top of the stairs I looked out over the ocean and saw a shape that I knew was Devon, still way out there, in the kelp beds, sitting alone on his board.

I stopped and stared.

This weird feeling came over me, like right that second I knew something bad would happen between me and Devon. Something that would change both our lives forever.

Then I felt a tug at my shoulder and when I turned around Olivia said: "You coming?"

I pop open my eyes in the pitch black of solitary confinement and suck in a huge breath, like I've been holding it all this time, imagining the summer and Devon and everything that's happened.

I pull against my straps to sit up, but I still can't budge. And for the first time I start wondering stuff about my cell.

How long have I been in here? Two months? Or two days?

And why can't I remember any guards coming in with a tray of food? Or at least doing a bed check like they always did at Horizons?

Then I start wondering something else.

What if it wasn't the police who picked me up, but people from Devon's revolution? Maybe when they found out I pushed their leader off the cliff they rushed the scene and threw me in their van and brought me to a secret torture chamber. And this is it.

Maybe Devon didn't die when he hit the sand. And they're waiting for him to get better so he can decide what to do with me.

My heart starts racing and I yell:

"Is anybody out there? Please! Help me!"

I listen for footsteps.

There's only silence.

I lay here breathing hard, trying to think, eyes shifting back and forth even though I can't see. If it really was regular policemen who brought me here, what if they're experimenting with some new psychological drug, and all my dreams of Olivia and the beach are really just a chemical hallucination?

Or what if this is death row?

I close my eyes and picture the summer again.

Devon paddling up behind us in the ocean that midnight. And two nights later, when I saw him stalking around Olivia's tent again. This time with a knife in his hand.

The more I lay here, thinking, the more I believe I was right with what I did.

I *had* to push Devon off the cliff.

Even if the police are testing new medicine on me. Or they're studying a criminal's brain. Even if Olivia and Mr. Red and everybody else never understand why I did it. If I'm never allowed to leave my cell again. And all I have left of my friends are hallucinations from solitary confinement.

Still.

All that matters is Olivia's okay.

And I saved her.

Like my mom saved me.

What Else I Know About Devon

How he stopped going to my tent after the kelp beds. And he stopped looking at me whenever we passed each other in the campsites or at the beach.

The Tuesday morning I woke up and went out of my tent and went to wait for Mr. Red so we could work, and Devon was sitting on my usual railroad tie, holding his knife. I stopped and he kept looking at Mr. Red's tent, even when he got up and walked away. And later that night when I came out of the bookstore with the first book Olivia ever mentioned, about the paralyzed guy, and Devon was standing on the sidewalk with his hood up, watching me.

The weekend day when he was out in the ocean on his trash Dumpster surfboard with a bunch of other kids Mr. Red was teaching to surf. And how he kept paddling for them and trying to stand and falling down. And then Mr. Red paddled over and gave him a boost and Devon stood up and rode the wave all the way to the sand and pumped his fist and all the campsite girls were together on the beach, watching, including Olivia, and it was the first time I saw her notice him, and my chest felt worried and jealous.

I ran with Olivia onto the Coaster train just as the doors were shutting, and together we fell into two empty seats in back, both of us laughing so loud people looked. As the train broke its stillness and started moving along the tracks she put her hand on my arm and said: "Now I *know* today's the right day."

"For what?" I said, still catching my breath.

"What I have to show you," she said. "Today's a showing day."

I didn't know what she was talking about, but before I could open my mouth she told me: "Don't stress, Kidd. You'll see."

I glanced at the scuffed train floor where somebody had carved OTNC POR VIDA in big block letters and under it somebody else had written GO BACK TO TJ, ESE!

"When you barely make a train like that," Olivia said, setting her bag on the empty seat next to her, "it's a good omen."

"I thought you didn't believe in that stuff," I said.

"Good omens?"

"Yeah. Or things being meant to be. Like in the story about one-hundred-percent perfect love."

She rolled her eyes. "You don't know much about girls, do you?"

I shrugged.

"The ones who claim they don't believe in fairy tales are the ones who believe the most."

"Really?"

"Really."

We both watched out the window as the train picked up speed, gliding us through the beach part of Encinitas and Cardiff. Outside our window passed the top of Moonlight Music, where Olivia played me her song, and the big white walls of the self-realization place and the part of the tracks where Devon once stood playing chicken with a train.

Olivia pointed at the campsites as they moved past and we looked at each other and smiled 'cause it's where we'd just come from and where we met, and I thought how it'd be if I stayed there the rest of my life, even when I had a wife and kids. Like, what if I just bought a family-sized tent and kept working for Mr. Red, and what if Olivia was the wife?

And then I thought something else. What if I'd been from Cardiff from the beginning? Would I be different?

I tried to decide about that as I looked out the window. The blue ocean going by, the sun's shiny glare floating on top. The surfers waiting for waves, sitting on their boards like we did the night of the kelp beds. Whitewash crumbling toward shore, where tiny kids stood with buckets and shovels, digging or building castles or burying each other.

What if instead of being born in a trailer in Fallbrook I'd been born as one of those little kids on the beach playing in the sand?

Were people who they were 'cause of their genes, or was it more to do with where they were born, and who their parents were, and what they saw growing up?

What if I never had to go to Horizons?

And what if I'd never met Devon?

The train moved along with my thinking.

• • •

Olivia had been away at SAT camp for the three days since I caught Devon watching her tent. According to her, as soon as she got back this morning she dropped her bags off in her tent and came straight to get me. She said she had an epiphany while doing an eight-page worksheet of sentence-completion problems. When I asked her what her epiphany was, she wagged a finger at me, said it had to remain a secret until we got to her favorite cliff spot at Torrey Pines.

The train dinged as we slowed to a stop at the Solana Beach Station. The doors slid open and a bunch of people got off and new ones got on and then the doors closed and we started going again.

I got a weird feeling maybe Devon was on the train now, but I looked all around and didn't see him. Eventually, I knew I had to warn Olivia about catching Devon outside her tent with a knife in his hand. But a train ride didn't seem like the right place.

"I'm so happy to be back," Olivia said.

"You didn't like your camp?"

"Try spending eight hours a day doing reading comprehension questions and essay-building strategies."

I tried to remember myself in school, sitting at a desk like everyone else, the teacher putting something on the board. It seemed like forever ago.

"Or studying five hundred new words a night. Getting tested on them the next morning." She shook her head and looked at me. "You know what 'clairvoyant' means?"

"I think so."

"'Able to see the future.'"

"Exactly," I said.

"That's the first part of my epiphany. I had a moment of clairvoyance. I was doing this one problem and all of a sudden I was picturing us at Torrey Pines, looking over the ocean and talking. Then I saw myself showing you what I'm supposed to show you."

"Me and you were there?" I said.

"Yep. And it was sunny like this. And you were even wearing those same cargo shorts."

I looked down at my shorts, one of the pairs Devon had stolen.

"PS, that's a joke," Olivia said, smiling. "You wear those shorts *every* day. Get it?"

"I don't wear these ones—"

"I'm kidding," she interrupted, and then she punched me in the arm, laughing. "You don't have to take everything so seriously, you know."

"I know," I said.

I thought about what Olivia had just said. About her picturing us together, even when she was away at camp. "You know that book you told me about?" I said.

"The One-Hundred-Percent Perfect Girl?"

"No, the one about the guy who had to blink his one good eye to write it." I still hadn't told Olivia I lost the book she'd just loaned me.

"*The Diving Bell and the Butterfly.*"

"Yeah. I think it really *was* a triumph."

"Oh, yeah?" She made a face and said: "That's a pretty random thing to bring up, don't you think?"

I shrugged, told her: "I read it while you were at your SAT camp."

"Seriously? You went out and bought it?"

"I liked it a lot," I said.

Olivia stayed looking at me for a while, then she put her hand over my hand and smiled.

Torrey Pines State Beach

The train dinged again as we slowed to a stop, and when the doors opened this time, Olivia grabbed her bag and my arm and said: "Come on, this is us."

She led us out of the station and onto a paved path toward a sign that said TORREY PINES STATE BEACH. But you definitely couldn't see any beach. It felt more like we were hiking into the mountains.

I watched Olivia walking slightly ahead of me, and I got this feeling. I knew I'd never forget this. Me and her walking together through trees and bushes. Going on a train together. Her putting her hand on mine.

But then another feeling interrupted me. Devon and his knife. Him staring at her tent door. Hurting her. Without thinking I blurted out: "Someone's stalking you."

She gave me a weird look and kept walking. "Someone's *stalking* me?"

"It's this guy I know from Fallbrook. You saw him surfing."

She stopped and looked all around us, like she was making fun of me. "Oh, my God. Where's this stalker now? Is he here? Is he watching us this very second?"

"I'm serious, though," I said. "He was by your tent before you left. In the middle of the night."

She shook her head and gave me a dirty look and started walking again. But I could tell she was worried.

"I don't know what he wants," I said, following her.

"How do you know he's stalking *me*? I share a tent with Jasmine and Blue, you know. And they're like ten times prettier than I am."

I thought about that as we turned onto a narrow dirt trail. It was true that Devon thought Jasmine and Blue were prettier. But this wasn't about how people looked. It was about Devon's revolution and him getting back at me.

Or what if Devon had changed his mind about Olivia?

What if he thought she was pretty now?

We came upon two old people sitting on a bench. The wrinkled man had a wooden cane across his lap and he was wiping his face with a cloth. The woman had on a white bonnet and as we got up to them she waved.

Me and Olivia waved back.

"Kidd, no offense," Olivia said, soon as we passed them, "but what were *you* doing wandering around in the middle of the night?"

"Me?" I said, trying to think.

"Yeah, the girls have seen you. Walking around the beach. What are you doing up so late?"

"Nothing," I said. "Sometimes I can't sleep."

I looked at her and thought: *Making sure nobody hurts you.*

She patted me on the back. "I'm giving you a hard time. But seriously, Kidd, the campsites are a safe place. What happened with us and those college kids, that's as bad as it gets here. And that was like a mile away. So is it cool if we drop the stalker talk?"

I nodded.

I didn't wanna make her scared. I just knew I had to bring it up.

As we got higher the trees and bushes we passed grew thinner, and so did the trail. I watched for spiderwebs since I'm so scared of spiders and tried to put Devon out of my head. Maybe Olivia was right and I was worried for nothing. Maybe he was just putting on an act to scare us. He'd done it before, back when he was still living with me at Horizons.

Olivia's Epiphany

Olivia led me through a slight break in the bushes to a small grass clearing where below us the giant blue ocean sparkled in the sun and drifted in the sideways wind like grass blowing. We went to two flat rocks near the edge of the cliff and sat next to each other.

It was the most amazing view.

"This is where I go sometimes," she said. "By myself."

"I can't believe how far you can see."

"Yep." She patted the rock I was sitting on. "Usually this one's empty."

I smiled.

We both stared at the ocean.

"Did you know the waves are supposed to be huge this weekend?" she said. "Like the biggest they've been in years."

"Mr. Red will be happy."

She nodded. "Do me a favor, by the way. Don't go any closer to the cliff. It's a straight drop."

"I won't," I said, looking at where the cliff ended. We were so high up it made my stomach feel weird.

"Last year these two kids from La Jolla High jumped. They made a suicide pact. It was in all the papers."

"They died?" I said.

"Instantly. That's an insane drop."

I thought about why two people would jump off a cliff together. It seemed like the worst possible way to die, slamming into rocks, breaking their backs landing on the sand.

I snuck a look at Olivia.

She was staring at the water, her lips slightly apart, her perfect blond hair coming out from under her hat and blowing in the breeze. She reached in her bag and pulled out a Chap Stick and put some on her lips and then stuck it back in her bag.

"Okay," she said, and she looked at me. "Now, for what I came here to show you."

"It's not the view?" I said.

"Unfortunately, there's more," she said. Then she shook out her hands and said: "God, I wish I wasn't so nervous."

She picked up a little stick off the ground and spun it around in her fingers and looked up at me. "So, there's a reason I mostly hang by myself and why I almost passed on the campsites this summer." She paused for a sec and said: "There's a reason why I've never had a real boyfriend."

I stared in Olivia's eyes, waiting for her to say more.

"How's that for an awkward transition?" she said, tossing the stick at me.

Her eyes were sadder than I'd ever seen them.

"So anyway," she went on, looking at the ground. "I was born with this rare skin disorder called Sturge-Weber syndrome. Ever heard of it?"

I shook my head.

"Well, that's because *nobody's* ever heard of it. Except the people who have it. It's congenital and neurological, which basically means it's with you right from the start. My case isn't nearly as bad as some people's, so there's that. But it's manifested on my face and scalp as port-wine stains."

"Stains?" I said.

She sat there a minute, playing with a new stick. "A bunch of really ugly birthmark-looking things."

Olivia wasn't looking at me as she talked. She stared at her stick or the ocean or the top of my head, but never in my eyes. Which showed how hard it was for her to talk about.

"When I was eight, my doctor showed me a magazine picture of some Russian guy named Mikhail Gorbachev. I remember my mom was sitting next to me with tears in her eyes. And the doctor was so awkward. He just showed me the picture and explained what the man had, and then he looked in my ears and down my throat and declared me completely healthy otherwise. But that night my mom held my hair to the side in front of the bathroom mirror, and we both stared at the pale pink mark going down my cheek, the mark I'd been staring at for as long as I could remember. She said it was a port-wine stain, same as the Russian man had. That's what the doctor had been trying to tell me.

"But mine was so much lighter. And smaller. You could barely see it when Mom covered it with her makeup every morning before I went to school. I figured the doctor had made a mistake."

Olivia turned and tossed another stick at me.

I watched it hit my shirt and bounce onto the ground.

She picked up a rock this time and stared at it. "As I got older, though, the stain got bigger. And darker. I started measuring it every Sunday night with a ruler. I took pictures. I kept a journal of how it was changing. By the time I got to high school it was the shape of California and it was almost eight inches long, if I counted the part on my scalp. And you could see it no matter how much makeup I caked on. That's why I always wear this stupid hat now. So people don't have to be disgusted by me."

A tear went down Olivia's face, but she quickly wiped it away. "My dad gets frustrated with me. He says there are millions of people worse off. And I know he's right. But is that supposed to make it easier when I look in the mirror? All I see is this huge, gross stain."

"You're not gross," I said.

She wiped another tear and gave me a tiny sad smile. "There's a doctor in New York who's come up with this experimental laser treatment. Supposedly the results are really promising so far. My dad said he's gonna take me. But he wants to wait until more people have had the procedure. Just to make sure. Next summer, he tells me, before I go off to college."

"They can remove it?"

"According to all the articles I've read. In the meantime, though, I feel like I'm just going through the motions until my real life starts."

I remembered my therapist telling me that same thing when I first got to Horizons. She said I wasn't taking an active part in my own life. And in order to make progress I had to stop going through the motions. I didn't mention it to Olivia, though. I just let her talk.

"Anyway," she said. "That's why I brought you here. For some reason I feel like I need to show you."

"Okay," I said.

She took a deep breath and closed her eyes, pulled off her ski cap and set it in her lap. I could see a small patch of pale purple on her cheek, coming out from under her long blond hair.

She opened her eyes and looked at me, more tears going down her cheeks. She moved her hair to the side and turned her cheek toward me.

I saw the entire purple shape now.

It was less than the size of my palm and it went up into her hair and disappeared. I looked at it for a few seconds, then I looked at Olivia. Her bottom lip trembling. Her face wet with tears, and her eyes looking out over the cliff at the ocean.

My chest got a painful feeling, and I knew right away what it meant.

I loved Olivia.

More than my body could hold.

More than anybody would ever know.

She reached into her purse for a small Ziploc bag, pulled a wet pad out that smelled like rubbing alcohol. She wiped the pad across her mark, taking off all the makeup that was over it. The mark got darker, and you could see a couple smaller, paler marks around it, like somebody had splashed her face with juice.

"I realize there are worse problems to have," she said. "But I don't have any of those problems. I have this one. And it makes me feel so incredibly ugly."

"You're not ugly, Olivia. You're beautiful."

"Thanks," she said, patting my arm. "I actually hate this part of me even more than my face. That I sit around feeling sorry for myself. But I can't seem to snap out of it."

I tried to think up other things I could say to make her feel better. 'Cause it really wasn't that big. And the rest of her face was so perfect. And who cares anyway. If anything the mark made me like her more. But nothing I thought of seemed like it would make her feel better so instead of saying anything I reached up and touched the mark with my fingers.

More tears came down her face, and as I traced her purple mark she closed her eyes and started making little hiccupping sounds like she couldn't catch her breath. She let go of her hair and some of it fell over my hand. She put her fingers over my fingers, and together we traced around the smooth skin.

Neither of us saying a word.

And she cried.

And I started crying, too.

'Cause I realized I was touching what hurt Olivia most, what made her feel sad and less real than other people. And that's exactly how I felt, ever since my mom left and I found her letter, and in this small way me and Olivia were the same.

After a while she pulled back and looked at me, her face like a rainy street. Then she leaned in and kissed me.

It was just a peck on the lips, but it was the first time I'd ever been kissed by a girl and it made my whole body feel light, almost too light to stay on the ground. She looked at me and smiled through her tears. And I smiled through mine. And then she closed her eyes and leaned in to kiss me again, only this time she kissed me the real way.

Everything became so spectacularly bright around us and then sucked into itself and disappeared.

And here we were together in this sun-drenched sky, stick figures floating on top of blue ocean water, on her dad's foam surfboard, rising silently over thick swells with nobody around, and now it was pouring rain on us, water raining down on water, all around us, the sound like somebody telling my brain to "shhh," thick drops washing away my mom's letter and washing away Olivia's mark, making us both new and real and meaningful. And now we were spinning in wide circles on our rocks, like a Disneyland ride, our faces pressed together, eyes closed, her hands in my hair and mine around her back, both of us holding our breath. Her lips softer than a feather on your cheek and her suntan-lotion smell the only thing keeping me from slipping off this Torrey Pines cliff, from falling down its face toward the awaiting rocks like a suicide pact. And now the old man with the cane had climbed on top of the bench beside us, and he was dancing like a miracle, he was pointing at me and saying: "Don't you understand what's happening, young man? It's a miracle. We've been saved. *We've been saved!*"

When I opened my eyes, though, it was just me and Olivia on our two rocks on the cliff.

And she was looking at me.

And I was looking back.

She leaned her head against my forehead and I swallowed and breathed and listened to the ocean moving below us, thinking for the first time since what happened with my mom and dad and Horizons that I belonged in my own life, and how that's what I'd tell anybody who asked, including a therapist.

Olivia hugged me tighter and I thought into her ear how a mark was just a scar and how everybody has them, except brand-new babies, like she explained in my tent.

And my chest felt so full as I was thinking about us, touching foreheads, it felt like it was bursting with meaning and thankfulness, and for the first time in my life I thought maybe I'd be okay.

If Olivia Really Liked Me or Not

All you can do in prison is think. And since I woke up I keep thinking about the same thing, over and over. Our kiss on the cliff, and whether or not Olivia liked me in a boyfriend-girlfriend way or just as friends.

If I can know the answer to that question I'll know if I was right or wrong about what happened on the campsite cliff with Devon and why they were alone together. . . .

Maybe: Her holding my hand on the walk back to the train after we kissed, and sometimes looking at me and smiling, like it wasn't a mistake. And how by showing me her stain it felt like she was saying something about us.

Maybe not: How Devon said eventually Olivia would realize we were too different. Like, she did so great on the SAT, and I could probably never get into college. Her hair is long and blond and shiny and mine is dark and short and stiff. Her skin is sparkly white and mine is a muddy brown. Her parents are rich and mine were poor and now they're gone. She grew up in Cardiff and learned piano, and I was born in a trailer in Fallbrook without instruments.

Maybe: Her saying how alone she feels, like me. And how she always hangs out by herself and has never had a real boyfriend. And how we were both going though the motions.

• • •

Maybe: She made that song for me and played it in the music storeroom. How on the way out the owner winked at me and said that in all his time knowing Olivia it was the first time she'd ever allowed another person in the room while she played.

Maybe not: How she always tells me goodbye three campsites away from her in case her parents are around. Or that time her dad drove up next to us and Olivia pretended she was telling me something that needed to be fixed in the girls' bathroom.

Maybe not: How smart Olivia is, and how she has all these theories about the books and stories she reads. And all I can think to say is that I like it.

Maybe not: Her being so sad about her cheek stain and feeling bad about herself and feeling ugly, but that doctor will be able to fix her with his laser. And she'll be normal. And she'll start her real life. But my stain will never get fixed 'cause it's on the inside. And lasers can't reach there.

Mr. Red came by my tent super early in the morning, and whispered through the wall: "Hey, Kidd, you awake? It's me."

I got up and unzipped my tent door and pretended to yawn like I'd just opened my eyes. But really I'd been up for hours trying to write in my philosophy of life book about me and Olivia and what happened at Torrey Pines. Right before Mr. Red showed up, though, I'd had an epiphany of my own.

It didn't seem like I'd ever be able to write about Olivia. But maybe that was okay. Maybe she meant more than what I could put in my book.

It was still dark outside and Mr. Red had a brown paper bag in his hand. "Sorry to bug you so early. But you remember at the start of summer when you asked me to explain how I felt about surfing?"

I nodded.

"And you remember how I said it was too hard to put into words?"

"Yeah."

Peanut lifted his head and looked at Mr. Red and then put his head back down and closed his eyes.

"Follow me," he said.

We went to Mr. Red's favorite place to check out waves and he pulled out two stashed beach chairs and set them up right in front of the old part of the fence and we both looked over the cliff at the ocean.

The waves were huge.

Mr. Red reached in the bag and pulled out two bagels and

two cups of coffee. He handed me one of each. I smelled the coffee and took a sip.

He pointed at the water. "Nothing better than this, bud. Big waves in warm water."

I watched one rise up like a wall then curl over itself as it broke in an uneven line toward shore, sending a thick white spray into the air.

"This is my favorite time, too," he said. "Real early in the morning, before anybody's awake. Before the wind picks up. It's called morning glass."

I nodded and bit my bagel, let Mr. Red go on.

"When you're out this early," he said, "you can be picky. I sit way outside, wait for the biggest wave of the set."

He sipped his coffee and adjusted his sombrero, a concentrated look on his face. "First I watch awhile from up here. Figure out where the best break is. The sweet spot. When I get down to the water I use something onshore as a marker. The steps or the old part of the fence."

We both watched another huge wave barrel toward the shore and pound into the water like the sound of thunder.

"It's mornings like this, Kidd. When I have the ocean to myself. When I get a couple hours of big surf, the sun coming up over my shoulders. Riding that last one in to shore and seeing how much the beach has filled up."

Mr. Red tossed his empty coffee cup into the bag and wadded it up. "Almost makes it all worth it."

"You going now?" I said.

He nodded.

I drank more of my coffee and watched the surf.

He stood up. "By the way, Kidd, I'd like to take you to dinner tonight."

"You would?"

"See what Olivia's up to. I'll treat both you guys. And we'll have one other person with us. A special guest."

"Who?" I said.

"It's a surprise." He turned and looked at the ocean, said over his shoulder: "It's kind of an important day today."

"'Cause the waves are big?"

He turned back to me, shaking his head. "It's my son's birthday." He lifted off his sombrero, ran a hand through his hair, then put it back on. "Would've turned eighteen."

I just sat there nodding and looking at him.

I didn't know what to say.

"Anyway," he said. "Ask Olivia. We're going to my favorite spot, Las Olas."

He ducked through the brush and headed in the direction of his work shed, where he kept all his surfboards.

Me, Olivia and Jasmine sat on the same towel on the beach, watching Mr. Red paddle for one of the biggest swells of the morning. He quickly popped to his feet, dropped to the bottom of the wave and then cut back, riding up the face, where he sprayed water in the air.

"Whoa," Jasmine said.

"Look how small he seems," Olivia said. "Compared to the wave."

Mr. Red carved up the wave's face some more then dropped all the way down into the barrel for a few seconds, letting the wave break over his head. When he shot back to the top this time he launched into the air, grabbing the side of his board, and landed on his feet on the other side as the wave crashed toward shore.

Everybody on the beach cheered as he lowered to his stomach and started paddling back out.

"He's still one of the best in Cardiff," Jasmine said.

"And he's almost forty," Olivia said.

"Exactly."

I peeked at Jasmine and Olivia, watched them watch the few Cardiff surfers who were brave enough to take on the big waves. It was the first time I'd ever hung out with Olivia and one of her friends. They'd come by my tent just after Mr. Red left and asked if I wanted to go watch.

Olivia winked at me after Jasmine said hi.

Now here we were. The three of us.

"My mom said Red was ranked in the top ten in high school," Jasmine said.

"Then he just quit, right?" Olivia said.

"After he turned pro."

"Why?" I said.

"My mom thinks it had something to do with his wife," Jasmine said. "And how she put so much pressure on him. You know he got a divorce, right?"

"Then he shows up here, doing maintenance," Olivia said. "It's kind of strange."

As they went on about Mr. Red's past I suddenly got a bad feeling and looked down the beach.

Devon was sitting on the sand, too.

By himself.

Staring at us.

He smiled and flipped me off and then turned back to the ocean.

I looked at the girls, to see if they noticed. But they were still talking about Mr. Red's old life.

Devon stood up and brushed off the back of his jeans. He looked at me again and made a slashing motion across his throat and pointed at Olivia.

My stomach dropped.

"You're with him every day," I heard Jasmine say. "Did he ever say why he stopped doing contests?"

I watched Devon walk down the beach the other way, disappearing behind a crowd of people.

"Kidd?" Olivia said. "Jasmine asked you a question. What's down there?"

"Sorry," I said turning to Jasmine and Olivia. "I thought I saw someone."

"Who?"

I looked at Olivia for a second but didn't say anything.

"No big deal," Jasmine said. "I just asked if Red ever talks about why he stopped surfing contests."

"He's never mentioned it," I told her. "But I know he still loves surfing. He was explaining it to me just this morning."

"Well, he's still the best around here," Jasmine said.

Me and Olivia nodded.

We all looked toward the water again, just as Mr. Red was paddling for another wave. He popped up quick and ripped down the face of it. I wanted to look down the beach again, for Devon, but I could feel Olivia's eyes watching me.

So I kept my focus on Mr. Red.

Seeing Maria Again

Soon as they sat us at one of the tables in back of Mr. Red's favorite restaurant, Las Olas, the waitress came over and said the fish of the day and asked for our drink orders. Me, Olivia and Mr. Red got Cokes, but I didn't even look up when I said it. I just kept staring at Mr. Red's special guest.

Maria.

I couldn't believe she was actually sitting across from me.

Her hair was much longer. And she had on a dress, which I'd never seen her wear before. But whenever she turned to me and smiled, it made me remember how much I loved her.

I had to admit, though, seeing Maria also made me remember a few bad things. Times I was so depressed I refused to get out of bed or even turn away from the wall. When she'd sit so patiently at the edge of my mattress, trying to talk to me. And I wouldn't answer. Or when I didn't eat for a whole week 'cause I thought all food was poisoned. Or when Maria had to turn my journal over to my therapist 'cause it listed all the ways I could hurt myself. Or reading the letter from my mom, over and over, day and night, until it fell apart in my hands and became dust on the rug by my bed. And how I started wailing on this guy Marcus 'cause he was vacuuming our bedroom as part of his chores. And the police came.

Seeing Maria reminded me of something else, too.

Devon.

Back when we were still best friends.

When he was the only resident in the whole house I talked to.

I looked up, and the waitress was still standing there and Mr. Red was saying: "This is a celebration, Maria. *Somebody* has to get a drink."

The waitress had her pad out, pencil ready.

Maria shrugged, said: "Apparently I'm not having iced tea." She glanced at the menu. "How about a margarita."

"Rocks or blended?"

"Rocks. No salt."

The waitress wrote it down and moved to the next table, where a young Mexican couple was sitting across from their daughter's high chair.

Maria reached across the table for my arm. "It's so great to see you again, Kidd."

"You, too, Maria."

It was the third time we'd said this to each other.

"How long's it been?" Mr. Red said.

"Let's see," Maria said. "My last day was January fifteenth of last year, and we're in August."

"A year and a half," I said.

Maria smiled. "The worst thing about getting laid off was losing touch with my guys."

"What's it like working in a foster house?" Olivia said, reaching up a hand to cover her mark. For the first time since I met Olivia she wasn't wearing her ski cap. And you could tell how self-conscious she was.

"Well, Horizons isn't an ordinary foster house," Maria said, looking at me. "I was a Counselor II, which meant I stayed on three and a half days a week. But we also had some amazing therapists who came in every day to work one-on-one with you guys, right Kidd?"

"Yeah," I said, picking up my fork and looking at the prongs.

Maria must've realized I didn't like talking about Horizons in front of Olivia 'cause she said: "Anyway, enough about me. How's the summer been, out here by the beach? You guys are living the life."

"The waves were giant today," Olivia said.

"Lemme guess," Maria said. "Red was out there showing off."

Olivia smiled and looked at Mr. Red.

"Cardiff doesn't get too many days like today," he said. "You gotta take advantage."

The waitress came and set down our drinks and took our food orders. When she left, Mr. Red held up his Coke and waited for everybody else to do the same.

"To Ben," he said.

Maria winked at Mr. Red and clinked his glass. The rest of us clinked glasses, too.

"Who's Ben?" Olivia said as me and her sipped our Cokes.

"Red's son," Maria said.

Mr. Red smiled. "Would've turned eighteen today. His knucklehead buddies probably would've taken him to a donkey show in TJ. Something stupid like that." He laughed a little. "I'd have been up all night worried."

Olivia looked shocked.

"How come you never talk about him?" I asked Mr. Red.

"Nobody asks." He smiled at me, then looked at the label on his Coke.

It was quiet for a few seconds. I wanted to ask what happened to Ben, but I decided it would be rude.

Maria broke the silence by complimenting Olivia on her green sundress, and Olivia said where she got it from. As the two of them went on about clothes and shopping I tried to picture Mr. Red with a son. I thought how he'd probably have been working at the campsites this summer instead of me, which made me feel guilty.

And if I was never here, in Cardiff, Devon never would've come here, either, which meant he never would've seen Olivia.

I peeked across the table at her holding her Coke, talking about the UTC Mall. I watched her mouth move and looked at her perfect face. When we met up before dinner I asked how come she didn't have her hat. She shrugged and said it was because we were going to dinner. And she didn't want to be rude in front of my friends.

Which seemed like a big deal.

She sipped her Coke and then looked up at me and smiled.

I smiled back.

And right that second I made myself a promise.

No matter what happened. To me or Devon or both of us. I would always protect Olivia.

I would never let somebody hurt her.

"So?" Mr. Red said to Maria.

"What?"

"How is it?"

"The margarita? I've had better."

Mr. Red turned to Olivia. "You know, I took Maria here on our first date. She ordered the carne asada fajitas, right, Maria? They came out sizzling and steaming and everybody watched the waitress set them down at our table."

"Ahh, isn't that sweet," Maria said, rolling her eyes. "He remembers. Of course Red does take *all* his first dates here."

"Not everyone gets the fajitas," he said.

They both laughed a little and right then the waitress and a busboy came with our food. They set down the plates and as soon as they left we started eating and having different conversations. We talked about my job this summer with Mr. Red, and Maria said how impressed she was that Horizons let me out of my contract, which is what they give every Horizons kid for their therapy meetings. Mr. Red gave me a look and stayed quiet and I didn't say anything, either. Maria told everybody how grown-up I looked, and how handsome, which made me feel self-conscious, especially 'cause Olivia was staring at me with this big smile.

Olivia talked about her sister choosing to spend the

summer across the country at a college called Brown doing an internship and how her sister's academic success made her feel tons of pressure.

Mr. Red talked about how he used to put his son on his surfboard, back when he'd just started walking. How he'd paddle the two of them around on days when the ocean was flat, so his boy would feel comfortable in the water.

Maria told us about her new job as a high school counselor in National City, and how challenging it was, and how little support she got from the principal.

When we were done eating the waitress came back and cleared our plates and then left to get our check.

Mr. Red reached across the table and grabbed Maria's half-finished margarita and put the glass under his nose and smelled it.

Maria made a face. "Red?"

"Maria?"

"Is that the best idea?"

Mr. Red held up the margarita glass and studied it. He looked at Maria.

"What's going on?" Olivia said. She obviously didn't know Mr. Red used to be an alcoholic.

Maria smiled and said: "Oh, nothing. Red's just trying to steal my drink."

Mr. Red winked at her. "Eighteen, Maria. That's a big one."

"I know it is," Maria said. "But it doesn't give you the right to steal my drink."

Mr. Red smelled the margarita one more time and then pushed it back across the table, in front of Maria.

She looked relieved.

The waitress came by with the check. Mr. Red grabbed it and put down his credit card without even looking to see how much it was.

After dinner we all stood by Maria's car, saying bye. She hugged Olivia and told Mr. Red she'd see him in a couple days for the grunion run. Then she asked if she could have a minute with just me. They said of course and started toward Mr. Red's Bronco.

Maria leaned her back against her car door and smiled. "Look at my good friend, Kidd Ellison."

Her eyes were a little teary, and I knew she was remembering Horizons and all the things that happened between us.

"Are you okay?" I said.

"Of course," she said, wiping both eyes with the back of her hand. "I'm just so happy for you."

I smiled, not knowing what to say back.

She rubbed my arm. "You've come a long, long way."

"Thanks," I told her, but I knew she thought I'd come farther than I actually had, which made me feel like I was lying to her.

She pulled a tissue from her bag, dabbed at the corners of her eyes, one eye at a time. "We had a tough stretch a couple years ago, didn't we?"

I nodded and looked at her Converse.

My mind automatically flashed through even more memories I'd hidden from myself. The night watch pinning me down on the cold bathroom tile 'cause I wouldn't stop banging my forehead against the shower wall. Blood all over everything. Maria holding my hand as the doctor pushed a needle in my arm. The morning I threw all my clothes and furniture out the window and Maria found me naked and asleep in a neighbor's backyard.

I could feel her staring, so I looked up at her and tried to think about nothing.

"Mr. Red's taught me a lot," I told her. "Like plumbing and how to build a fence. He's even helping me get a job at the zoo next summer."

"I know," she said. "We've been talking on the phone."

"You have?"

She nodded. "Red's constantly bringing you up. Kidd this, Kidd that. He *adores* you."

"He does?"

"Claims you're the hardest worker he's ever met."

She dabbed her eyes again and shook her head. "I'm just so amazed Horizons agreed to let you work here for the summer. Do you understand how much that says about your progress?"

I smiled on the outside.

Inside, though, it felt like I was gonna be sick.

"And this wonderful girl you've met," Maria went on. "She's beautiful. I always dreamed you'd get to a place like this."

The more nice things Maria said, the worse I felt. My stomach full of poison. My legs going numb. My chest not letting my lungs breathe deep enough.

'Cause none of it, not one single thing she was saying, was true.

It was all lies.

Things I made up.

And what would Maria say about me once she learned I was lying this whole time?

My heart was beating way too fast. Like I was gonna have a heart attack. "Maria?" I barely whispered.

"Yes?"

I looked at her for a few seconds.

Trying to breathe.

Trying to think.

"What's wrong, Kidd?"

I shook my head. "I'm so scared."

Her face got a surprised look and she said: "You're scared? Why, honey? You're doing so great."

A lump went in my throat, and I told her: "I'm gonna mess it all up. I already know it. It doesn't even matter how much I try."

She took my arm, said: "Kidd—"

"Something's wrong with me," I said, thinking about Devon's throat slash and me going in the current and the mark on Olivia's face. "I know I'm gonna mess up. And then what's gonna happen?"

She grabbed both my wrists and pulled my hands away from my face. She looked deep in my eyes and said: "Kidd, it's okay. I promise. We all feel like that sometimes. I know I do."

"You do?"

"Yes! God, yes. Sometimes I feel so overwhelmed I can hardly move. You remember how devastated I was when I found out I was losing my job."

I nodded.

"But I bet you didn't know I cried the whole drive home. Or that I didn't answer my phone for four days."

My throat lump got even bigger.

I felt awful Maria was trying to help me and it wasn't even her job anymore.

"I was depressed," she said. "I didn't think I'd ever find a job I liked again. But you know what?"

"What?"

"The world was gonna keep on spinning no matter how long I lay in bed." She put her hands on my cheeks. "And I *did* find another job, Kidd. Eventually."

She took her hands off my cheeks and we just looked at each other.

"I think that's a key word to remember," she said. "'Eventually.'"

A car came into the parking lot and went in the spot next to us. We both watched the lady get out and close her door and hurry toward the restaurant.

I kept looking that way, even after she was inside. It helped me start breathing regular. But I still knew I was lying to Maria. About how I was in Cardiff. None of it was true. I was the same.

"The fact is," she said, "you probably *will* mess up at some point, right? The trick is to regroup. Learn from your mistakes. Trust you'll get past it. Eventually."

"Okay," I said.

And I thought if that was a lie, too.

Maria smiled at me. "Maybe that's what it means to be human."

I nodded and told her okay again. And I remembered all the talks me and Maria used to have at Horizons, and how she was the only one who could make me feel even a little better.

"Now, come here," she said.

I moved into her waiting arms and we hugged and she said: "I'm proud of you, Kidd."

"Could you please not say that, Maria."

"I know," she said. "You never liked praise, did you?"

I shook my head.

"Okay. I'll keep it to myself."

The lump started leaving my throat.

We separated and she looked at me, said: "You okay, Kidd?"

I nodded.

"You sure?"

I nodded again, cleared my throat. "Could you not tell Mr. Red, though?"

"About what?" she said. "You and I were just talking. It's nobody's business but ours."

"Thanks, Maria."

My heart was slowing its beating.

She opened her car door and put one foot inside and looked back at me. "I'm gonna see you in a couple days, okay? For that fish thing Red gets so excited about."

"The grunion," I said.

"Yeah, that. I'll probably be a little late. It's my sister's birthday. But I promise I'll be there. Eventually."

She winked at me and smiled 'cause she said her word again. Then we both waved and I watched her get the rest of the way in her car and close her door and pull out of the Los Olas parking lot while I wiped my face on my shirt.

Soon as we got back to the campsites I left Olivia and Mr. Red and went searching for Devon. My talk with Maria made me think I needed to find him as soon as possible.

I hurried down the stairs to the beach, looked along the shore all the way up to where the college kids used to hang out, near Olivia's lifeguard tower.

I went across the street from the campsites, to the train tracks. I went to the park, the grocery store, the gas station, under the freeway bridge.

But Devon wasn't at any of his regular places.

I stood in front of the gas station trying to think if there was another place to look. His throat slash kept playing in my mind, over and over. And Maria's words about being human. And my lies to her. And Olivia's face without her hat. I knew I could make everything better if I just found Devon.

On my walk back to the campsites I decided to ask Mr. Red for help. Even if I had to tell him everything about Devon's threats. Maybe we could go looking in his Bronco.

As I was cutting through the campsites I passed Olivia and Jasmine and Blue, who were talking outside Campsite Coffee even though it was closed.

My whole mind was on Devon, so I hoped I could just slip by without anybody noticing. But Olivia stood up and said: "Kidd."

I stopped.

She was wearing her ski cap again.

I looked around for Devon as she walked toward me, even though I knew he wouldn't be here.

"Thanks for inviting me to dinner," she said. "I totally loved your friend Maria."

"She thinks you're beautiful," I said.

"Really?" Olivia looked back at her girls. "That's so sweet. What's Red waiting for? They seem so great together."

"I know."

"O, we going?" Blue called from the front of the shop.

"Hang on," Olivia called back.

She turned to me. "We're about to walk the beach, but I wanted to talk to you about something."

The bad stomach feeling I had with Maria came right back. "What is it?" I said.

"I don't know," she said, looking at the ground.

My heart started going fast again.

My legs felt heavy.

"I keep thinking about this stalker guy you told me about. You were looking for him on the beach today, weren't you?"

"Not really," I said.

She looked back at her girls. "Maybe we should wait to talk until I get back." She glanced at her watch. "Can we meet at your tent in like an hour?"

I nodded. Her watch said it was almost ten.

She didn't hug me or wave before she went back. I tried to think if it was 'cause she knew I was looking down the beach for Devon, or 'cause Blue and Jasmine were behind us.

Me and Mr. Red's Talk

When I got to Mr. Red's tent I found Peanut sitting by the railroad tie waiting for me, which seemed weird.

I tapped on Mr. Red's tent door.

No answer.

Peanut stood up and barked.

"What's going on?" I told him.

He started walking away, looking over his shoulder like he wanted me to follow.

We ended up at Mr. Red's favorite place to check out waves. I ducked under the bushes after Peanut, and there was Mr. Red, sitting alone in one of his chairs, holding a glass up to his lips.

He saw me and Peanut and stayed frozen like that for a few seconds, just staring.

Then he tilted his glass and drank.

I looked at the bottle in his other hand and instantly knew it was alcohol.

"Busted," he said.

"What are you drinking?" I said.

"Finest whiskey a man can buy for fifteen bucks." He raised his glass like he was toasting me. "Tastes like piss." He was slurring his words and his eyes were drooping and his whole body was sort of leaning to the side.

"You okay, Mr. Red?"

He smiled and shook his head. "Why do you still call me 'Mr.'? Jesus, I've never understood that. Aren't we friends by now?"

I opened my mouth to say we were, but he waved me off and pointed at his other chair, still folded up and stashed in the bushes. "Pull that bad boy over here," he said. "I've been meaning to talk to you."

I grabbed it, thinking how everybody wanted to talk to me, and how I always assumed it'd be about something bad.

I sat down across from him.

Peanut came near my feet, his tongue going, eyes switching between me and Mr. Red.

"Ever wonder what this old guy's thinking?" Mr. Red slurred.

I shrugged, told him: "I thought you didn't drink."

"I don't." He took the last sip out of his glass and filled it back up. "And don't be asking me to pour you a glass, either, Kidd. I refuse to serve minors."

"I don't want any."

"Well, that makes one of us," he said.

I watched him take another long drink and then turn to the ocean. You couldn't see the big waves in the dark, but you could hear them. The thunder sound of water crashing on water.

Mr. Red was drunk 'cause of his son. I knew that. But I kept trying to think why I felt so guilty about it. Like the whole thing was my fault.

Peanut laid down but kept his eyes open.

Like he wanted to watch over our talk.

It was quiet for a couple minutes, except the ocean. Then Mr. Red took off his old sombrero, put it on his knee and ran a hand through his floppy blond hair. "Jesus, big guy, I'm drunker than hell."

"Should you stop?"

"Of course I should stop."

He poured another glass and took a sip and looked at me for a while, shaking his head. "He was just doing a couple tricks on his skateboard, big guy. Him and his knucklehead buddies. At the mall."

"Who?" I asked.

But I knew.

"Was trying to ollie down some stairs. Like he had a couple hundred times before. This time he slipped, though. Bumped his head on the cement." Mr. Red downed the rest of his drink. "According to his buddies it didn't even seem that bad. They all laughed it off and kept skating. Including Ben."

I stared at Mr. Red's beat-up sombrero, trying to imagine having your son die.

I pictured my mom's letter.

The corner peeking out from under my pillow.

"I felt the little bump on his head when he got home. Told him to shake it off. Tossed a bottle of aspirin in his lap. We ordered pizza and watched a baseball game on TV. Then we went to bed."

Mr. Red's glass was balanced crooked on his knee.

Some of his whiskey was dribbling out.

"Went to his room the next morning. His mom was on her way over. But I couldn't wake him up. Grabbed his shoulder and shook him. Called his name, over and over. Ben. Come on, buddy, you gotta get up. Mom's gonna be pissed. But I couldn't get him up."

Mr. Red's glass slipped from his hand and fell to the dirt.

Peanut lifted his head.

The three of us stared at the fallen glass.

Mr. Red took a swig straight from his bottle, and wiped his mouth with the back of his hand. He smiled at me.

I felt so sad for him and his son. It didn't seem fair that someone like Mr. Red's kid was gone, and someone with problems like me was still here.

Right then Mr. Red's Bob Marley song started playing on his phone. He pulled it out of his pocket, looked at who it was, and put it back.

"Wanna hear the crazy thing about this life?" he said.

I nodded.

"You can be here one minute, talking like me and you, watching the Padres, and then you're gone."

He snapped his fingers. "Takes two seconds, Kidd."

Even though Mr. Red was smiling, there were tears in his eyes.

"All this stuff we do every day," he said. "All we think. It's hanging on by a thread."

I looked at the ground, picturing a kid who looked like Mr. Red falling off a skateboard. Picturing Olivia's face mark. Devon's gun against his own head. My dad punching my mom. Pushing me against a wall. Me caught in the ocean current.

Even though Mr. Red was drunk, I knew he was exactly right. We could all die in two seconds. With barely anything.

Why wasn't anybody watching over us? I thought.

Why wasn't someone making sure?

Then I considered my old philosophy, the one I thought back at Horizons. Nothing mattered. And nothing was worth it. And no one cared. I instantly felt my old sinking feeling.

I wiped my face on my shirt.

When I looked up, Mr. Red's eyes were closed and his entire body was leaning way to the side.

I hopped out of my chair and straightened him, the whiskey bottle slipping from his fingers and falling to the ground. Most of it spilling in the dirt.

Peanut barked and barked.

Until Mr. Red opened his eyes and looked at Peanut.

Then he looked at me and said: "How'd you get over here so fast?"

He chuckled under his breath and slouched back in his chair, his eyes closing again. "Hey, Kidd," he said, his face losing its smile. "I always wanted to ask you something."

"Okay," I said, putting his bottle straight.

"It's a serious question, though. Can you handle serious?"

"Yeah," I said, turning his wrist so I could see his watch. It was already after eleven. I was late to meet Olivia.

"You know when I had a meeting with those supervisors last summer? Your Horizons people . . ."

I looked over my shoulder, thought if I should hurry and meet Olivia and then come back or if I should keep listening to Mr. Red's slurred words.

Peanut stood up, watching me.

"I wore a tie," he said. "You picture that? Me in a tie?"

"Mr. Red," I said. "Can you wait here a minute?"

"I can wait here forever, bud." He laughed and said: "Nowhere else to go."

I told Peanut to stay and ducked through the brush and ran to my tent.

Olivia was already standing there, waiting.

"Kidd," she said, soon as she saw me.

I went right up to her. "Sorry I'm late."

"I just got here." She took both my hands and looked in my eyes. "Listen, I realized something on my walk."

"What?" I said.

She squeezed my hands and let them go. "You genuinely care about me."

I nodded.

"Probably more than anybody besides my parents. So this all comes from a good place, I know. But can we agree on something?"

"Okay," I said, getting ready for something bad.

"Can we please not talk about anyone following me?"

I looked back at her, said: "It's just, I want you to be safe—"

"I'm fine, though," she interrupted. She reached up and shook me by the shoulders. "Don't you see that?"

I nodded.

She let go, said: "Honestly? You're starting to scare me. And I don't want to be scared at the campsites. I've been coming here since I was a little girl."

I didn't say anything back. Olivia just didn't understand. She'd lived her whole life in safe places. But I knew about the string Mr. Red said was holding things together. And how easily it could break. And I didn't want that to happen to hers.

"Okay?"

"Okay," I said.

She patted my arm.

"I have to go help someone," I said. "Can I just see you tomorrow?"

"Actually, I wanted to talk to you about that, too— Wait, who do you have to help?"

"Mr. Red. He fell asleep in his beach chair."

"Need help?"

I looked at Olivia, wondering if Mr. Red would want anybody else to see him drunk.

Before I could tell Olivia no thanks, she said: "Lead the way."

I turned and started toward Mr. Red's secret spot on the cliff, listening to the sound of Olivia's footsteps behind me.

Mr. Red's Question

When we got to Mr. Red, his head was leaning *way* to the side, almost touching his sombrero, which was upside down in the dirt. His whiskey bottle was back in his hand, too, even though it was empty.

His phone played the Bob Marley song again, and Peanut stood beside him, nosing his leg.

Me and Olivia rushed over and sat Mr. Red up straight.

"Oh, my God," Olivia said. "Is he totally wasted?"

"I think he's just tired," I said, thinking Mr. Red wouldn't want anybody to know.

"No, look." She pointed at the whiskey bottle.

"Oh, yeah," I told her. I shook his arm and said: "Mr. Red. Wake up."

He didn't wake up.

I automatically thought of his son and shook him harder. And said his name again.

Olivia grabbed his phone off his lap, just as it stopped ringing, looked at the caller ID. "Who's Bill the Deacon?" she said.

"Mr. Red's friend."

She put the phone back down, and right away it started ringing again. I picked it up this time and shook Mr. Red, but he still didn't answer.

"He's passed out," Olivia said.

I flipped open the phone and said: "Hello?"

"Red?" a deep voice said. "Where's Red?"

"He drank alcohol," I said.

There was a short pause and then the voice said: "God-damn it! Okay, lemme speak with him. Is he there?"

"He's here, but he's passed out."

"Who is it?" Olivia said.

"Where's 'here'?" the voice said.

"The campsites. In Cardiff."

"Be there in fifteen," he said. And then he hung up.

"Who was it?" Olivia said again.

"This guy who's part of Mr. Red's alcohol program."

"Oh." Olivia looked back down at Mr. Red. "Do you think this is because of his son's birthday?"

"Here," I said, putting his sombrero back on his head. "We should carry him to his tent."

She nodded and we both put one of his arms over our shoulders and started moving him slowly down the campsite path, toward his tent. His legs barely doing any of the work. Peanut following right behind us.

"Don't you think, though," Olivia said as we struggled along, "it's because of his son?"

"I think so."

She shook her head. "How does anyone get over something like that? Losing a person so close to you?"

I looked at Olivia, wondering what she'd say if I told her how I lost my mom.

We finally made it to Mr. Red's tent, and I held him up while Olivia unzipped his door. We got him inside and laid him on his futon pad. Besides a small dresser there was nothing else, not even a picture of somebody. For the first time ever I saw Mr. Red as a lonely person. Even with all his women.

He blinked his eyes a couple times and looked up at me, said: "Can you picture it, big guy?"

"What?" I told him back.

"A tie on me?"

"You're home now," Olivia said. "Everything's gonna be okay."

Mr. Red looked at her, and then he looked back at me. You could tell he was too drunk to care what was even happening. "I just always wanted to ask about that," he slurred.

"About what?" I said.

His breath was pure alcohol, which I knew the smell of from my dad.

"Should I get him water?" Olivia said.

"Good idea," I said, lifting his head and sliding his pillow underneath.

She went out of the tent.

Mr. Red coughed and reached out his hand, like he was feeling for his whiskey bottle.

"It's gone," I said.

He grabbed his sombrero instead, laid it on his chest. "A nice kid like you, big guy," he said. "It just kills me to think of it."

"I don't know what you're saying, Mr. Red."

Olivia came back into the tent with a bottle of water and touched it to Mr. Red's hand.

He took it and drank a little.

Then he handed it back to Olivia and pointed at me. "Why'd you swallow all those pills?"

I stopped what I was doing and stared at him.

I turned to Olivia.

Mr. Red let his hand fall to the mattress, said: "They told me in that meeting we had."

"What meeting?" I said.

"I always wanted to ask," Mr. Red said. "But it's not my business. So I'm sorry."

I kept staring at him.

My skin tingling.

Mind emptying out, like a whiskey bottle in the dirt.

"It's just a thread, son. Why would anybody destroy it themselves?"

"What pills is he talking about?" Olivia said, touching my arm.

I shook my head. "I think he's drunk like you said."

Mr. Red mumbled a little more about the pills, but his words got too slurred to even understand. And then his eyelids slid the rest of the way down his eyes. And his breathing got heavier like he was passed out again.

"It wasn't me," I said under my breath, even though he was no longer listening.

"It wasn't me."

I backed away from the bed a little and stared at Mr. Red. Tried to think why he'd say that.

Olivia was still looking at me. "What was he talking about?" she said.

I shook my head, told her: "He mixed me up with another person."

Mr. Red had one arm over his eyes now. His sombrero on his chest. I made myself a deal.

I could think about everything later. After I found Devon. After I did what I had to do.

"You okay?" Olivia said.

I looked at her and nodded. "I'm worried about Mr. Red."

She nodded.

Me and Olivia waited like that, together.

In Mr. Red's empty tent.

Not really talking.

Until Bill the Deacon showed up a couple minutes later and said he'd take over.

I walked Olivia back to her tent, sensing it was weird between us, 'cause we were barely talking. But I had no idea what
to say to make it normal.

She stopped three campsites away from hers, like usual.
Peanut bumped into the back of my legs.

We stood there looking at each other, and she said: "I've
known Red for years. I never would've thought he had a drinking problem."

"I know," I said.

She smoothed down the flaps of her ski cap and said:
"Know what's strange, Kidd?"

"What?"

"I don't think people can truly know one another. I mean,
really *know*."

I shoved my hands in the pockets of my cargo shorts, considering that. Even though she'd brought up Mr. Red, it felt
like she was talking about me.

"We only reveal what we want other people to know, right?
It's like we create these fictional characters for the public. And
inside we're somebody totally different."

"You think everybody does it?" I said.

"I'm not saying it's a bad thing," she told me. "It's just how
it is. Everyone's a puzzle that's impossible to solve. 'Cause we
never have all the actual pieces."

I stood there nodding, wondering if we could even solve
ourselves.

We were both quiet for a few seconds, and I watched Olivia

lean down to pet Peanut. Her ski cap back on and her straight blond hair coming out the bottom. Sundress and flip-flops. Rubber bracelets.

Even if I could never solve Olivia, I thought, I had enough puzzle pieces to know I loved her.

"So I'm gonna be at this college fair tomorrow," she said. "And then my parents are taking my grandpa out to dinner for his birthday. So I won't be around."

"Okay," I said.

"And I think I might know something I'm not supposed to know. I heard my mom talking on the phone this morning. It sounded like my grandpa and dad might take me on a surprise trip to New York."

"Really?" I said.

At first I was happy for her, thinking she could find out about that laser treatment for her mark. But then I realized something. It was almost the end of the summer already, so me and Olivia didn't have that much time left. And what if her trip made it even less? What if it made it nothing?

"Anyway, it's not for sure yet."

"But you heard them say it?" I felt like I was never gonna see her again.

"I'm pretty sure that's what I overheard. Time to get my acting skills together, right? Pretend I'm super shocked if that's what they tell me tomorrow."

"Will you be back at the campsites?" I asked.

"That's the thing," she said. "I don't know when we'd go. I have school coming up, and I know my dad would never let me miss. We'd probably go soon."

I looked at the ground, nodding, feeling my depression

oozing back into my veins. It was worse than after I almost drowned in the riptide.

"Hey," she said, lifting my chin.

I looked up and tried to smile.

"I got an idea. We should watch the grunion together. That way, if I go to New York we'll at least have one last time of hanging out."

"Okay," I said.

"And you know what I was thinking?"

"What?"

"Maybe we could watch from that part of the cliff where we just found Red?"

I nodded. "He said I could use his chairs."

"Awesome," Olivia said. "It's a date, then. I'll come get you the day after tomorrow."

"Okay," I said.

"I better go, though," she said.

But then she paused, like she was thinking. "You think Red'll be okay?"

"I hope so," I said. "I'll check on him soon as I wake up."

"Good," she said.

She waved at me real quick and walked the rest of the way to her campsite, toward her tent.

As she stepped in and zipped the door back up, I thought how she didn't hug me again. And how this time there was nobody else around.

I jogged along the tide, looking for Devon, knowing everything was falling apart. The summer had been going so perfect. I met a girl. I had freedom. And a job. A tent. A dog to hang out with. But now it was all coming to an end. I had no idea what would happen to me.

The only way it could be okay, I promised myself, was if I found Devon and did what I had to do.

I went all the way to the lifeguard tower and back, but he wasn't on the beach. I went across the street to the train tracks and walked on the rocks between the rails. Devon wasn't there either.

I went to the park and looked all around.

Then I froze.

Devon was just sitting there, near the basketball court. The exact spot I'd been the first time I saw Olivia on the swings.

"Hey!" I yelled from across the park.

Devon looked up.

A smile going on his face.

There was nobody else in the park. Just me and him. And I started walking toward the basketball court.

He stood up and pointed at me. "I wouldn't do that, Special."

I kept walking.

"Trust me," he said. "I honestly wouldn't come too much closer."

I slowed down, said: "What do you even want?"

"World peace."

I stopped.

Stood there.

"You know what I'm talking about," I said. "What do you want with Olivia?"

"Don't you understand?" he said, shaking his head, holding out his hands. "These rich people, Special. From the time they're born they get everything. And we get nothing. We live in shacks and survive on bread and water. Somebody has to take action, Special. Somebody has to *do* something."

"You don't live in a shack," I said.

"Figure of speech, dude."

"You live under the freeway with homeless people. I saw you."

He started laughing. "You honestly think I'm that stupid?" he said. "Like I haven't known this whole time you've been following me?"

I started walking again.

"I really wouldn't do that," he said, and this time he pulled a gun from the back of his jeans and held it by his side. "Don't make me cap your ass, Special. These bullets are reserved for rich folks."

"I know it's fake," I said as I neared the basketball court.

"Is it?" He looked it over, let it drop back to his side. "Or is this a completely different gun? What if the fake one's still at the bottom of the ocean?"

"You went back and got it."

"You willing to take that risk?"

I stopped at the opposite sideline from him to think.

A big smile lit up Devon's face.

We were only a basketball court away from everything that was gonna happen.

"Why don't you trust me, Special? I swear to God I know what I'm doing."

"You want to hurt people."

"Only the upper class."

"They're people, too."

"People who hold us down. Who believe they're superior. Who send us to die in wars that make them money."

I shook my head. "Hurting rich people isn't gonna help anybody."

He smiled, said: "That's always been the problem between us. Ever since we met. You don't trust me."

I stared at him.

"And this whole time, man, all I've cared about is what's best for people like us."

"You don't care about me."

"I care about you the most," he said. "You're my only best friend." He looked down at his gun.

"You pulled me into that current. You tried to drown me."

"I tried to save you."

I shook my head. I felt so scared and frustrated my whole body was completely tense. My muscles ached. I had to tell myself to breathe. It seemed like the whole night was crashing down on me at once. Lying to Maria. And Mr. Red drinking and bringing up pills. Olivia saying she was gonna leave me forever.

And now Devon.

Holding a gun.

Lying about saving me.

"Look at you standing there," he said. "All pissed off at me. When you should be focusing on more important issues."

"Like what?"

"Like the fact that you know you're gonna ruin everything. All your stupid rehabilitation. Your superficial love affair with the deformed rich chick. Your one chance at a real life."

"Olivia's not deformed."

He sighed. "Aren't you tired of this, Special? Playing this idiotic role? The polite little punk who calls everybody 'sir' and 'ma'am.' The dummy who's too scared to tell his own girlfriend his honest opinion about anything. Why not embrace who you really are?"

"This *is* who I am."

He shook his head.

"Okay, then who am I?"

"You're exactly like me, Special. You've seen some bad shit and you're poor. So they tried to hide you away from the world. In a freak show like Horizons. That's why we've always been so close. 'Cause we've had to fight this thing together."

"I'm nothing like you."

He brought his gun up and cocked it and let it fall back to his side. "Do I really have to break it down for you? 'Cause I will."

"I don't care *what* you do."

He shrugged with his smile. "Your dad was a poor, spineless junkie who beat the shit out of you and your mom."

I shook my head.

"Your mom was a lonely wino who forced her own son to sleep in bed with her."

"Stop," I whispered, a lump already in the back of my throat.

He shook his head. "No, your dumb ass needs to hear this. How your mom tracked down your dad in broad daylight. Broke into some other woman's apartment. Found him on the couch, watching cartoons. How she shot him in the face, Special. Shot him three times."

"Stop talking," I said.

"Then she blew her own brains out. You guys made all the papers, didn't you, Special? You had your little two seconds of fame."

A tear went down my face, and I wiped it off.

I pictured Mr. Red snapping his fingers and saying people could die in two seconds. I felt so sick I wanted to die. Right now. With Devon's gun. I didn't care.

"But here's what you don't understand," Devon said. "When your mom put the gun in her mouth that day and pulled the trigger, she wasn't trying to save you, like she said in that stupid letter she hid under your pillow. She was trying to get *away* from you."

I pointed at Devon. "Don't say that."

"She was trying to escape from you."

"Don't say another word."

"What are you gonna do?" he said. "You've never actually *done* anything in your entire life."

I charged across the court, tackled Devon and socked him in the neck. His gun went flying. I tried to wrestle down his arms, but he slipped out of my grip and grabbed the gun and bashed it against the back of my head.

I fell to the ground.

When I opened my eyes he was standing in front of me, smiling and breathing hard, pointing the gun at my forehead.

"Well, well, well," he said. "Look at Special showing a little fight for once in his life. Maybe we could've used you in the revolution after all."

He backed up a step and recocked the gun. "But it's a little too late for that now."

I sat up, breathing hard.

Staring into the barrel of his gun.

"I'd end this little melodrama right here, but I need you to witness one more thing." He started laughing. "Want a hint? It involves a certain disfigured blonde. I'm gonna do her just like your dad did you and your mom."

"If you ever—"

"What?" he interrupted. "What are *you* gonna do, Special?"

I didn't say anything.

My heart was pounding a mile a minute. Warm blood trickling down the back of my neck from where he hit me.

"Now, I want you to close your eyes for me," he said.

I kept looking at him.

"Close them!"

I closed my eyes, waited for what else was gonna happen. Picturing his finger bending the trigger. The explosion. My thoughts and everything else disappearing. Like being hit by a train. This body dead. Forever.

But there was no explosion.

Just the quiet park.

I peeked open my eyes, spotted Devon sprinting out of the park.

I jumped to my feet, chased him across the road, yelling his name. I chased him past closed storefronts and the railroad crossing, toward Birmingham. Chased him down Manchester and Montgomery. When he cut across Liverpool and hopped a fence I hopped it, too, chased him through somebody's backyard. He leapt over the back fence, into a dirt alley. I was right behind him.

He ducked into another yard and a dog came loping out of a garage, barking, and lights went on in the house. I chased him over the opposite fence, through another yard and back into the street.

He kept looking at me over his shoulder, smiling like it was all a video game, like when we were kids at Horizons.

I ran as fast as I could to catch up, but I felt myself losing ground, losing everything.

He cut up Oxford.

By the time I rounded the corner he was gone.

I stood there for a second, in the middle of the road, sucking in breaths and looking around.

But there was no sign of Devon.

Anywhere.

I jogged up and down the entire street. Put my head over fences, checking people's yards. I looked down back alleys, into house windows, behind bushes. I ran all the way up to the gas station, peeked my head under the freeway bridge. But Devon was nowhere.

Since there was nobody under the bridge at all I went down there, looked around for something of Devon's. I sifted through abandoned clothes, broken bottles, fast-food wrappers. I kicked up blankets.

Then I noticed something.

The book Olivia had given me. The one by the Japanese author with the "100% Perfect Girl" story. It was just sitting there, leaning against the cement. Devon had stolen it right out of my tent.

I picked it up and looked at it, brushed off the dust. Then I walked onto the bridge and sat there trying to catch my breath, staring at the passing cars, my feet dangling over the edge.

I fingered the swelling on the back part of my head, trying to think about everything that had just happened, and what Devon said about my family, and him hitting me and pointing his gun, and Olivia saying we only had one more time together.

I gripped the book in my hands and watched the freeway cars, so worried about my life and worried how everything was gonna end.

I went to Mr. Red's tent early the next morning, waited with Peanut as usual, but he never came out. When I tapped on his tent there was no answer. Just to make sure, I unzipped his door a little and peeked inside.

Just his empty futon mattress.

I tried to work like everything was fine, but I couldn't. It felt weird without Mr. Red. And my mind wouldn't stop flashing back to me and Devon's fight. I kept hearing his words echoing through my head, again and again. Kept feeling the gun smashing against the back of my head and blood dribbling down my neck.

I did some of the regular jobs like cleaning the bathrooms and sweeping outside Campsite Coffee and emptying all the trash barrels. But one sentence from Devon made it impossible.

How he said my mom did it to get away from me.

To escape from me.

I kept thinking back to us in our old apartment. And there were signs she loved my dad more than me. Every time he left she'd get so depressed and never leave her bed. She'd forget to take me to school. Forget to go shopping for food. Sometimes I'd go in and check on her, and she'd wave me away.

What if Devon was right, I thought.

What if she didn't do it to save me, but to get away.

I stopped working, put away my gear in Mr. Red's shed and went in Campsite Coffee. I tried looking at magazines. Found an article in the paper about the grunion and Lea even cut out this picture they had from last year: the silver fish completely covering the sand and everybody standing around in the dark, watching it.

I stared at the picture and listened to Lea explain it. But I couldn't concentrate. My mind kept going back to Devon's words.

After I thanked Lea, I left the coffee shop and went looking for Devon. I searched the rest of the day, and most of the night, but I never found him.

When I got back to my tent I tried to write about Olivia leaving, but I had writer's block again. I couldn't even put one word.

I pulled out the book she'd given me, turned to the story about the 100% perfect girl and read it over and over.

Peanut snoring by the door.

The ocean sound outside my tent.

Eventually I shut off my flashlight, closed my eyes.

The only reason I could fall asleep was I knew Olivia wasn't staying the night at the campsites. She was safe somewhere else, with her family.

On the morning of the grunion I woke up early, and even though it was the weekend I went to Mr. Red's tent with Peanut. I tapped on his door and peeked inside. It was still empty.

I was just standing there, worrying that something serious might've happened to him, like maybe he was in the hospital, when I heard his voice behind me.

"There he is!"

I spun around, saw Mr. Red walking toward me with a RadioShack bag.

"Mr. Red."

"Big guy. Long time no see."

"Are you okay?"

"I'm alive," he said. "Listen, I just went by your tent. I have something for you." He handed me the bag.

I reached inside, pulled out a brand-new iPod. I looked back up at Mr. Red. "What is it?"

"What does it look like?"

"An iPod."

He gave me a thumbs-up. "Way to put your clues together."

"But it's not my birthday or anything."

"I know. It's my way of saying thanks." He pulled off his beat-up sombrero, ran his fingers through his hair and put it back on. "I appreciate you looking out the other night."

I nodded and checked out the iPod.

"Already downloaded a bunch of songs at the store," he said. "My own personal selections. Should be good to go."

"I've never had one before."

Mr. Red smiled, took the bag from me and crumpled it up. "Go ahead and test it out."

I pulled it out of the package, put the plugs in my ears and he showed me how to make it play. His Bob Marley phone song came on. I looked up at him, smiling.

"You like that, right?" He peeked down at his watch, then pulled one of the buds from my ears. "Listen, I wanted to apologize."

"It's okay."

"No, I'm supposed to set an example. And the other night. Man, I really took a step back."

He held out his hand and I shook it.

"Bill the Deacon had me in meetings all day yesterday. It helped, I think. A guy can't do everything on his own, Kidd. That's what I realized. Sometimes I'm gonna need to lean on friends. Like you and Bill."

We let go of our handshake.

I thought if I should tell Mr. Red about Devon now. And his gun. And how he said he was gonna do something to Olivia. I opened my mouth to explain it, but for some reason I couldn't get the words out.

He reached down to pet Peanut. "This old dog gets uglier by the day, doesn't he?"

I looked at Peanut.

Mr. Red was scratching him behind the ear. Then he stood up and looked at his watch again. "Okay, big guy. I'm off to get a haircut."

"You're cutting your hair?" I said.

He nodded. "Cleaning up my act. Got a day date with Maria."

I looked up at Mr. Red. "You do?"

"We're going on a long walk in OB, before she heads to her sister's birthday party." He slipped his hands in his pockets, said: "You might be surprised to hear this, but I'm gonna ask if we can get back together."

"You're gonna be with Maria again?"

He nodded. "If she'll have me."

"She will," I said, feeling happy for the first time in two days. "Everybody at Horizons always said how in love with you she is."

"Yeah?" He nodded his head. "Let's hope I didn't wait too long."

"You didn't," I said.

He stood there a second, like he was thinking, and then he said: "A guy said something in one of those meetings yesterday. Said people like us, the ones in the meeting, we tend to push away the people we love most. Without even knowing we're doing it. He said it's our way of protecting them."

Mr. Red looked at the ground, shaking his head. "But a man shouldn't push away his woman, Kidd. He should *take care* of her."

I pictured Olivia and felt proud 'cause that's exactly what I was gonna do.

"From now on," he said, "I'm gonna try to be that better kind of man."

He shook my hand again and got in his Bronco.

After he backed out of his spot, he waved and drove toward the campsite exit.

. . .

In the time I had left before me and Olivia's last time together I did two things.

First I went to a bunch of stores looking for a sombrero for Mr. Red. I figured since he got me an iPod I could get him a new hat.

It took me a long time to pick one, though, since I didn't know what he liked. His old one was so worn out you couldn't tell what it used to look like. I went to five surf shops and looked at them. The only one I skipped was the store where Devon got caught shoplifting.

The last place I checked was this store called Hanson's in Encinitas. It was next to the train station where me and Olivia caught the train to Torrey Pines Beach.

Right when I walked up to the rack of hats this one sombrero fell to the ground in front of me. I picked it up, trying to picture it on Mr. Red's head.

A saleslady walked over and said: "Excellent choice."

I thanked her and took the sombrero to the counter and paid for it.

Just as I left the store I saw a Coaster coming. I ran up to the platform and caught it. I don't even know why. I rode it all the way to Olivia's stop, hiked the same footpaths, sat on the same rock, and looked out over the same section of ocean.

I put on my new iPod and pushed play and let the music go all over my thoughts.

I took out Olivia's book and reread "The 100% Perfect Girl" two more times. I was finally starting to realize what I thought.

When I finished reading I opened my philosophy of life book to a blank page and took the cap off my pen.

I sat there awhile, thinking about me and Olivia's kiss and the story she told me about her port-wine stains and how she didn't wear her hat to dinner. I thought about bad stuff, too, though. How I'd probably only see her one more time. And how after that we'd go back to our separate lives. And then I thought about Devon saying he was gonna do something to her. And how he wanted me to watch.

I started getting worried all over again.

Maybe it was good Olivia was leaving. I only had to watch her one more night.

For some reason I flipped back to the beginning of my philosophy of life book, started reading the first entry about me and Devon looking for a place to pee. It was so weird to read what I'd written to myself, and how I used "Dear Kidd," and how it made me remember what was happening at the time I wrote each thing.

As I read through the rest of my book, I realized how much calmer it made me. And less alone. It was like reading letters from a friend. I stopped thinking about Devon and his threats, and I stopped thinking about Olivia leaving me. I stopped worrying.

I just sat there, listening to Mr. Red's music.

And reading my old words.

And when I got to the very end something amazing happened. I became inspired.

I looked out over the beautiful blue ocean and started the Bob Marley song over. I turned to a blank page. And for the first time since I met Olivia I actually wrote about her in my book. The words just flowed out of me.

And fifteen minutes later, when I took a break to read it over, I didn't even wanna tear it out.

I just kept writing.

'Cause it was exactly what I wanted to say.

I was on the cliff with Olivia, both of us in hoodie sweat-shirts and flip-flops, waiting for the grunion to run like all the papers and news-show people talked about. Mr. Red and the campsite surfer guys and Blue and Jasmine, and everybody's parents, were on the sand so they could be right there when it happened.

Me and Olivia looked down at them, and all the other random people, and I pictured those fish already swimming together in swarms under the choppy ocean water, way out past the kelp beds, having no idea about the swarms of humans waiting for them onshore.

"This is such a great spot," Olivia said. "It's like having box seats on Broadway."

"I know," I said.

Olivia sat in one of Mr. Red's chairs we'd set out. We'd put them right near the old part of the fence so we could still see the beach and the waves and the sand when it turned silver.

She reached in her backpack and pulled out a shopping bag, tapped the chair next to hers. "Come sit," she said.

I sat next to her.

Peanut was on the ground by our feet, looking toward the ocean like he knew the fish were coming, too. I watched him breathe, wondering if dogs sensed more than just thunder-storms. He looked up at me, his tongue going over his crooked yellow teeth.

I wished I could teach him to sense Devon.

"This is for you," Olivia said, holding out the shopping bag. "It's not a big deal, but I thought you might like to have it."

I took the bag and set it in my lap.

I was about to look inside when she put her hand on mine and said: "And I wanted to tell you something."

"Okay," I said.

"I was right about what I heard," she said. "My dad and grandpa are taking me to New York."

I nodded and smiled. Secretly, though, my stomach was aching. It didn't even matter that I'd been expecting this.

"They set up a consultation with that doctor I told you about. The one who does laser surgery."

"You must be happy," I said. I tried to feel happy, too, since I knew this meant she could start her real life. But I also knew her real life didn't include me.

"You have no idea." She smoothed down her ski-cap flaps and said: "The doctor has this computer program that shows what you'll look like after his treatment. I'll get to meet the future me."

"I'm happy for you," I said, trying to ignore how sad I felt.

I reached down for my philosophy of life book, opened it to the folded picture of last year's grunion run. I pulled out my tiger whisker and put it in her open hand.

"What's this?" she said.

"The tiger whisker I got from the zoo. They said it gives you good luck wherever you go."

She took it out of her palm with two fingers and studied it.

"You should have luck when you meet that doctor."

"That's so sweet," she said. "But what about *your* luck?"

"It already worked for me," I said, thinking of our kiss at Torrey Pines. And her song. And every single time we'd ever hung out.

I stood up, went to the fence and looked down at everybody.

"Thanks, Kidd. I mean it." She walked over, stood next to me by the fence, rubbed the back of my arm.

We both looked at the ocean for a while and then she said: "I was thinking about you while my family and I drove back to Cardiff this afternoon."

"You were?"

She nodded. "You and I are different in a lot of ways, obviously. But we have similarities, too."

I looked at her, remembering when I'd thought the exact same thing.

"We both have scars we let keep us on the outside." She let go of my arm. "I mean, there's a reason you're the first boy I've ever shown my face to. I knew you'd understand. I trusted you."

"I trust you, too," I told her.

Olivia smiled, and we both turned back to the ocean. I thought about our similarities. How we had scars. But then I thought how she was gonna go fix hers. And mine would still be there. I could picture Devon saying that's how come we weren't really the same. She'd always have money to fix things, he'd say. And since people like me and him had nothing, our scars would be forever.

I wondered if I should feel ashamed about being in the group with nothing.

Or if I should be mad, like Devon.

And right as I was thinking that, I glanced down on the beach and couldn't believe my eyes.

Devon was waiting there with everybody else.

Staring at the ocean.

I had no idea what I should do. Olivia didn't want me to scare her, but at the same time, he was right down the cliff from us.

I took Olivia's hand and softly led her back to our chairs and we both sat down. She looked at me funny. But then she noticed the bag she'd given me and said: "You ever gonna look in there or what?"

My hands were nervous about Devon as I opened it, pulled out a card. I opened the envelope and read it to myself. It thanked me for making her feel pretty, she hadn't felt that way since she was little. It said she had no idea how to categorize us, but she knew meeting me this summer was the best thing that happened in a long time.

"You mean it?" I said, looking up at her.

"Of course I mean it," she said. "But that's just the card. There's also this amazing picture I took of you. I had it blown up and framed."

I stood up and went to the fence, looked for Devon. He was still just standing there, staring at the ocean from the exact same spot, like he was in a trance. Like he wasn't thinking about anything else.

I felt calmer.

Maybe he'd never think of up here, and at least me and Olivia could have this one last time together. And then she'd be safe in New York. And I could deal with Devon on my own. And if anybody got hurt it would only be me or him.

I scooted my chair closer to Olivia's and sat down. I felt

inspired, like when I was listening to music on Olivia's rock at Torrey Pines. I told her: "Hey, Olivia."

"Hey, Kidd."

"I know you're excited to meet the future you," I said. "But I wanted to say. The current you is beautiful, too. The current you is the most perfect girl I've ever met."

She got a serious look on her face and said: "Kidd, that really means a lot to me."

I could tell by the way her eyes looked in mine.

Something was happening with us.

It felt important and less nervous.

She pulled off her ski cap again, never looking away from my eyes. Took my fingers and put them on her stain again, and without even thinking I leaned into her diamond-earringed ear and whispered: "You're the most perfect girl I've ever met."

She leaned in and kissed me.

And this time I tried to kiss her back as good as I possibly could, thinking it would say how much I loved her and how much I'd miss her when she started her new life and how thankful I was she picked me when there were so many other guys at the campsites, all of them with regular parents, living regular lives, in the same group as her.

But then, out of the corner of my eye, I saw Peanut stand up and start growling.

And I knew.

I looked over Olivia's shoulder, saw Devon staring at us through the bushes. The shopping bag Olivia gave me fell to the ground.

We kept kissing, but at the same time my whole body was going tense and I was trying to think.

I had to save Olivia.

I had to make him hurt me instead.

Devon crashed through the bushes and pointed at me and said under his breath: "Get away from her."

When I didn't get away Devon marched forward grinning and stopped right in front of us.

Peanut started growling.

Devon reached for Olivia, but I jumped in front of her at the last second and grabbed his sweatshirt. I shoved him by his hood toward the part of the cliff where the fence was still old, me still clutching my philosophy of life book, and Olivia screaming "Oh, my God, Kidd! What are you doing!"

"I can't let anybody hurt you," I told her.

"Kidd! You're scaring me again!"

When I looked back at her something wild leapt in her eyes, out-of-control flames that no amount of fireman's water could've ever extinguished or even slowed down.

"I have to make sure you're okay," I said.

"Why do you keep saying that? Nobody's hurting me."

But all I saw was Devon's back against the part of fence that wasn't new, and him grinning in my face and telling me: "So, here we are, eh, Kidd? You knew I'd show up."

His laugh.

Me looking all the way down the cliff, to the sand. Remembering my mom sitting me down to have a talk. Her explaining about my dad and my genes and how I could be my own person.

"You still don't get it, do you?" Devon said. "All these people here, man. They think they're better than us."

Peanut growling at us and one of his ears standing in a point like it was hearing something too high for humans.

"Kidd, stop!" Olivia said. She took two short breaths and told me: "Just—Just come back here a minute. I wanna talk to you."

My philosophy of life book dropping to the ground with all my answers.

"Please," Olivia said in a tiny voice. "Kidd."

"I'll do it," I said to Devon, my face in a frown.

"You won't," he said.

"I will."

"You won't."

"I have to," I said, and I drove him harder into the weak part of the fence until it broke like I knew it would break and I shoved him down the cliff and watched his body bounce-tumble-fall-stretch-fetal-thud into the thick sad sand and lay motionless, and everybody who was once waiting for grunion was now racing to my side and touching my arm, my back, my leg, and looking up the cliff at Olivia and then everything turned black and I felt slippery fish going on me and I heard Mr. Red screaming my name and screaming for everyone on the sand to back away from me. . . .

I **wake up suddenly** 'cause I feel the pain in my body, and I'm sure I'm broken on the beach sand.

But I'm not.

I'm still strapped down on my cot in my prison cell.

And Olivia's not here.

And Devon's not here.

And Mr. Red isn't holding my head and crying and telling me it's gonna be okay.

Telling me to just hold on.

The ambulance is on its way.

I suck in a huge breath like I've been holding it. And I try to think why things are so mixed up in my mind. Why I felt my body hitting the sand this time. And breaking. And why Mr. Red's voice was trembling and his face was over mine.

For the first time since I woke up here, in prison, I'm not really sure what happened on the cliff.

Did Devon push *me*?

Am I the one who fell down the ice plant to the sand? And where am I now if I didn't push anybody?

And what did Devon do to Olivia after I was gone?

Or did both of us fall?

I get so worried about what happened I start hyperventilating in my prison cell. There's not enough oxygen going to my brain. I feel everything slipping away until I'm no longer thinking anything. I'm just trying to breathe. I'm just trying to hang on like Mr. Red said. . . .

Philosophy 5:
About How a Man Should
Take Care of His Woman

Dear Olivia:

I'm just sitting here right now, on your rock at Torrey Pines, near the cliff where those kids had their suicide pact, but don't worry, I'm not going by the edge.

All summer I've been trying to write about you and all summer it's never worked. I tried after you jumped from behind that tree to scare me, and after that midnight walk when you told me about the writer who blinked his words, and after those college guys said stuff about you by the lifeguard tower, and after you played me your piano song, and even after regular times like us walking past each other at the campsites or while I was sitting outside Mr. Red's tent, waiting to start work, and you'd wave.

But I never kept anything I put 'cause I always thought it had to be as good as you and it never was.

Today, though, I'm on this cliff thinking about you and listening to Mr. Red's iPod, and I'm having one of those things you always have, an epiphany. Maybe it's impossible to make words measure up to the person you like, especially when you like them as much as I like you. So I've decided something. What if I just write you a letter instead. Even if it's one that just stays here in my philosophy of life book, and you never actually see it.

So here's the letter.

Dear Olivia (I already put this part, I know):

Today I was on the Coaster and I had a daydream about the future. It was me and you and we were older and we were living at another beach campsite, one way away from here. But I didn't have a job with Mr. Red like I always thought, I worked at a zoo since I like animals so much. And instead of living in a tent we had construction people build us a house, right there on one of the campsites. And you were in medical school to become a doctor. And Peanut was still our pet, even though he was like a hundred thirty years old in dog years. And on some nights you'd read to me from whatever book you had, even if it was just a school one about diseases. Or you'd play a song for me on this keyboard I bought from Moonlight Music, and you wouldn't even have to sneak it.

In my train daydream you never wore your ski cap, either. 'Cause your port-wine stain had mostly been lasered away. And even though there was a tiny bit left you finally realized no mark could ever make you less pretty to me, even if it was one that covered your entire body. And we had a son named

Ben and nobody ever hurt Ben and nobody ever hurt you 'cause they knew I'd never let anything happen.

I woke up in the middle of my daydream when the Coaster dinged and it was my stop and I had to hurry and get off. So I don't know what else happened. But as I stood there, watching the train start going again, toward its next stop, I got a smile as big as my face could do 'cause I was thinking how it was probably the best daydream I'd ever had. . . .

Dreams from Solitary Confinement

A strong wind lifts me up off my cot, moves me toward the prison bars, where I suck in my breath and slip through. I rise up into the pre-morning sky, into the clouds, the dark less dark now 'cause the sun's so close to coming up.

I'm flying like I do in all these solitary dreams, watching the world pass underneath. But this time I know where I'm flying from.

Fallbrook.

I'm tracing the exact path I took the night I ran away from Horizons.

I see where the hitchhiking car stopped for me and I hopped in and we drove toward the coast. I see the stoplights we went through and the freeway on-ramp we took. I hear the news-station voices on the radio. I see the man let me out and our handshake and his finger pointing in the direction of Cardiff by the Sea.

I seem so naïve in this version of me, just out of Horizons, in my old clothes, walking that long stretch of beach looking for Mr. Red, not understanding anything about who I am or what I will soon discover.

I fly away from the old me, lower onto a towel on the sand again, where Olivia's waiting. Like she's been waiting in all my dreams. The sun starting to climb into the sky over her shoulder, fingers of light gripping the campsite cliff and slowly pulling itself up.

Olivia doesn't notice me land, though.

She's too busy holding open my philosophy of life book and saying the first part of the secret letter I wrote her.

Her face swollen like she's just been crying.

Listening to her voice saying my words gives me the strangest feeling, like everything's off balance or upside down. My stomach nauseous with butterflies.

For some reason it makes me picture Devon against the old part of the fence again. The sound of it snapping. And then I'm shoving him.

But then it's me who's falling.

It's me waving around my arms, searching for anything to grab, crashing to the sand.

I try to push away these confused feelings by concentrating on the beach around my towel: the seaweed laying in clumps, the stairs going up the cliff, the ship now listing over whitewash waves near shore.

Olivia's voice:

. . . have a job with Mr. Red like I always thought, I worked at a zoo since I like animals so much. And instead of living in a tent we had construction people build us a house, right there on one of the campsites. . . .

She trails off and looks at me.

Like she's noticing what's suddenly happening with my body. The dull pain throbbing in my chest. Pulsing down into my thighs and calves and feet and toes.

I try to stretch, but the pain's so intense it feels like I'm breaking into tiny pieces.

Olivia's face changes as she watches.

Her eyes go wide.

Her jaw drops.

Her mouth forms the words: *Oh, my God.*

My mind is so jumbled that in a single motion the sun rises the rest of the way into the beach sky, a hundred times faster than possible. It stops directly over me and Olivia and our spot on the sand, brightening everything like it's now the middle of the day.

"Kidd?" Olivia says in a worried voice.

I look at her shocked face.

My body aching all over. Even just opening and closing my eyelids, flexing and unflexing my fingers and toes.

And when I turn my head to the side, to look at the stranded ship, it's no longer a ship, it's a framed picture of me squatting on the campsite fence. And when I look down at the seaweed laying on the beach sand, it's no longer seaweed but the black-and-white pattern of a tile floor. And the stairs going up the cliff are no longer stairs but a design on a wall.

Olivia's now running to that wall. She's pushing a red button and shouting into the intercom: "Please, somebody come in here! Hurry!"

I try to open my mouth, to ask her what's happening, but inside it's dry like cotton and my teeth feel tight and my tongue's swollen. I make a moaning sound, but it's weak and doesn't sound right.

Olivia is now grabbing my hand and lowering herself to a squatting position so her crying face is right in front of mine, and she's saying my name, over and over:

"Kidd, are you awake?"

"Kidd?"

"Can you hear me, Kidd?"

I'm staring back at her, realizing there's something in my

mouth. A tube. It's taped to my face. And there's an IV taped to my arm. I feel a tube between my legs, going into me, which makes it feel like my pee is everywhere.

I reach up and tug at the tube in my mouth and can feel it all the way down my throat. When I rip the whole thing out I gag and an alarm goes off.

Olivia is holding the tube in her hand now, saying: "Kidd, can you hear me?"

"What's happening?" I say in a whispery hoarse voice that doesn't sound like me.

"Oh, my God. You're awake."

Over Olivia's shoulder the sun is no longer a sun, it's a bright light on a white ceiling. And instead of sitting on a beach towel in the sand, I'm laying in a bed in a room, and what was once the constant hum of the ocean is now the buzzing of monitors and machines. Things hooked up to my body.

I'm not on the beach.

And I'm not in a prison cell.

I'm in a hospital 'cause I've been hurt.

Olivia jumps away from the bed when a man in a white coat rushes into the room.

Two women hurry in after him.

Olivia's shouting that I'm awake.

She's pointing at me.

I'm so confused as I watch other people rush into the room, too. Gather around my bed. Their worried voices blending together, one lady in scrubs holding Olivia back.

I've never been so scared.

Unsure.

Unable to think.

The man's face behind the doctor becomes Mr. Red's face. And one of the women by the door becomes Maria. She's covering her mouth and staring at me with tears in her eyes.

My last Horizons therapist is now holding my hand and talking in her calm therapy voice.

A doctor is lowering an oxygen mask over my nose and mouth. My breaths into it are too fast 'cause I don't understand what's happening.

My ears, though, are now adjusted to all the voices overlapping around me:

"Give him room."

"Devon, can you hear me? Are you feeling any pain?"

"Is he okay?"

"We're gonna need everybody out."

"Honey, do you know what day it is?"

"Who does he think he is right now?"

"Sir, you're going to have to–"

The doctor shining a beam of light in my eyes, one at a time, saying: "Push a baseline of morphine sulfate, one milligram per hour."

"Can you wiggle your toes? Move your hands?"

"Honey, I need you to look at me."

"He can't hear anything."

"Please. All of you."

"Do you know how long you've been out, Devon?"

"His name's not Devon. It's Kidd."

A nurse pulling the cap off a needle, pushing it into a tube on my IV bag.

"This should take away the pain."

"You've been out just over three days. It's Wednesday."

My therapist is pointing from her eyes to mine so I'll focus on her. She's telling me to remember back to when we first started. When we worked so hard to limit Devon's presence. When she had me go to him inside my mind, tell him I had to live my own separate life.

"You hang in there," she's saying, "and I promise you, honey. We'll get you back to that point. And beyond."

What is she saying?

Who does she think I am?

My mind is jumping all over the place as I watch the doctors and nurses now clearing everybody out of the hospital room. Including my Horizons therapist.

Olivia breaks through the circle of people, puts her face up to mine and says: "Kidd!"

One of the nurses is trying to pull her back by the arm, but Olivia's pushing away and saying: "Kidd! Can you hear me?"

I knock the oxygen mask from my face, tell her in my hoarse voice: "What's happening to me?"

Another doctor's now pulling Olivia, too, but she's holding onto my bed frame. "You jumped! You thought you were somebody named Devon. And you jumped off the cliff."

I watch her tears, the way she's fighting against the doctor and nurse. "You tried to kill yourself."

And when I hear her say those words, I tried to kill myself, my mind suddenly races back through tiny pieces of my life:

My mom sitting me down on my birthday, the day after

my dad broke my nose. Saying how I don't have to grow up to be like him. I can be somebody else.

My Horizons therapist explaining how I have a death drive, just like my dad. Explaining the time I was on the roof threatening to jump and when I swallowed the bottle of pills and when I banged my head on the shower wall so many times the water in the tub turned pink.

Waking up under the freeway bridge. In the middle of the night. Surrounded by litter and abandoned clothes and the sound of freeway cars above me. The black girl sleeping on my arm.

In the clothing store dressing room, laughing at the stressed worker, sneaking out the back. Her yelling that I didn't pay.

Marching back down the beach, to the rich college guys, aiming my fake gun in the short one's face, telling him it's not so funny anymore, is it?

Swimming out into the riptide. So ashamed Mr. Red said I could be anything, I wanted to drown. Then he'd never learn how I really am. And he wouldn't stop liking me.

And now I'm turning back to the picture Olivia framed.

Me on the cliff fence. Balancing. Laughing.

Me where Devon's supposed to be. No other person behind me. And I'm flooded with its meaning. That I am Devon. Like my Horizons therapist has always tried to say. And I always tried to forget.

Like my face in the picture. How my mouth is smiling. But my eyes are serious. They're secretly thinking how I can never let myself hurt Olivia the way my dad hurt me.

My mind begins slipping away 'cause of the stuff they put in my IV. The hospital room is blurring back into beach around me. Waves crashing behind my back, the staircase reforming on the cliff. The seaweed back in clumps around my towel.

Only Olivia stays the same.

A strong ocean wind rises up and tries to lift me. But I fight it this time, hard as I can, like Olivia fought the nurses pulling her away. I reach down for her hand and she grabs on. The rest of my body slowly floating in the air, turning upside down.

But my eyes never going off Olivia's eyes.

Wait for me, I tell her.

I will, she says back, crying, our fingers starting to slip. *I promise you, Kidd.*

We lose our grip and the wind sucks me back into the ocean sky, above the morning campsites, above the train tracks and the park and all of Cardiff.

It's me just hovering now, in the overcast, looking down. Olivia a shape on the sand now. And my tent and Mr. Red's tent and Peanut waiting by the railroad tie.

I think how I've ruined everything.

Like I knew I would.

But just before I'm swept back toward my prison cell, even though I know it's not real, I hear Olivia's voice.

She's standing by the tide now, facing the ocean, holding my philosophy of life book in front of her. She's reading the rest of the words I put in her letter.

As I listen, I try to think if the Devon part's gone. And I wonder if people who ruin everything ever get to start over.

And if they can learn how to lean on people, like Mr. Red said.

And if they can get better.

. . . After the train faded in the distance, though, Olivia, so did my smile. 'Cause I thought of something serious I wish I could tell you.

Real life isn't always your daydream. I believe that's the point of what that author was saying in his "100% Perfect Girl" story. Even though the couple doesn't end up together after they lose their memories, they still get to meet each other, and they still get to experience what love is. And even the ending, how they don't fully recognize each other when they pass on the street. There's still a glimmer of something between them, right? And they both turn around to look. What if that's what it means to know you've experienced love? That look? Maybe that's even more important than ending up together.

I wonder if it's the same with us, Olivia. I know you were a great girl before I met you. And I know you'll be a great girl whenever I stop knowing you. You'll go off to New York and that doctor will fix your port-wine stain and you'll have more confidence and you'll meet new friends in college and get a great job and have an amazing life. And I know I won't be a part of it. But maybe one day we'll pass each other in the street. And we'll have that glimmer. And we'll both know.

This guy I used to be best friends with once told me a girl like you could never actually stay with a guy like me. He said eventually you'd have to go back to your regular life 'cause girls who grow up with money don't end up with guys who grow up with nothing. And for the longest time I hated how he'd say that, and I hated trying to decide if it was true. But ever since I read that story I've been thinking about it in a different way.

Even if I never see you again, Olivia. Starting tomorrow, after we watch the grunion. Even if that's the last time I ever get to talk to you, and be next to you, and watch you laugh. Even if my ex-friend turns out to be right.

Still.

I believe I'm the luckiest person in the world. 'Cause I got to meet a pretty girl like you. And I got to hear you talk about all your books. And we rode the train together and took long walks and held hands and we even kissed on your secret rock at Torrey Pines. Where I am right this second. And just knowing you for these two and a half months. It's made me think differently about myself. And it's made me feel like I mean something in the world. And how maybe I could even have a future. Like regular people.

Like a regular person.

ACKNOWLEDGMENTS

I'm incredibly lucky to work with Steve Malk and Krista Marino. Steve, thanks for everything you've done for me as an agent and friend. It's an absolute honor to be one of your people. Krista, thanks for believing in me. And my books. And making us both better. You're the reason I've found my little place in this world.

Thanks also to Beverly Horowitz and Dominique Cimina and all the great people at Random House. Thanks to Matt Van Buren and Quan Long and Brin Hill and Sandra Newman and all the amazing teachers and librarians I've had the pleasure of meeting. Thanks especially to my folks, Al and Roni de la Peña, who have inspired me with the remarkable things they've accomplished in their own lives over the past few years. You guys make *me* proud.

And last, thanks to Joshua Ytuarte, a kid I met at Connell Middle School in San Antonio, Texas. Before my presentation I was warned he'd be the most disruptive in the group. And he was. At first. But as soon as I started talking about how I wasn't a great student in junior high and high school, he started paying attention. I watched him. After the session he asked to speak to me privately. He told me he was born in prison and that he'd been held back in school. Twice. But he wrote about San Antonio gangs.

He asked if I'd like to read the first half of his book. I said sure. But we were in a hurry to get to the next school.

He sprinted off.

Ten minutes later he ran up to me with thirty printed pages. He was sweating, out of breath. I took the pages and shook his clammy hand. He called me sir.

That night I read the pages. They were beautiful. And ugly. And sad. They were full of heart.

This Mexican kid, who was a thug, who was not pretty, who was too big for his grade, too old—he made something with his hands, and his head. And it moved me. It reminded me of the incredible power of words.

I Will Save You is **MATT DE LA PEÑA**'s fourth novel for young readers. He attended the University of the Pacific on a basketball scholarship and went on to earn a Master of Fine Arts in creative writing at San Diego State University. De la Peña currently lives in Brooklyn, New York, where he teaches creative writing. Look for his first three books, *Ball Don't Lie, Mexican WhiteBoy,* and *We Were Here,* all available from Delacorte Press.